THE ISLAND GOD

UNHOLY ISLAND BOOK THREE

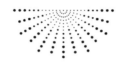

SARAH PAINTER

Siskin
Press

Published by Siskin Press Limited

Cover Design by Stuart Bache

ALSO BY SARAH PAINTER

The Language of Spells

The Secrets of Ghosts

The Garden of Magic

In The Light of What We See

Beneath The Water

The Lost Girls

The Crow Investigations Series

The Night Raven

The Silver Mark

The Fox's Curse

The Pearl King

The Copper Heart

The Shadow Wing

The Broken Cage

The Magpie Key

The Unholy Island Series

The Ward Witch

The Book Keeper

The Island God

For Dave. Always.

WELCOME TO UNHOLY ISLAND

Lindisfarne, or Holy Island, is a tidal island in the county of Northumberland in northern England. Visitors can gawp at the impressive remains of its ancient priory, established in 635 AD – a beacon of religious learning and salvation in a cruel world, enduring as a place of pilgrimage and piety throughout the years. When the priory was abandoned as part of the dissolution of the monasteries in the sixteenth century, religion gave way to military concerns. Henry VIII demanded fortifications against the Scots, and a castle was built on the highest point on the island.

Unholy Island sits a few miles northward, in an area that has been Scotland and then Northumberland and then Scotland again throughout recent history, but in ancient times was just the Old North. Unlike Holy Island, it escaped royal and monastic notice, and has endured without much external interference.

Unholy Island is a mile further out in the cold sea than Lindisfarne, but it has a similar causeway. Stable enough for vehicles twice a day, if you stick to the window of opportunity provided by the tide. Holy Island is also accessible on foot, the final destination for the famous pilgrimage of St Cuthbert's Way. The more distant position of Unholy Island means that only the strongest or most foolish would attempt to reach it on foot. Or the desperate.

On an average day, you can see Holy Island from the mainland, with the distinctive shape of the castle rising on its rocky hill.

Unholy Island is only glimpsed when the air is clear and the sun is high in the sky. It seems to have its own weather system, staying almost permanently shrouded in mist. Even for those who live close to the causeway on the mainland, it is easy to forget it is there at all.

The island community is very small and the visitor numbers are not large. Few people know about the island and those that do, those who bring delivery vans or visit to fix utility poles or water pipes or fibre broadband, don't really think about the place after they leave. It's not that they forget about it completely, it just passes from the front of their mind. In the case of the delivery drivers and the post office, this is a regular recurrence. A weekly knowing and then unknowing that becomes a familiar part of their mindscape and doesn't unduly trouble anybody.

There are tourists. Throughout the summer, a handful make the crossing. They walk the quiet beaches, watch the ringed plovers, skylarks and oystercatchers, birds which can still successfully nest as there aren't enough humans to trample their homes, and eat lunch in The Rising Moon. If the bookshop is open, they squeeze between the packed shelves and browse the used stock and usually come out with a small stack of books. They might buy some home-made tablet from the general store or a painting of the waves from the owner of Strand House, and as the sun crosses the sky and the tide begins to turn, lapping at the edges of the causeway, they get back into their cars and drive back to the mainland. The sea reclaims the island and the visitors eat their tablet, read their books, hang their new artwork, but never really think about Unholy Island again.

CHAPTER ONE

Esme Gray had made a nest for herself on the sofa.
She was surrounded by piles of books and there was
a small table pulled close for her mug of tea and a plate of
biscuits. On her lap she had a notebook, pencil case and
three different colours of sticky note. Sylvie, the French
stove, was glowing happily, warming the room and drying
the damp February air. Rain was pouring steadily down
the windows, but it only increased Esme's sense of content-
ment. She was inside, safe and comfortable, losing herself
in the joy of learning.

Since the island bookshop had almost been burned
down by a disturbed young woman, twisted by blood magic
to the point of madness, the shop had opened up to Esme
in a way it never had before. She had lived on Unholy
Island for seven years and had seen books about herbal
remedies and Celtic myths in the backroom 'esoteric'
section. Now, the shop was offering her books about hexes
and cursed objects, transmutation and levitation, white
magic and protection spells. There was also an ever-
changing selection of myths and folklore, as if the shop was
eager for Esme to read all the stories that had been told of

spirits and shifters, gods and monsters, fortune, fate, and the follies of man.

Some of the books she was able to buy, and she had an expanding home library at Strand House, the bed-and-breakfast on the island, but others were definitely only given as loans and she took extra care with these volumes before returning them to the shop. There were other books, ancient leather-bound tomes with onion skin pages and covers mottled with years of handling that were only to be looked at within the stockroom of the shop, and only when Luke Taylor, The Book Keeper, was present. Discovering these rules had been a process over the last few weeks, with the bookshop letting her and Luke know exactly when they were getting things wrong. Its methods of communication included flashing the lights, humming quietly, shaking the bookshelves, and dropping the temperature in the shop until Luke and Esme's teeth chattered.

She had been taking notes from a chunky book about warding magic. She was the island's Ward Witch and knew the ritual that she had inherited from the previous holder of the role. Esme thought there was no harm in being as informed as possible, however. Besides, she wasn't a believer in tradition for its own sake. Just because some-thing had always been done a particular way, didn't mean that was the best or right way. You only had to look at the patriarchy.

By the time she finished her tea and turned the last page in the book, the fire was getting low, so Esme stood up, scattering stationery supplies, and added a log. Sylvie was a temperamental stove, sometimes sullenly refusing to draw and others burning with a fierce heat, but she made up for this by being the most beautiful blue enamel. Esme's predecessor had a French surname, and she assumed that Madame Le Grys had brought Sylvie with her when she arrived on the island. She wondered what her successor would find at Strand House that would make her wonder about Esme. Her paintings, she supposed. The seascapes that she felt compelled to repeat. She sold plenty to the summer visitors, but never came close to running out. Jetsam, the cat she had also inherited, was sleeping on the smaller sofa. He woke up and stretched, turning to present a view of his rear as he did so, and then curled up on the cushions and closed his eyes.

'Luke is coming round after he closes the shop. Be nice.'

Jet didn't move.

'I know you're listening. And I want you to keep your claws to yourself.'

Jet opened one eye.

Esme took a breath. This was a risky strategy, and one that might result in Jet attacking her feet all night long, but she went with it anyway. 'If you attack Luke, there will be no ham for a week. Or butter.'

Both eyes were open now. The cat stared at her with an expression of imperious outrage.

'I like him,' she said softly.

Esme couldn't tell if this honesty had melted Jet's feline heart or whether he just couldn't be bothered to waste his best fury upon a mere human. Either way, he dipped his head to his paws and went back to sleep.

LUKE TAYLOR COULD STILL SMELL the faintest odour of burning paper, which made no sense as Kate Foster hadn't got as far as setting light to the petrol she had sloshed over the shop. If any scent was still lingering in the shop, it ought to be petrol, but between professional cleaners, sanded and refinished floorboards, and replacing the sodden stock, there wasn't a trace of that. He assumed the scent had to be a figment of his imagination. He had dreamed of burning so many times since being hexed by a cursed book that now his senses were playing tricks on him.

He shelved the crime novel that Seren had returned to the shop that afternoon. She had swapped it for a romantic comedy which had daisies on the cover. 'I've heard it's filthy,' Seren had said cheerfully and Luke had looked everywhere, anywhere, except at her face. He had busied himself with writing down the details and willed the blood he could feel rushing to his cheeks to sod off. Swapping books was a perk for the islanders and Luke kept a careful note of them in the shop ledger that sat on the counter. There was another ledger that lived in the stockroom of the shop, but that was for the special collection of books and not for public view.

Rain was sheeting down the new front window, obscuring the world outside. The lights were glowing steadily and there was the faintest background hum that meant the shop was happy. He was getting to know the different ways the shop expressed itself and felt there was a growing trust. He had spent hours waxing and polishing the bookshelves and the old wooden counter, and he felt a sense of welcome when he walked back inside after going to the pub for a meal or to Esme's. If it wasn't for the concern over his twin brother, he would be utterly content.

After turning the sign in the window to 'closed' and locking the front door, Luke went upstairs to change his clothes and pick up the bottle of wine he had bought earlier. He and Esme were taking things slowly, and he was yet to spend the night, but he was happy to wait. He could feel a certainty about their relationship, a kind of fated 'rightness' that calmed his natural impatience to get as close as possible as quickly as possible. They had time.

· · ·

ACROSS THE VILLAGE, in the cluttered general store that served the islanders with everything from cheese to light-bulbs, Matteo was straightening tins of chickpeas and tomatoes on the shelves and trying not to think about Fiona. She was single now, which meant he could think about her. There was no reason he couldn't. Except that it would be fruitless. Matteo had built a life for himself that insulated him from pain, but that was a side-effect. He had built a life to insulate others. He did not speak. He would not speak. He served the islanders and visitors and kept the shop clean and orderly. If somebody rushed in needing plasters and antiseptic for a cut finger, he could lay his hands on the supplies within moments. It might look like chaos, but he could find a jar of sun-dried tomatoes or packet of sewing needles, whatever was required, and there was a satisfaction to that. A job well done.

He didn't deserve that satisfaction, he knew. And he certainly didn't deserve a woman like Fiona. Even if, by some miracle, she was interested in him, he could not put himself in a situation where his guard might drop, even for a moment.

A memory flashed into his mind. A time from his past when he had lost control. The sickness that rolled through his gut was nothing to the block of black shame in his heart. So many times before that, he had hurt people, but that had been when he had not known the extent of his abilities. He did not like to think of those events and he felt bad, but he held a sliver of forgiveness for his younger self. He had not known. He had not been trained. He hadn't any control.

But on that bad day, that very bad day, he had lost control. Let go of his control, he reminded himself, not allowing a moment of denial. He forced himself to see it clearly and not to prevaricate or cosset. He had been capable of keeping his words in check, of not speaking, and he had known the possible outcomes and still he had used his voice. His words. He was entirely culpable and he would never let himself forget it.

HAMMER WAS NOT A HAPPY MAN. He rested the oars of the boat in the rowlocks and let himself drift as he picked up his binoculars. There was definitely smoke coming from Àite Marbh, the islet that lay to the west of Unholy Island. Nobody should be there.

Late the previous night, he had thought he had seen a light. It had bobbed and flickered as if somebody was carrying it through some trees and then disappeared. He had waited, watching for another ten minutes to see if it reappeared. When it didn't, he had convinced himself he had been mistaken. Now he knew he hadn't.

CHAPTER TWO

Tobias's first hint that something was amiss was Winter's sharp bark. His ears were pressed back against his skull and he let out a soft whine before another two short barks. They had been taking an early evening stroll along the coastal path that led from the castle to Coire Bay when Winter had pressed into Tobias's legs and let out his warning.

Tobias scanned the gorse that lined the path, the rocks that led to the sea, and then the horizon. Àite Marbh was a dark mass against the red glow of the setting sun. Tobias wasn't a superstitious man. Truth be known, he wasn't a man at all, but that didn't mean he didn't have instincts. At this moment his were telling him that he wasn't seeing everything that was there. He was used to seeing the layers of the world, past realities stacked upon each other, but the sense that there was something hidden amongst all these images was new.

DOWN AT THE SHORE, Hammer was hauling his boat onto the dry sand. He straightened and turned at Tobias's approach, and Tobias saw instantly that the man was shaken.

'There are lights,' Hammer said without preamble. 'Over there. I went to take a closer look.'

The islanders' habit was to avoid saying the name of the islet. More superstition, but Tobias didn't blame them. Human superstition was understandable. Their vision was so narrow, and he knew that deep in their subconscious they must constantly feel the press of the vast darkness stretching around their tiny flames. No wonder they clung to stories, searching for rules that would keep them safe. 'Did you go ashore?'

Hammer shook his head. 'Close enough to see some smoke. Someone has a fire.'

Tobias considered the possibilities. In the summer, a wildfire was possible. Unlikely, but possible. In the cold damp clutches of late February, it was inconceivable. Winter pressed against his side, not making any sound, but clearly picking up on his tension. 'I need you to take me to Àite Marbh.'

Hammer crossed his arms. 'It's too dark.'

'Tomorrow then. First light.'

'I don't know about that. No one goes there.'

'You can stay in the boat. Just get me close enough to wade ashore.' He felt bad, looking at the conflict drawn clearly on Hammer's roughly hewn face, but the dead island had been quiet for centuries and he had to make sure it stayed that way.

AFTER DINNER, Luke got up to clear the plates. Esme watched him move around her kitchen, putting things away and starting on the dishes in the sink.

'Leave those,' Esme said. 'I'll do them later.'

'You cooked,' he protested. He began rinsing the plates.

Having turned down a second glass of wine, Esme put the kettle on to make tea. 'You want coffee?'

He shook his head. 'I'll have what you're having.'

'You won't like it. Spearmint.'

'Ah, okay. What's the one that makes you feel like you're on fire?'

Esme thought for a moment. 'The one with ginger and turmeric?'

'Yeah, I think so. I'll have that, please.'

Esme would have thought that Luke would have avoided that particular feeling after touching a hexed book that almost made him combust. His fever had been so swift and so high, he had been in mortal danger, and he had said it had felt as if he was burning alive.

As if mirroring her thoughts, Luke added. 'It's weird that I like that sensation now.'

He had filled the sink with fresh hot soapy water and was making short work of the washing up.

'How do you feel? In general?'

'All better.' He turned his head to smile reassuringly. 'I promise.'

'You want me to stop asking?'

'I like that you care,' Luke said diplomatically.

With his hands occupied in the hot water, Esme stepped behind Luke and put her own hands around his waist. He went still as she ran her hands over his t-shirt, feeling the planes of his chest and stomach beneath. Their bodies were close, she was pressed up against his back to give her roving hands access, and her front felt alive with sensation. After a few minutes, in which she wasn't sure that Luke took a breath, Esme stepped away and finished making the tea. Luke resumed washing up.

They hadn't talked about it, but Luke seemed to sense

that she needed to feel in control in their more intimate moments. Kissing was going very well indeed, but they had yet to progress further. He seemed to be happy to let her conduct her experiments, never pushing.

Esme could feel her cheeks flaming and her own breathing didn't seem to want to calm down. She focused on brewing the tea. Luke might not be pushing, but her own body seemed to have a mind of its own. And that mind wanted to progress things physically. If only her brain would stop throwing up panicked roadblocks. Every time she contemplated getting naked with Luke, she felt a deluge of self-doubt that doused her libido like a bucket of iced water. Ryan's voice, mostly banished, would start whispering. She didn't believe that voice any longer, but a small part of her was still worried that if Luke saw her without her clothes, he would be disappointed. She had seen enough of his naked body to know that it was all hard muscle and angles. Hers was decidedly squashy.

Once they were both sat at the kitchen table with their mugs of tea, Luke stretched his legs out to the side. Esme knew he was avoiding crowding her, but she hadn't minded the way their knees had met underneath the table, his legs tangling in hers. She was determined to push Ryan's voice all the way down again, not to let him spoil her current happiness. Besides, if she didn't get braver with Luke, he might get tired of waiting. She gulped some mint tea.

'You look thoughtful,' Luke said.

'I found a glamour spell in a book. I was thinking it was the sort of thing that Kate Foster used.'

He shook his head. 'I don't understand why anyone would risk their health like that.'

'Easy for you to say.'

'What do you mean?'

Esme made a vague gesture with her hand, sketching Luke in the air. 'You look like you.'

He smiled slowly, then. The light in his eyes making his whole face ten times sexier. 'You like the way I look?'

'Don't fish. Every human with a pulse likes the way you look.'

'I don't think that's true,' Luke said. His face creased in concern, and his tone went from teasing to serious. 'Are you upset?'

Esme was about to say 'no', but she realised it wasn't true. She grimaced. 'Thinking about Kate Foster.'

'Ah.'

'I can't stop worrying that I could have helped her. But I'm angry with her, and sort of glad she didn't pull through and that makes me feel really bad.' Tobias had heard via DS Robinson that Kate Foster had died the previous week. She never woke up from the coma and had, apparently, suffered a massive seizure.

'She did really bad things before you ever met her,' Luke said gently. 'She was too far gone.'

He was trying to make her feel better, but Esme couldn't take the comfort. 'This is supposed to be a place of sanctuary. Everyone here has a past, but the island is a safe place. The island let her stay here. What if I let it down by not helping?'

'You feel like you let the island down?' Luke was speaking carefully, a crease between his brows.

'You think that's daft. I know it's a place, not a person.'

'I don't think it's daft, but I do think you are taking too much responsibility for Kate Foster's actions. You are not the only island resident, for starters. And it wasn't your fault. None of it. She literally took her own life when she swallowed that...' he trailed off. 'Whatever that was.'

Esme had assumed that Kate had cursed a small object

and that had been what she had swallowed. One of the books she had found in the hidden storeroom of Luke's shop had been entirely filled with lethal curses. Ones that were fused to objects usually took days to work to their full effect, but if ingested that time was sped up considerably. They hadn't been given details from the hospital, as they weren't family. Not that she expected the hospital would have recognised what they would have found. 'How do I stop being angry with her? It doesn't feel right now that she's dead, but she could have killed you. Destroyed the bookshop.'

'But she didn't. Because of you.'

THE NEXT DAY, Tobias and Hammer were silent in the boat. They hadn't left until long past midday, with Hammer insisting on food and then checking over his boat in what Tobias recognised as a delaying tactic. He understood that the man did not want to sail to the islet. He knew that every atom of his being would be rebelling against the thought, so he waited patiently while Hammer prepared and prevaricated.

A brisk wind had sprung up as soon as they took to the sea, blowing directly against them as if trying to turn their boat around. Winter was back on Unholy Island, safely shut in Hammer's boat house, although he had whined pitifully when they had closed the door on him. 'I'll not take him to that place,' Tobias had said, his voice leaden with a dread that had settled in Hammer's stomach.

Hammer used the motor to get them within reach of Àite Marbh, and then rowed them around to a landing spot where the islet dipped down to meet the sea.

He manoeuvred the craft until the hull scraped sand and then made to climb out.

'You don't have to,' Tobias said. He didn't have to raise his voice as the wind that had battled them for every inch of the journey had abruptly dropped and the air was eerily still. 'You can wait here.'

Hammer answered by clambering over the front of the small boat and onto the sand. Tobias followed, and they both hauled the boat further up.

A line of scrubby trees and bushes hid the rest of the islet from view, black against the pale grey of the sky. Tobias hadn't set foot on Àite Marbh in more than fifty years, and every part of his body remembered why. Goosebumps broke out across his skin and, ancient though he was, he felt a child's urge to run away. There was an emptiness here. An absence that was like a hole in the world.

He looked at the large man who was standing with him. Hammer was a fighter and a survivor. His face was a mask, but his skin was paler than usual and pulled taut across the cage of his skull. Tobias could sense the tension radiating from him as he scanned the environment, looking for the threat that he could feel in his bones.

Tobias spoke first, his voice leaden. 'Where was the smoke?'

Hammer pointed to the left and they began moving together, their footsteps loud in the uncanny silence.

After a few steps, Hammer spoke. 'It's so quiet.'

'No birds.' Other small islands like this were havens for seabirds. Handa and Skomer hosted enormous guillemot breeding populations, the Farne Islands had puffins and terns. 'Nothing lives here,' Tobias said.

Hammer's expression betrayed nothing, but Tobias sensed the big man's scepticism. It would be warring with the evidence of his senses, and Tobias felt compassion for him. 'This island might be called dead place, but it's the other way around. A place for the dead.'

They had been walking up an incline and now they reached the top of the rise. The hidden side of the island was revealed, a bowl shape with jagged rocks rising up on the side that faced the mainland. Laid out below was a small plain of low ground with a grassy mound roughly in the middle.

'There's nobody here,' Hammer said. He produced a small pair of binoculars from his coat pocket and scanned the area.

The air was still. The grass down the slope and across the mound unmoving. Tobias began picking his way down the slope to the middle of the island. Two large stones, planted upright five thousand years ago, marked the proper way to approach the cairn. This was a place for the dead. It always had been, since before there were beings sentient enough to name it as such. The mound was a monument and a resting place. Tobias knew that Neolithic kings slept inside, along with their wives and children. Their ghosts did not trouble him. Not even the smallest ones. There was something else he feared.

CHAPTER THREE

Hammer watched the mayor pick his way down the slope. There was a ring of higher ground enclosing a flat area, which contained a small grassy hill in its centre. It looked landscaped, not entirely natural. After a moment, he followed.

Tobias skirted the edge of the flat area and stepped between two large rocks before approaching the mound. Without thinking about it too hard, Hammer did the same. Something was very wrong in this place, and he was following his instincts. Hammer might not believe half of the weird things that were talked about on Unholy Island, but he had seen enough to know there was substance to the other half. And he knew that just because he didn't have all the information in a given situation, didn't mean he couldn't get hurt by it. He hadn't stayed alive this long without obeying his gut.

Once on the flat ground, they moved around to the west of the small hill. Tobias seemed to be moving with purpose, but before Hammer could ask what he was looking for, he saw it. A rectangle of black against the green grass.

ESME CLIMBED the stairs to her studio, intending to spend the day painting. By lunchtime she was feeling frustrated with her brushes, her pigments, the canvas and herself. The seascapes that she was always so compelled to paint calmed her. Usually, the act of creating sky and waves from brushstrokes, the layering of colour and unexpected interplay between those layers, drew a deep quiet that was like the meditation sessions with Bee. But even better as she wasn't supposed to be doing anything other than getting paint onto the canvas. There were no other expectations placed upon her and she was free to think or not think, suspended in time.

Today, however, something strange had happened. She had picked up her brush, expecting to add the final touches of paint to an almost-finished piece. A few highlights, mixed from titanium white and cadmium yellow, added to the places where the light caught the tops of the waves. Instead, without noticing, she had somehow loaded her brush with Brown Madder and Davy's Grey. Before she was fully aware of what her hand was doing, she had painted a dark shape in the middle of her calm blue sea. She took a step back from the canvas, one hand still clutching the brush and the other over her mouth. The islet loomed from the water where she had not intended to paint it at all. She felt sick looking at the brutal interruption to her carefully layered waves, but couldn't tear her gaze from it. The picture was ruined.

TOBIAS HAD BEEN STANDING in silence in front of the entrance to the tomb for over half an hour. Hammer kept scanning the bowl-shaped ground, expecting to see movement over the ridge at any moment. The middle of the island felt as dead as the beach where they had landed. The air was so still that he could barely feel it on his skin and there wasn't a sound other than his breathing. It wasn't natural. And his eyes were playing tricks. He couldn't help but see creatures appearing over that stark edge. His mind didn't conjure people but crouched skittering monsters, straight out of a horror film. Hammer didn't consider himself a man of imagination, but it appeared to be getting the better of him in this strange place.

Finally, Tobias turned from his position. His face was the same as it always was. A kindly looking old geezer. The sort of man with a tidy garden, adoring grandkids, and a freshly hoovered car.

He shook his head. Just once. And then walked across the ground to join Hammer.

'It's all right,' he said. 'Nothing has changed. I couldn't see anything.'

Hammer wondered what Tobias had expected to see, standing at the entrance like that, but he didn't ask. If the old boy hadn't fancied walking inside that weird old hill, Hammer wasn't going to be the one to challenge him on it. Apart from anything else, he didn't want to go inside himself and wanted, pretty fucking keenly, now he allowed himself to think about it, to leave the dead island as soon as possible. Hammer felt a strange disinclination to turn his back on the mound, but he made himself do it. He had been in car crashes and knife fights. He wasn't going to let a tiny hill with a door in the side freak him out. Besides, it was the quickest way to get the fuck out of this place.

They had taken three steps away from the hill when Tobias stopped.

'Hell's bells,' he muttered, and Hammer felt the hairs on his arm stand up.

He didn't want to turn back, but did it quickly. Like making yourself look at a knife wound to assess the damage.

The hill looked the same. An unnatural-looking shape, covered in unmoving grass.

'Did you hear that?' Tobias asked, his hand on Hammer's arm, as if holding him back.

Hammer shook his head.

Tobias was stock still, his chin lifted and eyes fixed on some faraway point as he listened.

Hammer listened, too. It was all eerie silence. A silence that was so wrong it made him want to throw up the bacon roll he'd eaten earlier.

The seconds ticked by and Hammer fought the urge to grab Tobias's arm and drag him back to the boat. He wanted to row them both the fuck away from this place and never come back.

Hammer refocused on Tobias. His spine was, impossibly, even straighter than usual. He looked like an octogenarian soldier, but his eyes were sad. 'I have to go inside.' Tobias sounded almost apologetic. 'You can wait here if you want.'

'I'll come with you,' Hammer said immediately. He wasn't being a hero. Nothing on earth could make him stay in this place on his own. He wasn't going to think about that very hard. It was just the truth.

The entrance to the hill was a neat rectangle, formed by horizontally laid stones. The vegetation on the hill shrouded the stone structure almost entirely, leaving just the edges of the entrance visible. The earth and grass of the hill was like the flesh and skin of a giant creature, the stone structure beneath, the skeleton. Hammer immediately wished he hadn't thought of it that way. Both men ducked as they walked through the dark doorway. *Into the belly of the beast.*

It wasn't a beast, though. It was a stone passage. Surprisingly neat and clean. Hammer didn't know what he had expected from a structure made five thousand years ago, but it wasn't this. He always kept a Maglite torch in the inside pocket of his jacket and he switched it on, playing the beam over the slabs that formed the passage and revealing openings spaced up ahead, presumably leading to other passages or chambers.

Tobias was in front of him, moving slowly up the passage and partially blocking Hammer's view. He raised a hand behind him and waved it. 'Turn off the torch.'

Hammer did not want to do that. He anticipated the total darkness, knowing he would be able to feel the pressing air in this strange place, but to be blind to it. His hindbrain stirred uncomfortably. He did not want to be blind in this place. But he trusted Tobias. And would be the first to admit that he was out of his depth. He clicked the button on the end of the torch.

Their breathing seemed louder in the dark. Hammer stared into the total black, willing his eyes to adjust. He waited for Tobias to speak. Waited for him to say that they could turn around and get out. But the longer he waited, the more he realised that he couldn't hear Tobias breathing, only himself.

Tobias had been just in front of him, his brain insisted. An arm's length away at most. And the passage was narrow. Hammer's shoulders brushed the stone on either side as he had entered, and he could feel it hadn't widened much.

As Hammer waited for some vision to return, he felt a deep conviction that Tobias wasn't there anymore. That he was alone underneath the ground. His breathing was loud, rasping in and out, and his heart was pounding. He couldn't remember a fear like this. It was as if the ground above and below was squeezing him.

He blinked and tried to regulate his breathing. Called on the old techniques to calm his limbic system. Nobody was fearless, you just learned to control it. Or use it. Hammer was largely self-taught, stuff he had learned through experience. He had learned quickly when he was young. As soon as he grew into the kind of figure that made people turn to him for help or for other men to challenge. Like he was challenging them to a fight just by existing. But there had been one guy. Ex-forces. He had been very smart and talked about the parasympathetic nervous system and the vagus nerve and taught breathing exercises. Hammer thumped his chest, now, trying to activate his, remembering too late that he was supposed to press on his chest, not hit himself. But all the trying to remember had distracted him enough so that he was able to take a breath. Panic over. Job done.

He was going to get out, he decided. He would tell Tobias and then he would turn around and get out. Or he wouldn't bother turning around, he would just walk backwards. Until he was clear of the hill. Either worked.

His eyes had adjusted to the dark and there was something up ahead. A rough rectangle of not-black. It had to be one of the openings in the passage. Perhaps the main passage continued that way and it was lighter because it led to another doorway? An exit. But Hammer knew there was a way out behind him. Much closer. And he didn't think he could physically take another step into the hill.

Besides. The grey rectangle up ahead told him one thing. Tobias was no longer in the passage.

CHAPTER FOUR

Tobias knew two things for certain – that Hammer was following him and that he was inside a burial cairn. He clung to those facts and tried to focus on his surroundings in order to anchor himself. He considered the cairn. The openings along the central passage led to chambers which held the remains of Neolithic kings. Not that they would have been called kings, then. Mayors of towns. No, not mayors, that wasn't right either. They were the heads of family groups. The natural leaders in the small communities of humans that had scraped an existence using stone tools and collaboration.

The stones were piled with regularity, an interlinking pattern that had held for thousands of years. It was a place for the dead. On the surface, it was common sense. Humans following their animal instincts to keep dead, rotting material away from their hearth and home. But Àite Marbh was more than that. Tobias remembered when the islands were born. It looked like they rose, but really the sea was receding.

Tobias had known this place when it was a hole in the world. He didn't remember how long he had been standing in the cairn. Time had stretched or folded. It had done something, he was sure of that. He was as certain about that as he was that Hammer was no longer behind him. Or that he was no longer in the same place. He felt something shift under his feet, and then the sharp shock of cold water. His physical body was catching up to what his mind already knew. He was no longer in the cairn on the small island of Àite Marbh.

Esme walked into The Rising Moon with Luke. It was the first time they had done so publicly. They had eaten together there countless times, of course, and had probably walked in together before, too, but this felt like the first time. They had been at the bookshop and had lost the last hour or so kissing and talking and kissing some more. Now, her lips still tingling and face flushed, they were walking into the pub as a couple. Her hand was in Luke's as they walked the short distance from the bookshop and he didn't drop it as they stepped into the pub.

A fire crackled in the large fireplace and the copper pots that were mounted along one wall glowed in the lamp-light. Fiona and Hamish were at the largest table, right in the middle of the room. Fiona was wearing a cheery red knitted jumper, and she glanced away from Hamish, who was sitting in a wooden high chair and had something yellow smeared across his face. Her greeting died on her lips and her smile changed to a strange, unfathomable expression and then back to a smile again in rapid succession.

'Hello,' Luke said easily and Esme wondered if he had noticed Fiona's confusion.

Everyone knew that sitting at the big table was an invitation to join in and that folk wanting solitude would choose one of the small tables dotted around the perimeter of the room. Luke squeezed her hand reassuringly and Esme saw Fiona noticing their clasped hands. She sat opposite Fiona and began studying the menu. Which was ridiculous, as she knew it off by heart. The specials were on a chalkboard on the wall and that was the only place a local needed to look. And *that* was only if they failed to pay attention when Seren explained the choices.

'And how are you, young man?' Luke was asking Hamish. In response, Hamish gave him a slow, level look that suggested he had his suspicions. Or it might have been incomprehension at being addressed as if he were a nineteenth-century gentleman instead of a toddler.

'He's a wee bit shy,' Fiona said, retrieving a plastic spoon that Hamish had flung onto the floor.

'How's he sleeping now?'

Fiona made a seesawing motion with one hand. 'Not bad.'

'It's worth it, I bet,' Luke said.

Fiona's answering smile chased the last of Esme's discomfort away. She was a reserved woman, but Esme had forged a friendship that she felt she could rely on. She had already told Fiona, in private, about her relationship with Luke, and she was bolstered by her presence.

'Do you have siblings?' Fiona asked Luke.

'Just my twin,' Luke replied, leaning back in his chair and stretching one arm behind Esme. They had agreed to go public, but it still made Esme feel strange. She leaned forward.

'Oh aye,' Fiona was concentrating on passing food to Hamish and catching pieces of bread and potato and apple that occasionally went sailing over the side. She was remarkably fast. 'No wee ones to look after while you were growing up, then?'

'No,' Luke said. 'It was just the two of us.'

Esme's discomfort was back. Talk of family was always difficult. She had come to terms with her own lack in that department, but it didn't mean she enjoyed thinking about it. And seeing the easy way Luke interacted with Hamish opened a small, secret door inside herself.

Thankfully, Seren arrived, rattling through the options with her usual efficiency. 'Venison casserole, please,' Esme said. She could smell the food from the kitchen, and her mouth was already watering.

'Same for me.' Luke was ignoring the way that Seren was staring at the position of his arm.

'And a glass of wine,' Esme added. She was leaning as far forward as possible, her elbows on the table.

Seren quirked one of her perfect eyebrows. 'Special occasion is it?' She looked at Luke significantly.

Esme knew that her face was no longer just flushed, but probably the same shade as Fiona's knitted jumper.

Seren had moved away before Esme had time to formulate a response.

'Rat-dit!' Hamish announced, abruptly shoving the bowl on his tray table. He arched his back as if wanting to physically distance himself from the food.

Esme thought it was comical until she realised she had been doing the same thing by leaning forward away from Luke's arm.

'Rat-dit?' Luke asked, his voice competing with Hamish's, as the boy was now chanting the word with increasing volume and urgency.

Fiona transferred the food from the highchair and onto the main table. She calmly tore a wipe from a packet, and wiped Hamish's hands and face with practised movements, before delving into her bag to produce a board book.

'Rabbits,' she explained. 'Here you go,' she passed the

book to Hamish, whose chanting immediately stopped. A beatific smile broke out across his face and he grabbed the book, waving it triumphantly.

'Sorry,' Fiona said. 'Talk amongst yourselves. I'll just have to...' She helped Hamish to open it and began reading upside down, Hamish turning the chunky pages.

'So,' Luke said, turning to Esme. His eyes were crinkled and his lips curved in a warm smile. 'How are you coping?'

'Great. Good. Fine.'

'Uh-huh?' Luke cut his eyes to his arm on the back of her chair and the gap between it and her body. She was still leaning her elbows on the table, her body rigid with tension.

There was a pause in which she didn't move.

'Too soon?' Luke asked after another moment. He withdrew his arm and Esme felt her stomach dip. She had disappointed him.

He smiled at her, no sign of anger, and she allowed herself a breath. It was Luke. She didn't have to be afraid of disappointing him, of his disapproval. He wasn't Ryan. She wondered how many times she would have to remind herself of that fact, whether the shadow of her past would ever detach and float away. I have no need of you, she whispered in her mind. *Go away.*

The door opened, letting in a blast of fresh air. Matteo walked in, raising a hand in greeting.

'Usual?' Seren asked.

Matteo nodded and came to sit at the table. He hesitated before taking the chair next to Fiona. She was bunched up next to the highchair, reading the rabbit book for the third time in a row.

Hamish was distracted by the newcomer. He splayed a hand onto the pages and stared at Matteo.

Matteo stared back. After a long moment, he pulled a

sudden, surprisingly silly face, tongue lolling out and eyes crossed.

Hamish didn't laugh. He continued his long hard stare, same as the one he had given Luke.

Matteo shrugged and smiled.

'He'll warm up,' Fiona said with an apologetic smile for Matteo. 'Won't you, wee man?' She addressed Hamish, who shoved the book away and held his arms up in the international gesture for 'lift me up'.

Seren returned with two plates of venison casserole. Then, digging into the wide pocket in the front of her apron, she produced a small pot of yoghurt and placed it onto Hamish's tray. He immediately dropped his arms and lunged for the pot.

'What's it like having a twin?' Fiona asked Luke, while peeling the lid on the yoghurt.

Luke shrugged. 'I don't know anything different.'

'You always had a pal to play with, though.' She was watching Hamish attack the yoghurt with his plastic spoon and Esme saw the worry on her face. 'I always felt bad for Euan.'

'Whatever happens, he's got you,' Luke said.

'That feels like one of those kind lies,' Fiona said. Then, she added, 'Sorry. Sorry, that was blunt, it's just...'

'I know. You worry. You want what's best for him.'

'And Hamish has you and a big brother,' Esme added. 'Euan dotes on him.'

Matteo was writing in his notepad. He showed it to Luke and Esme was able to read it.

Do you have a psychic link?

'With Lewis?'

Luke didn't seem at all thrown by the question and Esme wondered if it was one of the top ten conversational gambits for identical twins. She supposed that people were probably fascinated by the phenomenon and that undoubtedly led to intrusive queries.

'I used to think so,' he said and smiled at Matteo. 'When we were kids, I was convinced I knew what he was thinking, and he definitely seemed to know what I was thinking, feeling, whatever...'

'Not anymore?' Esme asked.

Luke laughed, a little self-conscious. 'No. I mean, it's impossible. Back then, we were just similar enough and living in the same situation and with the same people, so it was easy to pretend.'

'You pretended?'

'No, I mean... imagine. It was easy to look at each other and guess what the other was thinking, and it felt like a connection. That is having a connection, I suppose. But since we've been apart, living different lives, it doesn't feel like that anymore. I'm sure most siblings can tell what the other is thinking. It's just familiarity.'

'I wouldn't know,' Esme said. She was aiming for light and airy but Luke's eyes crinkled in sympathy.

BEE ARRIVED while they were finishing their meals. Fiona had released Hamish from his highchair and was following him around the pub, holding his hand as he toddled about and making sure he didn't get too close to the fire. He babbled away happily, occasionally shrieking or laughing. It was a pleasant sound and made the pub feel homely.

Bee nodded a greeting and ordered quickly. She fell into a conversation with Matteo about hardy plants. Matteo wanted to get things growing in planters at the front of the shop and wanted advice. He was distracted, though, his eyes following Fiona and Hamish as they moved around the room.

Esme put her knife and fork together on her plate and finished the last of her wine. She wanted to ask Luke if he was all right. He had been quiet since the subject of Lewis had been raised earlier, and she wondered if he was thinking about him. As far as she knew, there had been no further communication. Luke had shown her the message that had said 'stop looking for me' and Hammer's follow up request for 'proof of life'.

She leaned in and spoke quietly. 'Are you thinking about Lewis?'

He gave her a sad smile. 'Not as much as I should.'

'You've done everything you can.' She put a hand on his arm and squeezed gently.

'Have I?' Luke shook his head. 'I don't know...'

She thought he was going to add something else, but the door flew open and Hammer strode in. He was a commanding presence at any time, but was wild-eyed and accompanied by a distressed-looking Winter. The black labrador had his head low, ears back and his tail tucked between his legs. He let out a low whine.

Everyone in the pub looked at him and the strange sight of Winter without his master. All conversation stopped.

Hammer almost growled the words, his register so low it made them difficult to make out. 'Tobias has gone.'

CHAPTER FIVE

B ee stood up. 'What do you mean?'
Seren appeared from the kitchen, a tea towel over one shoulder and carrying Bee's meal. She stopped at the sight of Hammer and Winter.

Hammer pushed wet hair from his eyes and looked around at them all. 'We went to Àite Marbh.'

There was a collective gasp and Fiona tsked loudly as if Hammer had sworn.

Bee's expression was tight-lipped, but her eyes burned.

'We were together. This close...' Hammer stretched out an arm to demonstrate. 'And he just disappeared.'

'On the islet?' Bee snapped.

'Inside,' Hammer said, meeting her gaze. 'There was a mound, a hill. We went underneath.'

'Oh shit.'

Esme looked at Bee. She didn't think she had heard the woman swear before.

Hamish, probably picking up on the sudden tension, began to cry. Fiona lifted him up for a cuddle.

'What is it?' Esme was watching Bee carefully. If any

of them would know, it would be her. Or one of her sisters. 'Where is he?'

'Between,' Bee said after a pause. 'If I had to guess.'

AFTER THAT, Bee left in a hurry, and Esme and Luke went soon after. Esme found she couldn't stand to be around the group and their questions. Questions without answers.

Leaving the pub with Luke, she knew she didn't want to be entirely alone either. Luke offered to stay with her and she accepted. 'Just for company,' she added awkwardly.

'I know,' Luke said. 'Until you say otherwise, I won't think anything else.'

Back at Strand House, she had offered various beverages and snacks, but Luke had turned it all down. He looked as spooked as she felt, and they agreed to head upstairs.

'I'll stay until you fall asleep and then I'll go home,' Luke said, when Esme came out of the bathroom. She had brushed her teeth and changed into flannel pyjamas.

'You can stay,' Esme said. 'I won't make you sleep on the floor.'

He looked at the double bed.

She looked at the double bed, suddenly uncertain. She trusted Luke, but the urge she had felt for him to stay with her, for the comforting solidity of his presence, was dissolving in the face of the reality. Could she really sleep with a man so close by? Would her subconscious feel a threat and wake her up with one of her nightmares? She hadn't really suffered for years, but what if they came back? He would see her shouting and sweating, a wild and mad woman. Her flannel pyjamas felt gossamer thin, and he was suddenly very close, even though he hadn't moved an inch.

Luke seemed to sense her discomfort and he moved to the other side of the bed, sitting on top of the covers and arranging a couple of pillows so that he could sit upright. He flipped the duvet open on the other side, inviting her to get underneath.

Esme tore her gaze from his legs. His long, jeans-clad legs were on her bed. He was wearing navy wool socks. His Viking god body was filling the left side of her bed. Her duvet cover was white with tiny spring flowers embroidered all over it. The blanket at the end of the bed was a crocheted rainbow. Her mind seemed to be intent on cataloguing the familiar items, as if trying to reassure her that the world hadn't changed. That things were safely the same.

'We can go back downstairs to talk, if you want,' Luke said. His tone was gentle and easy, and his eyes were kind.

Esme felt the tension flow out of her chest. The small inner voice that she thought of as her true self, the one she had been nurturing and trying to hear, told her that she was safe, that all was well. And that she really wanted Luke Taylor in her bed. She flushed, telling her true self to pipe down and not start trying to run before she could walk. 'That's okay,' she said. 'I'm shattered.'

He smiled, bigger this time.

She got into bed and he flipped the duvet back over her legs. 'You can lie down. If you want.'

She wanted him to hold her, but didn't want it to mean anything else. She felt numb from the news about Tobias and startlingly awake because Luke was in her bedroom, inches from her flannel-clad arm.

'I can't get my head around it,' Luke said. 'How can he be just gone?'

Bee had explained to Esme before that there were other worlds, other realities, that were layered up alongside our own. 'This is all metaphor,' she said. 'It's hard to talk about because we don't have the right language in this world.'

Apparently, some of these realities were far away, and some were very close. And there are physical places in our world where the membrane between the realities is very thin. When Bee said that Tobias had 'gone between', Esme guessed that she meant that he had slipped through the membrane and into another reality.

'I know this is a stupid thing to say, but I need to say it anyway. Shouldn't we tell the police or something?'

Esme turned to her bedside table to take a sip from the glass of water she kept there. She was glad he couldn't see her expression. 'I don't think they can help,' she said.

The tiredness that had been dogging her all day swooped in. She had intended to prop up her pillows and sit up next to Luke, but now she found she didn't want to be upright for a moment longer. She laid down, curled onto her side, one hand underneath her cheek. Speaking quietly while facing away from him, and not sure whether he would even hear her, she let the quietest part of her say the thing it most wanted. 'Will you hold me?'

MATTEO LEFT The Rising Moon at the same time as Fiona. He held the door for her and she was grateful for the simple kindness. Hamish was wriggling in her arms, fussy and tired. 'I need to get this one to bed,' she said at her front door.

Matteo smiled and nodded. His eyes were soft and Fiona had the distinct impression that he wanted to speak. She waited for a beat, giving him the opportunity, but

Hamish was reaching for the front door, arms outstretched and pulling her off balance. She shifted her stance to avoid falling, and Matteo backed away. He raised a hand in farewell and turned to walk to his shop.

Inside, Fiona focused on Hamish's bedtime routine. Warming his milk, dressing him in soft cotton pyjamas, reading his favourite stories. Finally, she wound the dial on the chunky plastic music box. It projected waves and fish onto the ceiling and played a lullaby. Euan had liked it as a baby, and she was glad she had kept it.

Closing the door softly, she went to the living room to sit down. Euan had emerged from his bedroom and was sprawled on the sofa, all gangly limbs and one arm stretched up behind his head. Fiona had an acute understanding that she was straddling two stages of motherhood. And then the realisation that, despite all of the protective thoughts she had thrown up – not to get too attached, that Hamish didn't belong to her, and that his real mother might change her mind and ask for him back – she felt like he was hers. She felt motherly toward Hamish and there was no amount of rationalising that would prevent it.

'You all right, love?' She focused her attention on the half-boy-half-man prone on the furniture.

He rolled his head, and as soon as he saw her face, he sat up. 'What's wrong?'

Fiona sank onto the nearest seat and prepared to explain the inexplicable to her firstborn.

WINTER STUCK to Hammer's side all the way back to the boathouse. He wasn't a small dog and a less solid man would probably have been knocked over by the dog pressing against his legs as he walked. The moon was almost full and he didn't need his torch for the path from the village to Harbour Bay.

The stove was banked up and Hammer woke up the fire to chase the damp chill of the evening. He thought Winter would be more comfortable in his own home, but the idea of staying in Tobias's house was unthinkable. Better to consider this a strange one-off aberration. Nothing permanent.

He didn't feel hungry, but warmed up a tin of stew on the stove. He opened a second tin and emptied it into a bowl, which he put down for Winter, along with a dish of water. He would need to get dog food, he supposed. Maybe he ought to pick up supplies from Tobias's house. His mind rebelled again at this line of thought. Tobias would be back tomorrow. Winter would be back with his master, in North House where they both belonged.

There was a knock on the door and Hammer opened it quickly, expecting Tobias to be standing there, ready to take his dog and his rightful place in Hammer's life. Constant.

It was Bee. Her long hair was braided, as usual, but strands had escaped, forming a halo around her face. 'I need you to tell me what happened.'

'I already did,' Hammer said, but he stepped back so that Bee could enter.

She shook her head. 'You come outside. Winter, stay.'

Winter whined softly, but when Hammer stepped outside to join Bee, he left his position of leg limpet and allowed Hammer to close the door. He left it ajar, making sure that Winter could come outside if he really wanted to. He knew what it was like to be imprisoned and it didn't sit right with him to do it to anyone, even a dog.

Bee took a few paces away from the doorway, and it struck Hammer that she didn't want to speak in front of the dog. He had clearly been on Unholy Island for too long, as it didn't even seem odd.

She stuck her hands into her pockets, face serious. 'What were you doing on Àite Marbh?'

And there it was. The question he couldn't really answer. He was the enforcer on the island. He was prosaic. There when heavy things needed to be lifted or a rowdy tourist escorted out of the pub. He was there to provide an air of menace so that just his presence ensured there wasn't any trouble. And, if there was trouble, he was there to deal with it. This was above his pay grade, and he felt a stab of resentment.

'I saw a light. Moving.' He pointed to the islet. Its dark silhouette was deepest black against the night sky. His gaze skidded away, unwilling to look at it for long.

'Like someone using a torch?'

He nodded. 'Then there was smoke.'

'And Tobias volunteered to go with you?'

'He saw the fire,' Hammer said, hating his defensive tone. 'It wasn't just me.'

'Okay,' Bee said. 'You decided together to go to Àite Marbh.'

He couldn't maintain eye contact with Bee's pale blue stare. 'Yeah.'

'And you didn't think to ask what I thought?' The words were crisp.

'No.' Hammer didn't embellish. He wasn't a big one for talking at the best of times, and this was one of the very worst. He felt bad enough about Tobias going missing on his watch, he wasn't going to compound it by making excuses.

'And then what happened? Exactly.'

Hammer tried to recount the trip to the islet. The

mound. The doorway. Tobias being there and not there in the blink of an eye.

'Did you see anything else?' Bee was still searching his face, her gaze intent. 'Could be anything at all.'

'No.'

Bee's lips tightened. 'No lights or creatures or things that might have seemed like hallucinations?'

He shook his head.

'Even a strange smell or sound. Anything out of the ordinary?'

'It was very quiet.' Hammer remembered now. The eerie stillness of the small island.

'And Tobias went in first?'

'Yeah. I was going to wait outside, but I followed him. He was right in front of me.' Hammer held up his arm to demonstrate. 'I could touch him.'

'What happened?'

'And then I couldn't.' Hammer let his arm fall. 'He was just gone.'

CHAPTER SIX

On the morning after Tobias went missing, a fog rolled across Unholy Island. It coated the land, hugged the village buildings and hid the pathways. The familiar landmarks of the island, the castle and causeway and the ruined church, were all disguised in thick grey robes. Bee liked fresh air and always slept with her bedroom window wide open. She woke up to find the thick mist in her bedroom. An uninvited guest that hung in a sullen miasma around her bed and made everything beyond murky and indistinct. She closed her window and got dressed quickly in clothes that were slightly damp. It was going to be a long day.

Luke woke up in Esme's bedroom. He remembered lying down. Esme's sleepy voice telling him it was okay if he wanted to sleep where he was and him saying that he would just wait for her to fall asleep and then he would go. He had pulled the pillows down and wrapped his arms around her, listened to her breathing as it became deep and regular. And he must have fallen asleep.

He was still fully dressed, but had shifted underneath the duvet during the night. Esme had pushed her half of the duvet down in the night and was curled up against his body, her head on his torso and one arm flung around his waist. Her wavy brown hair was spread across his chest, and his hand itched with the urge to touch it. His other arm was stretched underneath her and he stayed completely still, worried about waking her up and how she might feel when she realised she was cuddled up to him.

A loud yowling sound from outside the bedroom door reverberated loudly, shattering the early morning quiet. Esme opened her eyes and lifted her head. 'I shut Jet out,' she said, wiping the side of her face self-consciously.

'He's not best pleased,' Luke said.

Esme's cheeks were flushed pink, and he wondered if she had ever looked so pretty. He knew that part of his body was responding to waking up and was pressing against his jeans. He hoped, fervently, that Esme hadn't noticed.

Her gaze flicked down and he sat up quickly, hoping to hide any evidence. 'Shall I let him in?'

'Better had, he won't stop...' Esme was back on her side of the bed, the duvet pulled up to her chin.

Luke swung his legs off the bed and crossed to the door. Esme's cat didn't seem particularly grateful to him for opening the door, but he stopped yowling at least. Luke scowled at the little bastard as he leapt onto the bed and rubbed the top of his head against Esme's chin.

'I'll go and make coffee.' He scrubbed his face, trying to fully wake up.

'Tea for me, please,' Esme replied, focusing on the furry interloper.

Downstairs, Luke realised he was smiling as he made the hot drinks. He was still worried about Tobias, of course, and it was no time to be happy, but he couldn't help it. He had stayed the night in Esme's bed. Whatever worries her conscious mind threw up, her body had relaxed enough to sleep next to him and to curl up close. He wrapped his arms around his own torso, remembering the feel of Esme's arm across his middle, the weight of her head on his chest.

Through the window, the garden was obscured by a thick sea fog. It pressed against the glass as if it wanted to come into the warmth of the house and was oppressively, obnoxiously grey. He turned away from it, thinking of the woman upstairs. However bad the weather, however worried he was about Tobias, he knew one thing for certain: he was exactly where he wanted to be.

With some relief, Bee discovered that the fog hadn't got further than her bedroom. She walked downstairs and found Diana in the main room of The Three Sisters' house. The plants grew energetically and bloomed all year round, and Diana was talking to a particularly vigorous fern. She had small secateurs in one hand and was patiently explaining to the plant that it needed to stay beneath the ceiling or its leaves would go black.

'We have a problem.'

Diana put the secateurs onto the nearest surface and gave Bee a reassuring smile. 'I doubt that.'

'Tobias has gone.'

A beat. The tiniest frown appeared on Diana's smooth and healthy skin. 'What do you mean, gone? To the mainland?'

Bee shook her head. She found she couldn't form the words.

'That's not possible,' Diana said after another moment.

Bee sank onto a floor cushion, legs crossed. The damp cloth of her shirt was sticking unpleasantly to her skin.

Diana joined her on the floor. Kneeling close so that she could look into Bee's eyes. 'Where?'

'I don't know.' She needed time to think. She would close her eyes and look inside, see what answers were waiting.

'We could look,' Diana said. She didn't mean meditation, though. She meant the three mirrors that waited, shrouded, in the room next door.

'It won't help,' Bee said, closing her eyes. It never helped. When you had foreseen as much as The Three Sisters, you realised that knowing made no difference. You could look ahead and see the path as clear as day, but the present would unfold in its own night-time way. And the end would come just as sharp, just as final.

'Shall we tell Luce?'

She opened her eyes. Lucy. Their youngest sister. Strong, unpredictable, hedonistic. Feral.

'Not yet,' Bee said.

'She's fond of Tobias,' Diana warned.

Was she? Bee hadn't realised that Lucy was particularly aware of any of the island's residents. But, she supposed, Tobias was different. And perhaps even the basest heathens had a god.

AFTER LUKE HAD GONE HOME to open the bookshop, Esme went upstairs to look at the painting she had ruined the day before. The dark shape squatted in the middle of her seascape, just as awful as she remembered. The longer she looked at it, the darker it seemed to get.

She was distracted by the sound of her landline.

Hurrying down the stairs to answer it, she almost tripped on Jet.

Fiona's voice was very welcome. 'Do you want to come round for a wee bit?'

Jet had followed her to the dining room, his tail raised in the air and expression indignant. Esme could still see the dark shape from the painting in her studio behind her eyes, feel it pulling at her as if it wanted something. She said she most definitely did and went to get her shoes and coat.

Fiona's living room was a comforting jumble of cushions, cups, toys and books. Domestic normality helped her to stop seeing the dark shape of the islet, but it couldn't stop her from feeling like a failure. Tobias was gone, and she wasn't doing anything to find him. 'I just feel so bloody useless,' Esme said, not for the first time.

Fiona passed a blue plastic block to Hamish and made a sympathetic sound. 'I know, hen.'

'Why did he go into the cairn? Why even go to the islet?'

'Bee said he saw something. A fire.'

'I know,' Esme said. And she did know. Tobias was the mayor and he had probably felt that he had to go and investigate. She wondered if he had been frightened.

'He's not gone forever,' Fiona said. 'He wouldn't leave us.'

Esme wanted to ask how Fiona knew, but she was scared to press the issue. It would be nicer to just accept her comforting words.

'I just wish there was something we could do.'

'Ock,' Hamish said. Esme realised that he was addressing her. He held out a pink block. An offering.

'Thank you,' Esme said, accepting it.

'Ock!' Hamish said a moment later.

'He wants you to hand it back,' Fiona said. 'Sorry. He probably won't stop now.'

No sooner had Hamish accepted the pink block back, he shouted 'ock!' in triumph and offered a yellow version.

'Is there anything you can do?' Fiona asked, not looking at Esme. 'As the Ward Witch?'

'I don't know,' Esme said, feeling wretched again. 'I've been reading books from the shop and there are spells for finding, but I don't know if any of them are real.' She wasn't going to volunteer that she had already tried one involving candles, a crystal and some chanting that felt like a meditation mantra. Tobias hadn't walked back into their lives, and now there was the fog.

AFTER SEVERAL ROUNDS of pass the block, Esme made her excuses and left the house. She could still barely see more than a couple of feet. Esme had seen plenty of mist in her time on the island, formed over the cold sea and blown inland by the warmer air currents. They called it a haar and expected several days to be lost to the blank damp over the summer. This fog seemed different, though. It seemed to have seeped from below the island and was now advancing up the walls of the stone buildings. Soon Esme couldn't see her own knees and felt as if she was wading in a thick grey sea. It cut sound, too, so the village was eerily quiet. Was the island expressing its feelings? After Alvis died, there was a terrible storm. Did the fog mean that Tobias was dead, too?

THE SKY WAS RED. It took a moment before Tobias realised that it wasn't the sky. It was the ground. It was dry and cracked, the redness was the earth itself. He wasn't in the sea anymore and that was bad. He didn't remember this place, and that was even worse. He knew his memory wasn't as pin sharp as it had once been, but he was good with places. Or was it faces? He knew he was good with one of the two.

He touched the ground and felt the fine grain of sand. He licked his lips and tasted salt. The red cracked earth stretched for as far as he could see in any direction, vast and utterly featureless. The horizon was a thin line of bright light. He couldn't see a sun, but he could feel heat beating down onto the top of his head, so he began walking across the barren plain. He needed to find shade.

CHAPTER SEVEN

After tea with Esme, her sitting in bed in her pyjamas and him in the clothes he had slept in sitting next to her, Luke had made his way home to open the bookshop for the day. He hadn't been sure whether it was the right thing to do. Tobias going missing felt as if there ought to be a day of mourning or something to mark respect, but Esme thought they should carry on as normal. She seemed to think that if they acted as though Tobias was just going to wander back into the village, then maybe he would.

The shop greeted him by illuminating soft lights. He patted the counter as he walked past and went upstairs to wash and change. When he took his phone out of his jeans pocket, he realised he had a new WhatsApp message. His mouth was dry as he tapped to open it. Nobody else he knew used WhatsApp. Below the message that Hammer had written – send proof of life – there was a reply. It was the address of a Wetherspoons pub on Otley Road and a time, three o'clock.

His heart had stuttered and begun racing at the sight of the message notification. His first hope – that it was Lewis, finally replying – was instantly snuffed out. The way the message was written, short as it was, didn't feel like Lewis. If his brother wanted him to meet at a certain time and place, he would have added some more information. Especially after all this time.

It was most likely to be from Dean Fisher, the criminal boss that Lewis had pissed off, or one of his minions. Maybe he was finally going to offer proof of life, or perhaps he was ready to make some kind of deal. Something that would result in Lewis's return. Or, this was his way of tying up loose ends. Maybe he was ready to get rid of the one person looking for Lewis Taylor.

He didn't need to wonder whether the three o'clock time meant that afternoon or not, and he wasn't about to reply to ask. This was the kind of message meant to let you know your position in the order of things. He was being told to jump.

It was almost ten. He tapped the address into Google and it told him the drive would take just over three hours. The lights in the bookshop flickered. 'I know you have a roadmap,' he said out loud. 'But Google tells me about delays.'

Esme was due at the shop at half eleven. They were going for lunch together and, before that, she was going to borrow some books on Neolithic burial mounds and any lore surrounding burial rites and rituals. Luke wasn't confident that she would find anything useful to solve the mystery of Tobias's disappearance, but he also understood her need to keep busy.

He had already packed his rucksack with overnight gear and explained to the bookshop that he was going away for a short time. It didn't reply, naturally enough, but there was a strange charge in the air that suggested that it was listening. 'I'm hoping to be back tonight, but if I'm too late for the causeway, I will have to stay overnight on the mainland. I will definitely be back tomorrow, though.' He hoped he wasn't lying to the shop.

Having rehearsed his speech out loud to a building, it ought to have been easy to say the words to Esme. But they seemed to stick in his throat.

He waited until she had finished browsing the section at the back of the shop and looking through the books in the stockroom. The bookshop obliged by displaying three textbooks on the subject, including a large volume with black and white photographs of tombs and accompanying diagrams. Esme piled them onto the counter. 'Is it all right to borrow these? I'm happy to pay for them...'

'It's fine.' The finances of the bookshop were precarious to say the least, but the lack of rent really helped matters. And Luke's monetary needs were small. If Dean Fisher was hoping to extort more cash from him, he would be in trouble. The thought darkened his mood even though he tried to push it away.

'What's wrong?' Esme had her hand on top of the pile of books and was immediately tense.

The lump in his throat had grown, so he showed her the message on his phone.

'You can't go,' Esme said, horrified.

Part of Luke was gratified by her protective reaction and the warm glow it ignited in his heart. The other part needed her to be okay. He didn't want to cause her distress and he could see that her hands were shaking. He caught hold of them, squeezing gently. 'It will be fine. I'm going to be careful.'

'You can't go now. What about Tobias?'

'There's nothing I can do about that,' Luke said.

She blinked and looked up, as if trying not to cry.

He squeezed her hands again, willing her to look at him. 'He's gone. There's nothing any of us can do about it. But this is something I can do. This is something I can fix.'

Esme's gaze snapped to his. She pulled her hands away and crossed her arms. 'I understand.'

'I don't want to leave you. Or the island while it's like this.'

'We'll be fine,' Esme said, and he hated the distant sound in her voice.

'I'll be back tomorrow at the latest.'

'But what does he want from you?'

'I don't know.' It was an honest answer, but it didn't delve into all the things he suspected. Dean Fisher knew that he had something that Luke wanted – information regarding his brother's disappearance. That was currency, and Fisher probably wanted to convert that into cash. Given Luke's financial situation, he was hoping he would be able to pay for the information in some other way. Hopefully in a way that didn't land him in prison or the ground. He chose the least alarming version of his imaginings to share with Esme. 'He probably just wants to talk to me.'

Esme shook her head, clearly not buying it.

'I have to go. It's a chance to find out what has happened to Lewis.'

Esme didn't say anything about how unlikely it was that Lewis was still alive and Luke was grateful.

Esme stared down at the floor. 'You said that Lewis was Dean Fisher's man. It sounds like you are offering to take his place.'

'No,' Luke shook his head. But he felt the shard of doubt.

'You are going to go anyway, aren't you?' She looked at him, then, and took a step back.

'He's my brother.'

Luke went to see Hammer. He knew that the island's enforcer would be likely to turn up at the carpark and stop him from leaving if he didn't. Or maybe insist on coming with him.

He knocked on the door of Hammer's home. It was an upturned boat that had been converted into a tiny house. A steel chimney pipe stuck out from near the apex of the curved walls, and there was a hefty padlock on the door that Hammer used when he was out. The fog had thinned to mist, and Luke glimpsed the rolling waves offshore.

There was a single sharp bark from inside and Luke remembered, with a stabbing sensation in his chest, that Winter was staying with Hammer. And why.

The door scraped open and Hammer loomed in the entrance. He looked like shit. Like he hadn't slept in a month.

He leant on one arm on the door frame and regarded Luke with a flat expression. 'You about to do something stupid?'

'Probably,' Luke said. 'I've been summoned to a meeting with Dean Fisher.'

Hammer looked momentarily confused, but the blank expression was back in place quickly enough. 'And?'

'I'm here to ask you not to stop me. I'm going to be careful. I won't bring any trouble to the island.'

Hammer shrugged and began to shut the door. 'Do what you want, Book Keeper.'

'Right.' Standing in front of the now-closed door, Luke

didn't know what to think. He had come ready for a fight. And a small part of him had been counting on Hammer insisting on joining him. With the man mountain following in his car, he would have known he had backup. Hammer had made it clear he was on his own.

CHAPTER EIGHT

Hammer realised he was scowling when Winter whined. He forced himself to stop. 'Ignore me, I'm being a grumpy bastard.' He stroked Winter's head and his soft ears until they both felt a little better.

In that moment when he had opened the door and seen Luke Taylor, his spirits had risen. He had thought that Luke was going to go looking for Tobias, that he would be asking to borrow a boat or for Hammer to take him across to Àite Marbh. Hammer would have said no, of course, and called him a bloody idiot, but it would have felt like they were in the thing together. That it wasn't just Hammer alone, the one who lost their mayor.

Esme hated that Luke had left, and she didn't think she would be able to focus on the books she had borrowed from the shop. She didn't feel like being alone, so even though she wasn't hungry for lunch, she walked to The Rising Moon instead of going straight home. Seren greeted her with the news that Bee was calling an emergency meeting.

Sitting at the big table in the middle of the room, she checked her phone for messages, even though she knew Luke would have barely crossed the causeway at this point. *Maybe he would change his mind, turn around and come back?* She didn't believe it for a moment. He had a real family, and they came first.

Fiona had left Hamish with Euan and was sitting between Matteo and Seren. Hammer arrived with Winter and Esme made a fuss of the dog, trying to distract herself, but he was more subdued than usual. Hammer sat on the other side of the table, and Winter pressed against his legs as if making sure he wasn't going anywhere. The place at the head of the big table, the place that Tobias usually sat, was empty.

'I swam out around the island,' Fiona said. 'I didn't find him.'

Everyone looked at the table or away from Fiona, not wanting to catch her eye. Nobody asked anything about the form she had taken to swim that far, and nobody questioned her ability to trawl the sea for a single body.

The door opened, and Bee arrived. Her hair was as neatly braided as usual, but her face held a wild-look. Esme felt she could see something unravelled in the older woman. It was possible she was projecting her own feelings. Tobias's absence had grown to a size and weight she couldn't ignore.

Bee took a spare seat across from Esme. 'Diana's not coming,' she said. She didn't mention Lucy.

'Did you look for him?' Fiona asked Bee.

'The future is no help to us,' Bee said.

Nobody asked any follow-up questions. If Bee had seen something about Tobias in her mirrors, she would have said.

'I looked in the sea,' Fiona said, bringing Bee up-to-date on their conversation. 'Nothing.'

Bee nodded. 'That's good.'

Esme knew that Bee didn't need to spell it out. No body meant that Tobias might still be alive. She looked around the table. 'Where is our Book Keeper?'

'Gone,' Hammer said. 'Mainland.'

'He didn't want to leave, especially not now,' Esme said, defending him. 'It's for his brother.'

Matteo wrote on his notepad and then pushed it to the centre of the table. Hammer took it first and then it was passed around until everyone had read what was written.

We need a mayor?

'Do you mean we should name someone as acting mayor while Tobias is away?' Esme asked. She refused to contemplate the possibility that Tobias's absence was permanent.

'Or are you asking whether we need a mayor at all?' Bee's tone was completely neutral.

Matteo shrugged, his face a question.

'We need a mayor,' Hammer said, surprising Esme. She would have assumed he would be anti-authority. He looked around. 'What?'

'Bee could do it,' Seren said. 'Just until Tobias gets back.'

'Will he come back?' Fiona asked the question that had been hanging in the air.

'I can't be mayor,' Bee said, rolling right past Fiona's question. 'It's not for me.'

'I think we'll survive for a few days,' Fiona said.

Esme felt the others tense. She looked Bee dead in the eye. 'Tobias will be back soon, won't he?'

Bee's lips compressed. She didn't speak.

. . .

LUKE MADE it to the Wetherspoons on Otley Road in under three hours. He drove past, scoping out the ample parking and the lack of any obvious threat. Not that he was sure what that would look like. A gang of headcases standing outside the pub, holding weaponry?

He drove to a garage and bought a takeaway coffee and a bottle of water. Hydrated and caffeinated, he went back to the Wetherspoons and parked facing the road. He was twenty minutes early.

Exactly twenty minutes later, a blue transit van pulled up on the main road. Luke watched the three men in the front of the van having a conversation. Then two of the men got out and stood on the pavement. One of them looked right at him and raised his chin. He had movie-star cheekbones, light brown skin and a sharp fade hairstyle. His white friend was taller, thicker-set, and pug-ugly.

Luke sighed. He got out of the car and locked it. Approaching the van, he wondered whether this was going to be the last stupid thing he ever did.

'Luke Taylor?' the well-groomed one asked.

'Yeah.'

'Get in the back.'

Luke thought about saying that he had assumed the meeting was in the pub and that he wasn't 'on board' with going to a secondary location. But he knew it would be pointless. That was exactly what he had been intended to think. And he doubted these men gave a flying rat's arse what he was and wasn't 'on board' with. The man opened the back doors of the transit and Luke got inside.

It was lined with plywood, with boxed-in wheel arches, and completely empty. Luke sat on the floor, preparing himself for a nauseating ride. They hadn't cuffed him or put anything over his head and he held onto these small mercies as the doors clanged shut, plunging him into compete darkness, and the van accelerated.

Luke was surprised they hadn't taken his phone away, but he wasn't going to complain. He texted Esme with an update and his current GPS coordinates. He didn't think he could rely on his phone staying with him for much longer, but it was comforting to think there would be an accurate record of where he was, at least for the next few minutes. And the glow of his home screen was a little bit of normality. Just seeing Esme's name made his breathing a little easier.

He was being, he knew, monumentally stupid, but he pushed that thought away. He was in it now. And he didn't feel as if he had any real choice. Lewis was his brother. His twin. His other half. There had never been a choice. His time on Unholy Island was starting to seem dreamlike and unreal. He wondered if it was the wards that Esme set starting to work now that he'd been on the mainland for a few hours, or whether it was just the nature of the weirdness of the place. He wasn't going to forget it, though. He was The Book Keeper.

The van took a corner and he had to brace himself. At that moment, a reply appeared from Esme. *Come home.* He stared at Esme's text and conjured her face, imagining her expression as she had typed out the words. He wanted to be back on the island. He wanted never to have left.

THE WOMAN STANDING in the middle of the main street had long, dark hair and was wearing a leather jacket and jeans. In deference to the freezing weather, she had decent boots on her feet and was wearing a grey woolly scarf, thick gloves and a knitted beanie. She had her back to Esme, and she set off for the far end of the village with a determined stride.

As Esme looked at the woman, she realised that she was finding it increasingly difficult to focus. The figure was a dark shape and, for a moment, her outline seemed to judder and jump, as if she was moving at a different frame rate to the world around her. At that moment, she turned to the side, as if she had heard something. Esme caught the glimpse of pale skin and a determined mouth.

Hammer had come out of the pub with her, Winter between them. They had stopped with Esme and she reached out to pat the dog's head.

'Who's that?' Hammer's voice seemed to be coming from far away.

'No idea,' Esme said.

'Fog has cleared a bit,' Hammer was saying. Had he asked her another question? She focused on his face. His eyes were worried.

'You all right?'

'Fine.' Esme forced a smile.

'He'll be back before you know it,' Hammer said.

'You don't have to sound so grumpy about it,' Esme said. She couldn't face having a serious conversation about Luke, couldn't bear to make anything more real than it already was. She had been aiming for a teasing tone but didn't feel entirely present in the conversation and was pretty sure she hadn't managed it.

'He's upset you,' Hammer said, brow furrowing. 'I'm gonna have to have words.'

'No you don't. He's our Book Keeper. And he's not done anything wrong.' Esme hoped that was right. She wanted Luke to come back from the mainland, but she knew the tie that had taken him away from the island wasn't going to be undone. For as long as Lewis existed, Luke would run when he called. She looked back up the street to where the woman had been standing, but she had gone.

CHAPTER NINE

The sound of the road changed and Luke could hear crunching. They were driving over small stones. A driveway? The crunching went on for a long time.

Then the van stopped. He heard movement, the front doors opening. The smell of petrol seemed to get stronger and Luke had a moment of pure panic, his mind spinning with the possibilities. Were they planning to set fire to the van with Luke inside? He rubbed the scars on his chest, his body suddenly on fire with the remembered sensation of being hexed. Then blinding light as the doors were flung open.

He blinked rapidly and climbed out of the van. His legs felt a bit wobbly, which was unsettling. The house that rose before him was enormous and old. Victorian, maybe, but Luke would be the first to admit he was no expert. There was a sweeping gravel driveway and large, well-trimmed shrubs and hedges. He couldn't see any other houses or hear road noise. They may as well be in the middle of the countryside.

Four stone steps led to a solid front door, flanked by wooden panels, a keypad and cameras. Luke wondered if those panels had contained stained glass at one point and whether the glass was boarded over for security. He caught sight of the edge of the door as he passed through. Metal core.

A woman in a black dress with a white collar was crossing the polished parquet hallway, carrying a tray. She swerved around their little group without acknowledging them.

He followed his chauffeurs into a living room that looked like something from a National Trust property. Floor to ceiling oak panelling, dark red curtains with swathes of material across the top of the windows, the name of which Luke had no clue, leather chairs, and lots of dark wood furniture. The window panes were criss-crossed with black leading, dividing the view of a flagstone terrace with a fountain and stone benches.

Sitting on a brown leather sofa, expensive shoes on a Persian carpet, was the man Luke assumed was Dean Fisher. He was stocky and sun-tanned with dark hair, greying at the temples.

'Have a seat,' he said. A broad Yorkshire accent at odds with everything else. It was an accent that Luke associated with bread adverts and honesty, not crime bosses and transit vans. He sat in the chair Fisher indicated. The two men from the van left the room, presumably to listen at the door in case their boss required anything.

'Drink?'

'No, thanks,' Luke said. 'Nice house.'

Dean shrugged. 'It's quiet. Missus wanted it and you know how that goes.'

Luke didn't reply.

'So. You're the good little brother.' He openly appraised Luke.

'We're twins.'

'Lewis said he was first out the chute.' Dean smiled without warmth. He was either trying to rile Luke or to establish dominance. Either was fine with Luke. His father had taught him many things, and one of the main lessons was how to wait and listen. He could still feel the fear coursing through his body, but he had spent his time in the van regulating his breathing and he was in better shape than he would have expected. Besides, if Dean Fisher was planning to put him in the ground, why had he brought him to his home?

The thought occurred that maybe he didn't mind Luke seeing his home because he was planning on burying him later, but he pushed that into a room of his mind and locked the door.

'I have a problem,' Fisher said after a short silence. 'It's why we're having this conversation.'

'I'm sorry to hear that.'

'Yeah, thanks,' Fisher replied, as if Luke had been speaking in earnest. He leaned back and stretched his arm across the back of the sofa, crossed one leg over the other. He was wearing a neatly pressed shirt that probably cost more than Luke's entire wardrobe, but the skin around his eyes was heavily wrinkled and had a yellow-ish tinge. Smoking or sunshine or spending too much time peering at his bank balance. Who knew?

'I no longer have access to your brother.'

Luke's heart squeezed. Did he mean he was dead? Was this the moment he found out, for sure, that his twin was gone forever? Was Dean Fisher about to show him a picture of his brother's broken body? 'Access?' was all he managed to say.

Dean's mouth turned down at the corners, just a little. 'An old friend wanted him, so I let him go.'

'You had Lewis...' Luke wanted to say 'captive' but he

found his voice wasn't working very well and he realised that his steady breathing was shot to shit. He focused on counting his inhales and exhales.

Fisher waved a hand. 'Old news. Had to teach him a lesson. He was very naughty, your brother. Bit of a pain in the arse, all being said.'

'What about the men you sent? The debt collectors.'

A smile. Real, this time. 'I told Lewis I would pursue the money he owed me. His debt passed to you, as his family.'

'That was settled.' Luke knew that Hammer had convinced the debt collectors to write off Lewis's debt, but he didn't know what they would have told their boss.

'Your friend paid up, it's true. And he agreed to keep an eye on you for me, just in case I needed you. Good thing, too, as it happens.'

If Fisher had hoped this to be a shock, he was disappointed. Luke knew that Hammer had agreed to watch Luke on behalf of Dean Fisher. It had seemed like a good way to ensure there weren't other teams dispatched to the island. 'You don't have Lewis anymore?'

'Keep up, son. No. I don't.' Fisher looked irritated by that fact. 'A Crow turned up early doors and took him off my hands. Wouldn't leave without him, which landed me with a bit of a situation. Until I remembered you, that is. A lookalike waiting in the wings—'

'Where is he?'

Fisher looked surprised at being interrupted, and then his expression went blank. 'Wherever the Crow Family want him to be.'

'The Crow Family?' Luke knew it made him sound stupid, but the question was already out. It hung in the air.

'Want some friendly advice?' Fisher asked.

'Not really.'

'Put up a nice gravestone for your brother. Have a service, all that. He's as good as gone.'

Luke couldn't believe that he had found the man who had been keeping Lewis, that he was sitting in the same room as him. Maybe he was even in the same house that Lewis had been kept, but that his brother had been moved on. Taken by another gang for whatever reason. It didn't sound like Fisher had wanted to let him go, and certainly not today, but maybe he had needed to use Lewis as payment or leverage. Like a bag of money being put from one criminal's boot into another.

'So.' Fisher clapped his hands together loudly. 'That's enough chitchat.'

Luke tensed.

'I need a little favour.'

'Why would I—'

'Don't finish that thought, son. Just nod and ask me how you can help.'

'I don't want to work for you,' Luke said. 'No offence.'

'I can understand your feelings.' Fisher nodded. 'But I'm not looking for a new employee. Just one job. One little favour and you're all done. Thing is, it's not just about the money. Your brother broke my trust. He stole from me. You understand why I had to punish him?'

Luke stayed quiet.

'And that punishment has been finished early. By my calculations, that means he still owes me a debt.'

Luke wanted to argue that the Crow Family taking Lewis early wasn't his fault. Or Lewis's. But he didn't think it would make the slightest bit of difference to Fisher, so he kept his mouth closed.

'And, as a show of goodwill, I'll consider your brother's debt paid to me, too. Done and dusted.'

. . .

BEE HADN'T BEEN HOME long after the meeting at the pub when she received a caller. Lydia Crow was standing on her front step, a wing of black hair visible beneath a warm hat and her cheeks pink from the cold. Bee didn't know how the woman had known which was her home, but she wasn't about to cede power by asking.

'You're late,' Bee said. If the woman had arrived earlier, perhaps their Book Keeper wouldn't have gone haring off to the mainland.

'I promised to come when you called,' Lydia said. 'Not to be on time. Besides, I brought a gift.'

Bee didn't let herself frown. 'I didn't ask you for anything.'

'I'll take him away then, shall I?'

A pause. 'The boy?'

'In the flesh. Undamaged. You're welcome.'

'He's here?' Bee couldn't stop herself from glancing over Lydia's shoulder, as if expecting to see Luke Taylor's twin looming out of the fog.

'In my car, sleeping like a baby. They were keeping him drugged up. Docile. He's not in any state to move right now, but give it a couple of hours and I'll bring him along to you. Right to your door.'

'I didn't ask you to do that,' Bee said.

Lydia smiled. 'I over-deliver. It's a curse.'

Bee waited, knowing there was more to come.

'Which means you owe me a favour, now.'

'I didn't ask you to bring the boy here, just to find him.' Bee crossed her arms.

'But you did ask me for a favour. You opened the door.'

'What if we were to agree, mutually, to close the door?'

'We'll see,' Lydia said. She looked around the street, at the small houses and the lingering fog, the sky and sea beyond. 'For now, the Crow Family considers our relationship to be ongoing. Officially speaking.'

'It's nice to have friends,' Bee said, keeping her tone just on the right side of pleasant.

Lydia smiled back. 'That's the spirit.'

MATTEO WAS DOING the crossword and sipping espresso when the sound of the shop bell made him look up. A woman wearing a leather jacket and blue jeans was browsing the shelves nearest to the door. Matteo wasn't very good at judging ages, but he would guess late twenties. She was small, but had a vigorous energy about her that suggested unpredictability. If she had been a teenager, he knew he would have laid money on her being a shoplifter. Or, he reassessed as he caught sight of the line of her jaw, the calculation in her eyes, the leader of a gang of shoplifters.

He mentally shook his head, wondering when he had started to have random thoughts about perfectly innocent tourists. Didn't they say you got more conservative as you got older? More closed in. Was this all it took these days? A leather jacket and heavy boots, and he was ready to brand someone a thief?

He knew that his prepared notes for tourists were stacked neatly on the counter, ready for him to use, along with the laminated map of the island that he used to point out directions. He went back to his crossword. At least he tried to, but there truly was something unsettling about the young woman and he kept finding his gaze drawn to her. Perhaps it was because her dark hair and pale skin reminded him of somebody else, someone he couldn't quite place at this very moment.

'Do you have any salt and vinegar?' Her accent was south London. It threw him back in time, to his old life.

He pointed to the top left section of his crisps display. It was a wire rack with baskets to hold the different flavours.

'This is an interesting place,' the Londoner said. 'Must get mobbed in the summer.'

Matteo smiled politely and held out his hand to make a seesaw 'so-so' gesture.

'Although,' the Londoner looked away from him and toward the door. Her expression was canny, as if she was looking beyond the door and around the village, the island. Thinking hard. It gave Matteo an unsettled feeling.

'I'd never heard of it. That's interesting. I mean, everyone has heard of Lindisfarne, but not this place.' She left a gap at the end of her sentence, eyes on his.

If she was waiting for him to fill the silence, she would be waiting for a very long time. Matteo smiled politely. After another beat, he pointed to the bag of crisps on the counter and raised his eyebrows. It was his 'is that everything' move and people usually understood.

The Londoner, and here he really had the feeling she was being deliberately obtuse, said 'What?'

He shook his head. He reached for his stack of cards, shuffling them while he waited for a more specific question.

'You don't say much, do you?' The Londoner had placed a hand on the counter as if about to drum her fingers. The cuff of her jacket slid up a little and he saw black ink. He could have sworn he saw it moving.

He had a card for situations like this. Most people didn't worry about a quiet shop assistant. They wanted to pick up their snacks and carry on with whatever visitors did on the island. Birdwatching. He shuffled until he found it and then placed it on the counter, facing the Londoner.

Her hand moved quickly and touched the back of his while he was placing the card. He pulled his hand away and looked into her eyes in surprise. In there, he saw something that made his stomach drop. Knowledge. She couldn't know. He had to be mistaken. He didn't know this woman and she didn't know him. It wasn't possible.

She glanced at the card. *I'm sorry I cannot speak.*

Matteo had laboured over the phrasing on this card. He had wanted to be polite, this was a place of business after all, but he hadn't wanted to use the word 'mute'. It used to be used all the time and he hadn't really minded, perhaps because his lack of speech was a choice, but he knew it was considered offensive in this day and age. 'Cannot' wasn't technically true, but in another sense it was completely accurate. He could not bear the consequences, so he was incapable of speaking out loud.

'A Silver that can't speak,' the Londoner said. She shook her head, expression incredulous. 'I don't know if that's divine punishment or the ultimate irony.'

It wasn't just a drop in his stomach, Matteo now felt vertiginous. Sick. Who was this woman and how the hell did she know he was a Silver? Speechless, and not just in the usual way, it took him a couple of short breaths, his heart hammering, before he was able to move. He picked up his pen and wrote along the top margin of the newspaper. *Who are you?*

'Lydia Crow,' she put out her hand. 'Pleased to meet you.'

Matteo shook her hand, dropping it as soon as was possible while still making it a polite interaction. His mouth was dry. He didn't want to give his name, but he knew there was no point in hiding it. She already knew he was a Silver, which meant she probably already knew his name. Perhaps this was a test of his honesty or to find out how deeply he was hiding. That would be leverage. He had to appear unconcerned. Maybe if she didn't think there was anything to hide, she wouldn't think there was anything to exploit. He wrote *Matteo*. His mind was whirling through the possibilities. She must have heard about him from somebody else, which might mean that his Family knew where he was. Or, she had found out another way and was now looking for a hefty payout in return for her silence. But who could have told her? Nobody knew. Nobody from his old life, anyway. He had been using a fake surname for years.

'You know who I am?' the woman asked, but it wasn't really a question. 'Our Families go way back, but I don't remember hearing about you. Black sheep? Or a lost lamb?'

While he had left the Family a long time ago and kept his distance in all senses, he still knew the name Lydia Crow. She was the heir to the Crow Family, the beloved daughter of Henry Crow. The last he had heard, Henry had stepped aside and his brother Charlie was running things. Henry had disappeared to the suburbs to have a normal life. He hadn't wanted little Lydia to be brought up in the Family business or to know anything about it. Rumour was he had wanted her to have the choice about her destiny, not be locked into it from her first breath. It was something Matteo had always admired. And, he supposed, the knowledge that Henry Crow had successfully retired from the Family, managed to move away from Camberwell where the Crows ruled the roost, and make his own life, had been something of an inspiration and a comfort to Matteo. Now little Lydia was a grown woman and it seemed she had made her choice.

Lydia Crow had paid for her crisps and left without

further conversation. Matteo wasn't fooled, however, and was not surprised when she walked back in an hour later. 'I've been asking around the island, but nobody wants to tell tales.' She sounded approving. 'So I'm back to the source.'

Matteo knew that nobody would have intentionally given him away, but the problem with keeping secrets secret was that nobody really knew what damage they could do with a careless word. His friends on the island might not be aware that his being a Silver wasn't information to be shared. Not that it mattered. Lydia Crow had known that fact and he had spent the previous sixty minutes wracking his brain for who might possibly have told her. After his initial panic, Matteo had realised that if his Family had been the source of the information, they would have already turned up to the island to persuade him to come home. Home, for them, meaning the Temple area of London around Chancery Lane. And 'persuade' being as easy as the head of the Family, Alejandro, opening his mouth and telling him.

What do you want?

This was another of Matteo's prepared cards. He had never imagined using it in a situation like this.

'What do I want?' Lydia Crow looked around the shop.

Through her eyes, Matteo saw the place anew. Instead of his cosy little kingdom, his neatly ordered shelves and the comforting kaleidoscope of packaging, he saw a sad little bolthole.

'I'm curious as to what you want. What keeps you in this place, away from the bright lights?'

He straightened up, deliberately ignoring the weight that settled across his shoulders. This was his home. His life. And he would be damned if he was going to allow a blow-in from the mainland make him feel bad. Even if she was the head of the most powerful of the London Families. He shrugged, careful to keep his expression politely neutral.

'I find this interesting,' Lydia said. 'But I'm not looking to make enemies.'

She must have read his thoughts in his expression, because she added. 'Yeah. You're right. I have enough of those to be going on with.'

She picked up a chocolate bar from the rack below the counter, seemingly at random, not moving her gaze from Matteo. Then she reached across to the till and propped a business card onto the keys.

Matteo didn't know if she expected him to accept that as a form of payment. He kept a price list on the counter and he pointed at the appropriate line.

Lydia smiled and turned her hand over. There was a two-pound coin in her palm, and she placed it in the middle of the counter. 'Keep the change.'

CHAPTER TEN

Luke had expected an abandoned warehouse or sketchy block of flats. Something with burned-out cars, gang tags, and an odour of piss and death. Instead, he was directed to meet Yuri in a chain restaurant near a cinema in the suburbs of Leeds. A couple of beefy men were standing outside the front entrance. One was smoking and keeping a keen eye on the car park, while the other was scrolling his iPhone. They clocked Luke as he approached and when he pulled open the heavy glass door to walk inside, the smoker threw away his cigarette and followed.

It was early evening on a weekday, so the place was quiet. An elderly couple circled the salad bar, and a couple of lone diners were dotted around the mostly empty restaurant. The host stand was unoccupied and Luke couldn't see any staff at that moment. The bodyguard stepped in front of Luke before leading him down to the far end of the room and the last booth. The window looked onto the deserted carpark where a plastic grocery bag was blowing in the wind. It was the opposite of an Instagram-worthy meal moment. A Crapstagram.

Enjoying the depressing ambience and shovelling a

wedge of meat-feast into his mouth was the largest and most-tattooed man Luke had seen in the real world. He didn't know why he bothered with henchmen as he could clearly pick up and crush any and all would-be attackers.

Luke was not a small man and used to towering over others. This man was a mountain. He would even make Hammer look petite. Still, the larger they were, the harder they fell. At least, Luke hoped that was true.

He had brown, frizzy hair pulled back in a ponytail and a beard that was shot with a few grey hairs. The eyes watching him from a craggy face were sharp and assessing.

'You wanted to see me,' Luke said.

Yuri didn't stop eating until he had finished the slice he had been working on. It didn't take long. 'You look well.'

Luke cautioned himself not to react. There was no reason for Yuri to suspect that he wasn't Lewis. He was going to say 'you look the same' but what if there was something really different about his appearance? Would it reveal that he hadn't met the guy before? Blow his cover? He was overthinking, he knew. He had to calm the fuck down. 'Fresh air,' he said, hoping he hadn't paused for too long. 'Living right.'

The man barked a laugh. 'That's not what I heard. But I guess Fisher's been looking after you better than I thought.'

'What can I do for you?'

'Just like that? You don't want to give me shit about my pizza?'

Luke's mouth was dry. 'Places to be,' he managed.

'Last time you told me I had taste buds of five-year-old little child.' Yuri leaned back. A crease deepened between his eyebrows. 'We have problem?'

Breathe, breathe, breathe. Luke forced himself to lean back a little, too. 'Not that I know of.'

Yuri didn't speak for a few seconds. He was still looking at Luke with a piercing gaze, evaluating him with a calm intensity that made the skin on the back of Luke's neck crawl. Eventually, he spoke. 'You know why you're here? I need to look you in eyes and hear it.'

Luke had no idea what he was talking about. If he said that, he would sound evasive, maybe turn the meeting acrimonious. 'Why do you want to know?'

The bright eyes hardened to chips of glass. 'Careful. It has been long time since we did work together. I want to know we still solid.' He thumped his chest.

'We're solid.' Luke said, hoping that was enough.

'You have been away for long time. Time enough to get chatty I think.'

'I hope you know me better than that.'

Yuri paused, weighing up his response. 'I guess Fisher isn't favourite right now. I think you know I'm better friend to have. There is still lots of work we could do together.' He shook his head, his eyes softening a little. 'I've been worried about you, my friend.'

Luke hadn't been expecting that. Yuri seemed to be genuinely concerned for Lewis, but he wondered when Yuri was going to get to the reason for the meeting. Lewis clearly had more history with the man than Dean Fisher was aware of. How many deals had his brother been involved in? How deep was the shit and who had taken his shovel?

'Fisher wants to make things right,' Luke said, hoping that was what Yuri wanted to hear.

'Is that so?'

'Yeah.' Luke couldn't help the sarcasm breaking through. 'He's the penitent type.'

'Penitent?' Yuri's face folded into a furious scowl. 'You eat dictionary?'

Shit. Luke controlled his own features. He had no way of knowing how Lewis spoke in this world.

'Always were snotty fuck,' Yuri said, and Luke could breathe again.

'You know why I'm here,' Luke tried.

'Because I told Fisher to send you,' Yuri said with some satisfaction. 'He knows I won't let product move until I checked on my friend. I told him. It's been long enough. Time to forgive and move on. Time to get back to business.'

'If you say so.'

Yuri looked at him, not speaking for a long and uncomfortable time.

Eventually, he shook his head, as if deciding Luke and Dean Fisher weren't worth his staring effort. 'I would have thought you be more grateful. Fisher going to think twice before burying you good.'

'I am,' Luke said. 'Thank you.'

'No need for thanks. Long as you have kept your mouth shut. Safe. You keeping our business safe and sound, we don't have problem.'

'Okay. Great.'

Yuri held up a meaty finger. 'You say it.'

'I haven't said a word,' Luke said, hoping he sounded trustworthy. Certain. Even as he had no idea what he was promising. 'You don't have anything to worry about.'

Yuri stood up, opened his arms. 'Come here. We hug now. You are still my brother.'

Luke stood, hoping this wasn't a trap, hoping that Yuri wasn't about to squeeze the life from him with his bare hands.

It was a good hug, all being said. If Luke hadn't been in fear for his life, it probably would have been even better.

'There,' Yuri said. 'All is good. You can tell Mr Fisher that I will allow his business to continue through the usual channels.' He wagged a finger. 'No more locking up my friends, though. Yes?'

'Thank you,' Luke said. He was filled with a rush of genuine gratitude and affection. This man, whoever he was and whatever terrible things he did, had prevented Dean Fisher from killing his brother.

DRIVING AWAY from the pizza restaurant, Luke's head started pounding. He realised he wasn't taking enough breaths and pulled over at the side of the road to get his head down. Little black spots danced in front of his eyes as he sucked in oxygen. One little favour, Fisher had said, but what were the chances that would be it? And how far would he really go to protect Lewis?

He didn't have Dean Fisher's home address, although he could probably find it given enough time with Street View. He wasn't interested in showing up unannounced and getting himself shot, though. Instead, he called the number he had been given.

'Yeah?' Fisher answered quickly.

'Yuri says it's business as usual. As long as Lewis remains a free man. He seems very fond of him for some reason.'

'Lewis killed someone for him,' Fisher said. 'They bonded over it.'

Luke couldn't speak. Fisher had to be lying. His brother was not a killer. Dodgy, yes. A thief and a conman and sometimes violent: yes, yes and yes. But a killer? Absolutely fucking not.

'He has a way of making friends, your brother. That's why I kept him around. Didn't know how Yuri would react if I chucked him in the canal. You sure you don't want a job?'

'I'm sure. Thank you. Lewis's debt is paid. We're both clear.' Luke was gripping the phone too tightly and he forced his hand to relax.

'As I said,' Fisher said, 'don't stress. You played your part, I've got my cash and had six months of Lewis's life. It is enough. This time, but...'

'Six months?' Luke interrupted. 'It's been eighteen, easily.'

'I told you. He was a pain in the arse. Took me over a year to find him. Lot of wasted time, lot of manpower. I should add that to the bill, really. You're lucky.'

Lewis had been ignoring him for a year before Dean Fisher grabbed him? That couldn't be right. He was about to tell Dean Fisher that he was misremembering the timescale, but shut his mouth in time.

'You change your mind about work, go to the Spoons and ask for Fred. They'll get a message to me. Cheerio, son.'

CHAPTER ELEVEN

Bee looked at the man sprawled on the brightly coloured cushions. A large grape vine had sent out exploratory tendrils and delicate green shoots had almost reached his leg where it lay near to the large pots of foliage at the side of the space Bee used for yoga and meditation. Warm lamplight fell upon him, illuminating the angles of his face and casting shadows into the hollows under his cheekbones.

It was like a scene from Gulliver's Travels. Luke's twin was, unsurprisingly, also tall and broad. An outsized man stretched out in the Sisters' calm oasis.

He had been unable to keep his eyes open when he had arrived, leaning heavily on Lydia's arm, and Bee had asked whether Lydia knew what had been used to drug him. She had also wondered at how the slight woman had managed to walk him all the way from the carpark. He dwarfed her. Bee supposed she was stronger than she looked.

'Not a clue,' Lydia had replied. 'And who knows what state they've had him in and for how long?'

The man's breathing was deep and even. As far as Bee could tell, it was a normal sleep, but she was no expert. She could call Esme, but she wasn't going to bother the witch unless there was a clear need. She needed to tell Luke first, by rights. He was the man's kin. At least he was safe and alive. With Tobias missing, she needed the Book Keeper on his game and not absent through grief. Or revenge. It was nice to have some good news for once. Bee was used to being asked questions that rarely had the answer the person wanted to hear. This time she would be able to open the door for The Book Keeper and produce his brother, alive and well. Ta-da.

Lewis made a noise in his sleep and turned onto his side, facing the door.

Diana appeared from upstairs. She met Bee's eyes over the hulk of manhood in their living room and formed a question with her face.

'Luke's twin.'

'I can see that,' Diana whispered. 'What is he doing in our house?'

Bee had integrated with the islanders, while her sisters kept to themselves. For the most part, this worked for everyone, but there were times when she wished Diana was a little more interested in the residents of Unholy Island. Her sister was already turning away, as if she couldn't be bothered to wait for the answer.

'He won't be here long,' Bee said. 'I'll move him.'

Diana's attention was on a calathea in a red enamel pot. She ran her finger down one of its large striped leaves and then touched her lower lip. When she spoke, it was offhand. 'Should I get Lucy?'

Bee suppressed the urge to shudder. 'Absolutely not. I'm going to get him out of here before she notices.'

Diana turned away, already finished with the subject and ready to leave. 'Make sure he doesn't damage any of my plants.'

· · ·

ESME HAD TRIED to keep busy while Luke was on the mainland. In amongst the textbooks on burial mounds, the bookshop had included a slim volume of retrieval spells. Bee had said that Tobias had 'gone between', so perhaps magic would be the answer to bringing him back? Kate Foster had been a stark warning of the dangers, but Esme was willing to take a risk for the sake of Tobias. Besides, she wasn't going to touch anything involving sacrifice.

She was halfway through the book and diligently making notes, but was finding it hard to focus. She couldn't stop thinking about Luke, worrying that something would go wrong. He was dealing with dangerous people. Bad people. And part of her couldn't believe he had walked into that world willingly. She knew he hadn't really had a choice, but part of her still resented the fact that he had left her and the island. Even while they were in crisis, while Tobias was missing, maybe worse, he had left. He had chosen his brother, and it was a salutary reminder that she wasn't his family.

She was just thinking that the causeway would be closing and that if he wasn't back in the next few minutes, he would have to wait until the next day, when she heard the squeak of her garden gate and steps on the path. She was out of her chair and opening the door before Luke had knocked. It was dark outside, and the air was cold. Esme didn't care, standing on the back step to hug him as tightly as she could. He was safe. Whole. Home.

Inside the warm kitchen, with the door bolted against the freezing night, she listened while Luke told her all about Dean Fisher and Yuri.

'So Fisher had already let your brother go? That's good, isn't it?'

'I think so. It means he was alive recently, at least. And Yuri seems to object to him being hurt or held, so hopefully that's an end of it.'

'Yuri is a friend? Of Lewis?'

Luke looked uncomfortable. 'I guess so. Something like that.'

'What's wrong?' Esme could see he was holding something back.

Luke looked at his hands. 'I got the impression they had worked together. Yuri seemed to like Lewis or felt like he owed him or something. He's the reason Dean Fisher held Lewis captive rather than just killing him after he caught him skimming.' Luke shook his head, still not looking her in the eye. 'I don't know what Lewis was into with Yuri, but it sounded serious.' He passed a hand over his face.

'I was so scared,' Esme said.

'Me, too.'

'I kept thinking. First Tobias. Now you.'

He flinched. 'I'm sorry. I'm sorry I put you through it. But I'm back. I'm not going anywhere.'

Esme wanted to tell him not to make promises he couldn't keep. The moment Lewis needed him, he would leave again. The knowledge was a stone in her stomach. 'It didn't feel like home,' she said instead. 'With you gone. How can that be true when you've been here less than a year? How can everything have changed that fast?'

He shook his head gently, looking a little confused. 'It's not bad, though, right? It's good that I belong. You want me here, don't you?'

'I do,' Esme said. 'But I'm scared of losing you. I'm scared that you will leave again and take my home at the same time.'

He frowned, and Esme knew that he didn't understand

what she meant. 'I never had a place to belong when I was growing up. I was always an outsider. A visitor. When I was in the group home, I dreamed of being adopted, but it was only ever foster care. Always temporary.'

'I'm sorry.' Luke wrapped his arms around Esme, holding her with just the right amount of pressure. She felt comforted, not caged.

'And now I have a home. I do belong. I will do anything to protect it and feeling like that scares me a little.'

'I know what you mean. I don't even like my brother a lot of the time, but he's my brother and I know I would do anything for him. Ultimately. It's like having your free will taken away, almost. Family has such a strong pull.'

'I wouldn't know about that,' Esme said. She tensed in his arms, feeling suddenly cold.

'You do,' Luke said gently. He stroked her back. 'The islanders aren't just your friends and neighbours, they are your family. They would do anything for you, I can see it.'

Esme didn't think that Luke should use the word 'family' so freely. It was difficult for those who had grown up with one to know the depth of her longing. She was a fully grown adult and had dealt with her issues as best she could, but if there was one thing that hours of meditation with Bee had taught her it was this: the small child that had longed for a mum and dad, brothers and sisters, cousins and aunties and a *place* in the world still lived inside her adult self. She could recognise when it was speaking, when it was crying in the dark and soothe it as best she could, but it would always be with her. Always be inconsolable, just as she had been when she and the child had been one and the same.

When she hadn't spoken for a few minutes, he shifted so that he could look into her eyes. 'Are you all right?'

Esme tried to smile reassuringly, but it didn't take. She

blinked back tears and pushed her tongue into the roof of her mouth to stop them from coming. An old trick. Crying children didn't get adopted. Her soul was hurting and she wanted to stop thinking like this. The past was in the past, and there was no point in revisiting the old hurt. She leaned in and kissed Luke, losing her sadness in the sensation of his lips. His jaw was covered in thick stubble, long enough that it felt soft to the touch, and his skin was warm.

He responded, hands in her hair, cradling her face and neck, kissing her hungrily like she was the single most important thing in the world. Sparks burst behind her closed eyes as her nerves lit up and desire bloomed until she was just feeling, not thinking.

Luke was the one to stop. They were breathing heavily and Esme realised that she had climbed onto his lap and was pressing herself against him.

His eyes were heavy lidded and glazed and looking into them made Esme want him even more. It was intoxicating. 'Let's go to bed,' she said. 'Right now.'

'Are you sure?' Luke's pupils were huge, his hands flexed on her hips.

'Yes. Make it all go away for a while. Please.'

CHAPTER TWELVE

The next morning, Esme woke up to find Luke's body pressed against her back, one of his arms curled protectively around her torso. She stretched, feeling at home in her own body in a way she couldn't remember ever experiencing before.

'Morning, beautiful.' Luke's voice was a low rumble and it set off a chain reaction of pleasurable sensations. Esme couldn't even bring herself to tease him for being suave.

She tried to reach for some water, but Luke growled and pulled her close.

'I'll have morning breath,' she objected, snuggling back against him for a delicious moment.

He kissed her neck. 'I don't care.' Then he moved and reached across her to retrieve the glass. 'But you've reminded me about mine.' He drank some water and then offered the glass to Esme.

Lying back down, facing each other, Luke's expression was warm and his eyes had a softness that she realised he reserved for her. A balloon of happiness inflated in her chest.

'Are you all right? About last night?'

'Definitely,' Esme said. She wondered whether they had time for a re-run before Luke had to go and open the shop.

A small crease had appeared on Luke's forehead. 'I don't want you to think I expect...'

She stopped him with a kiss. And then another. Answering him without words.

LEWIS AWOKE, disorientated and groggy, in the early hours. Bee told him he was safe and that he could go back to sleep. She knew that she had an unthreatening appearance, and was sitting up to guard him from Lucy's interest. Diana was in her room, keeping away. To a boy like him, she probably looked like a grandmother, and she hoped that was a soothing image for him. He glared around at the room for a little while, but then his heavy eyelids got the better of him and he fell back to sleep.

When he woke again in the morning, she made him coffee and toast. He asked her practical questions. Where was he? How had he got here? Bee said as little as possible. She was tired from sitting guard all night and the worry over Tobias's absence was dragging on her mind. She had more important things to deal with than babysitting a criminal.

'Your brother lives here,' she said. 'He has been looking for you and I called in a favour to find you. You can go and see Luke now, if you like.'

Now that she had confirmed he was alive and awake, Bee wanted the boy out of her house. The longer he stayed, the bigger the chance that Lucy would find him, and it was impossible to know how she would react.

· · ·

AFTER LUKE HAD LEFT to open the bookshop, Esme showered and got dressed. She returned to the book of retrieval spells, determined to make headway. Now that her mind was free from worry over Luke, she felt clear and focused. And there was a new confidence, too. In all her fears of getting closer to Luke, of opening herself up to the possibility of rejection, she hadn't realised one essential truth – the payoff outweighed the risk. She smiled as she replayed the previous night. Being with Luke. *Really* with Luke. Definitely worth it.

So much for focus, she thought, gently chiding herself to get back on task. The book had spells for finding small objects like lost keys and less prosaic ones for 'rekindling lost affection' or 'regaining memories'. There wasn't a spell specifically for returning a person, but there was one for a lost cat. 'Nothing ventured, nothing gained,' she said out loud.

Jet, who was stretched on the kitchen floor, stopped rolling for long enough to give her a slow blink.

Esme fetched a length of blue fishing rope. She kept a reel for garden use, but didn't see why it wouldn't be suitable for magic. It would be better if it was dark or a new moon, but Esme was pretty sure that her intention and focus were the main ingredients. She sat on the kitchen floor and drew a rough circle in chalk on the tiles. She placed pebbles at each of the four compass points. It ought to be candles, but something told her that she needed to invoke the island.

She held the rope in both hands and quietened her mind, conjuring the image of Tobias as clearly as possible. She pictured his kind face, tweed clothes, and the way he leaned on his walking stick when he paused on a walk to chat with her.

Then she began tying knots in the rope, making sure

she worked from the end furthest away towards herself. It was important that the knots were pulling Tobias to her and not pushing him away.

By the third knot, her eyes were firmly closed and the image of Tobias was getting more detailed. She could have sworn that she could sense the stones that she had placed around the circle. The island was watching, willing her on.

The knots were getting more difficult to tie. The rope felt slippery and uncooperative, as if there was a weight at the far end, preventing her from making the necessary loops. Her fingers burned as she struggled with the rope and finally her eyes flew open, the image of Tobias disappearing as if torn away. The stones had gone quiet.

Spring was still a long way off on the island, and Hammer had his jacket done up against the sleet-filled wind, thick boots and a woolly hat pulled low on his head. He had left Winter lying in front of his stove. The dog had barely lifted his head when Hammer had asked him if he wanted to go for a 'walk'. He thought that was the magic word for dogs, and was now wondering whether it was possible for a dog to have depression. What he knew, but was refusing to think about, was that Winter was pining for Tobias. It made him feel sad, but that translated to him wanting to kick the world in the bollocks. Anger was familiar. Anger felt safe.

There was a familiar figure on the street, increasing Hammer's annoyance with the world. That good-looking bastard Luke grinned at him with a shit-eating smile. 'Morning.'

'What the fuck are you looking so happy about? I thought you were off on the mainland? Didn't you go to play detective with the criminal pals of your waste of space brother?'

The smile didn't dim. It got wider, lop-sided and knowing. Hammer treated himself to a little daydream of punching Luke Taylor in the face. He was a resident now, it was true, and he had proved himself trustworthy enough. So he probably should restrain himself. For the moment. If he took a single tiny step out of place, though. If he even looked like he was going to hurt Esme...

'Lovely day for a stroll,' Luke said, one eyebrow raised.

There was a mocking edge to Luke's voice. More than usual. Hammer wondered if he had started to read minds. He grunted in response and made to walk on.

Luke seemed to be in a chatty mood, he reversed his direction to walk with Hammer. 'I'm heading to work.'

'Good for you,' Hammer replied.

'You're not heading there?'

'Why would I be going to the bookshop?'

'You look like a scholar.'

Hammer stopped. Something was off. He always found Luke Taylor annoying, but there had been an uneasy truce after he had helped him out with a situation. He knew the man didn't like owing him a favour, he wasn't stupid, and maybe that was playing on his mind. 'I might pop in, after all,' he said slowly.

Luke waited until Hammer started moving before joining him. Like he was being weirdly polite all of a sudden.

They turned down Widdershins Wynd in silence. The wind dropped in the shelter of the narrow lane, revealing the sound of gulls calling. The grey cloud had lifted and the sky was a slice of blue above the stone cottages.

Hammer waited for Luke to unlock the shop.

Luke was staring at the building like he had never seen

the place before. 'Never thought I would own a bookshop. It's a decent size, too.' He stepped to the side. 'After you.'

'You didn't lock up?' He spoke as he tried the handle on the door.

It turned and opened just as Luke said 'nah'.

Hammer hadn't been back in the bookshop since he had helped Luke to repair the floorboards. The smell of dry paper and warm wood filled his senses, and he felt the ever-present knot of tension between his shoulders loosen.

He eased through the narrow corridor to the front room.

'Bloody hell,' Luke said from behind him.

The lights were flickering.

'Be right with you,' a voice called from deeper in the building. Luke's voice.

Hammer turned in confusion. Luke was behind him, that strange 'aw shucks' grin on his face. But his voice had come from further away.

Luke appeared, trailing one hand along the shelves as he walked, as if soothing them.

He stopped when he saw Hammer and the man Hammer now realised must be his twin brother. 'Look who I found. A lost lamb.'

'Surprise,' Lewis said, raising a hand as if planning a little wave and then lowering it again.

Hammer wondered what he had seen in his brother's face. As far as he could tell, Luke looked blank. 'Well, isn't this cosy,' he said. 'I'll leave you two to catch up.'

'Don't go,' Luke said. 'Might need your professional opinion.'

Hammer hesitated. He didn't like Luke Taylor much, but he was the Book Keeper. If The Book Keeper was asking for help, Hammer knew that Tobias would want him to stand guard.

'We should go outside,' Luke said. He cast a quick look at the bookshelves. His hand patted the nearest one.

Lewis's face darkened. 'You saying I'm not welcome?'

'Pub,' Luke said. His voice was strangely robotic and his expression was still blank. Hammer knew he had been looking for his brother for over a year and guessed he was in shock. It didn't look like a happy surprise.

CHAPTER THIRTEEN

At The Rising Moon, Luke went to the bar and ordered three pints from Seren. He didn't want Hammer to leave and thought buying a drink would keep him for a few minutes at least. He didn't know why he wanted Hammer there, and didn't have the time or headspace to examine it.

Seren's eyes were wide and sparkly, her face alive with interest. 'Is that your twin?' Her voice wasn't quiet enough and Luke felt a jagged sting of irritation. Still, this was small community life and, besides, he liked Seren, so he managed to squash the words 'no, just a random stranger who happens to look exactly like me'. He carried the drinks to the table where Lewis and Hammer were sitting in silence. Lewis had one arm stretched over the back of the chair next to him and his long legs were sprawled out. Hammer looked, as always, like he was ready to pummel something.

Having spent so many months imagining the moment of finding his brother, Luke was disconcerted to find he didn't have anything to say. The obvious questions – where had he been for the twelve months before Dean Fisher had taken him prisoner, why hadn't he been in touch, and how the hell was he suddenly here – seemed stuck in his throat.

'You're angry,' Lewis said.

And you're a fucking genius, Luke thought. He took a sip of the pint he didn't even want.

'Ask me.'

That was it. The calm self-assurance. The nerve of him. He wanted to throw a punch, to be rolling around on the pub floor kicking and flailing at each other until one was in a headlock. But they weren't kids now. They were grown men and he should use his words.

'I think it's sweet that you've been worried,' Lewis said, a smirk lifting the corners of his mouth.

Luke lunged across the table and found himself held back by Hammer. 'No,' he said. 'Not in here.'

Luke shrugged off Hammer and left the pub. Outside, he sucked in lungfuls of freezing air, so cold it made his chest burn.

Lewis appeared, closely followed by Hammer. Which meant he was handily placed to create a soft (ish) landing for Lewis when Luke launched himself at his twin, fists flying.

He landed a decent starting punch, but then Lewis got one on his jaw, which snapped his head back. It gained him a few seconds and Luke found his legs swept out from under him. They went down on the ground, hard, and were grappling in the ungainly wrestling style that had characterised most of their youthful disagreements.

'Fucksake.' Hammer was watching them in disgust, but not intervening. Luke didn't blame him. He felt ridiculous. And furious. And currently, the fury was still winning.

After some more tussling, Luke felt some of the energy

drain away and some clarity of thought returning. This was not dignified. He imagined Esme walking along the street and seeing him like this. Rolling around, grappling with his long-lost brother, grunting and stupid. In a moment he saw two grown men fighting and realised that Esme might find it threatening. The physical violence of it. That was like a bucket of cold water being emptied over his head and he released his hold from around Lewis's neck.

He might have decided to stop fighting, but Lewis hadn't got the memo and he took Luke's going slack as an opportunity to flip on top of him and wrap his hands around his throat. Looking up at his brother as he felt his chest burn and the grip around his neck tighten, Luke wondered whether this was still like the fights they had had as teenagers or whether Lewis had changed. Before the dart of fear could lodge itself, Lewis was pulled violently backwards and his grip on Luke's neck released. Luke took a gasping breath and sat up.

Hammer had hauled Lewis backward and had him immobilised a few feet away. He had wrapped his thick arms around Lewis's chest and was managing to keep him up on his tiptoes. 'Enough.'

It was one word, but it seemed to break through Lewis's fugue and he saw his face relax, the manic look slink away behind his eyes to hide.

After a moment, Hammer judged him to be calm enough, and he let him go. Lewis turned and openly appraised the other man. 'Bet you're useful in a proper fight.'

Hammer stared back at him implacably.

Luke was on his feet now, and he nodded his thanks to Hammer.

'That's two,' Hammer said, holding up two fingers.

Luke knew he meant he now owed the man two favours. In that moment, it didn't seem the worst thing in the world.

'Pub?' Lewis said.

It was cold outside and Luke didn't know what else to do, so he shrugged and they trooped back inside The Rising Moon.

'I'M WAITING,' Luke said, once they had sat back down.

Lewis opened his mouth and, from his expression, Luke knew he was going to say something smackable. Instead, he closed his mouth and shrugged.

Seren arrived at their table. 'I've run out of venison, but there's fish.'

'We're not eating,' Luke said, still glaring at Lewis.

'Fuck we're not,' Hammer said. 'Fish and chips, please.'

'All round?' Seren asked, gesturing.

'Yes,' Hammer said, draining his glass. 'And three more pints.' He stood up. 'I'll come and get them.'

Luke expected Seren to snap at him, but she shrugged and walked back to the kitchen. Hammer ducked around the bar and began pulling pints.

Lewis was staring at the tabletop.

'Where have you been? Why haven't you been in touch?' Luke gritted his teeth for a moment and then forced himself to breathe in and out slowly. He consciously forced his shoulders down. 'I thought you were dead.'

For a long moment, Lewis didn't answer. Then, addressing the table, he mumbled. 'It's complicated.'

'I should fucking hope so. Unless you want an audience, you should tell me now.' Luke watched Hammer pulling a second pint. He was taking his time, but he would be back with them soon.

'I wanted to tell you,' Lewis said in a rush. 'But it was too dangerous. I needed to keep you out of it. Out of it all. You're a dick, but you're my brother.'

Luke's guts twisted. 'Tell me.'

'I got in a spot of bother with Dean Fisher. You know the name?'

'I'm aware,' Luke said dryly. 'And you owed money.'

Lewis's eyes widened for a split second before he smiled knowingly. 'Easy guess.'

'Very easy. I met a few of your old pals. Looking for their cash.'

Lewis absorbed this for a moment. 'Shit. Sorry.'

Luke shrugged. 'I handled it. With his help,' he jerked his head in the direction of the bar where Hammer was working on the third pint.

'Wait. They came here?'

'There was a rumour that you were hiding out on an island off the north-east coast. That's what brought me here in the first place. I was looking for you.'

Lewis leaned back in his chair. 'I think I might know how that rumour started.'

'You?'

He shook his head. 'I was detained for a few months. Guessing my landlord put it out that I was in hiding.'

'Dean Fisher. I know this part. He's been holding you for the last six months, after he caught you skimming funds. But I want to know about the year before that. Where the hell were you? Why didn't you call? Send a message. Anything.' The words 'I've been worried sick' flashed into his mind. They sounded like something he had heard on the TV or in a book. Something a concerned parent would say.

Lewis didn't answer for a beat, then he looked directly into Luke's eyes. 'Do you remember how things were? We weren't exactly best mates. We had our own lives.'

'Radio silence,' Luke said stubbornly. 'You disappeared. You didn't reply to my messages, you didn't answer your phone. You must have known I was freaking out.'

Lewis looked at the table, shoulders hunched. 'There was a lot going on for me. A lot of serious stuff with serious people. You wouldn't understand.'

'Try me.'

'Look. You weren't exactly top of my list. I had a lot going on. I don't know what else to say.'

'That's it? Charming...'

'I might have been in touch, I was thinking about it, but then I got locked up by my psycho boss...' Lewis trailed off.

The reality of it was beginning to seep into Luke's consciousness. His brother was here. Alive. And he had been kept god-knew-where by Dean Fisher. What had it been like? 'Six months,' he said. 'I can't even imagine being held...'

'You don't need to exact revenge,' Lewis said quickly. 'There's no retribution here. Trust me.'

'I'm not about to rock the boat. But someone kidnapped you. I'm surprised you are willing to just let that go... Does this mean you're finally growing up?'

A small smile. 'I hate that word.'

'Kidnapped? How about man-napped?'

'That's not better.'

'No.' Luke didn't want to smile. He couldn't shake the image of Lewis in a grimy bed or tied to a chair. A bucket in the corner of the room. Hungry. Frightened. Trapped.

'I brought it on myself, really,' Lewis said. 'Dean didn't have much choice. And he was being nice. He could've just buried me in the foundations of a carpark.'

Yuri wouldn't have liked that. Luke decided to keep the thought to himself for now.

'I've been out of it,' Lewis said. 'Dean's people kept me drugged up a lot of the time, which was probably for the best. I don't really remember leaving, either. I was in a car. Then I was here.' He spread his hands. 'Surprise.'

Hammer had finished and had moved to the other side of the bar to pick up the full beer glasses.

'Look,' Lewis said, shifting forwards and putting his elbows on the table. 'It was a bad time. It's over. I'm out. And I don't want to discuss it.'

'Right,' Luke said, his eyes on Hammer as he brought their drinks. 'That easy.'

He picked up a glass as soon as they landed and drained half of it.

'Family reunion going well?' Hammer said in his rough voice. Luke could swear he was enjoying himself. 'Causeway closes at four, so you'd better hurry up and say what you need.'

'You're not leaving,' Luke said.

Lewis shrugged. 'Got nowhere to be.'

'You're not staying, pal.' Hammer's expression closed down and Luke remembered the man looking at him in exactly the same way. It made him realise how much Hammer had mellowed toward him over the last couple of months. But he had something else on his mind. Turning to his brother, he asked: 'What did you mean?'

'What? When?' Lewis drank some of his beer and wiped his mouth.

'You said I was a dick.'

Lewis smirked. 'Well, you are.'

'I know why I'm pissed off with you. You disappeared, you bastard, and I've been going through seven shades of hell as a result.' Luke put his elbows on the table and looked his twin straight in the eyes. 'But what the fuck did I do?'

Lewis met his gaze. 'You know.'

Luke started to say 'I really don't', but then he stopped. Lewis couldn't be talking about that... There was no way he was still upset about that. 'Freya?'

CHAPTER FOURTEEN

Luke hadn't thought about Freya for a while. He had questioned her when Lewis had first disappeared, of course, and given her his mobile number in case Lewis got in touch with her first. He knew her as his brother's live-in girlfriend and had written over any other previous identity she might have held. Yes, they had technically been a couple for a few months. Nothing serious. But they had broken up long before she and Lewis became a thing.

Lewis was looking at him like there was something he was supposed to know about or apologise for. He had nothing. To avoid saying 'Freya?' again, he asked whether they were back together. Which, as soon as the words were out, he knew had been a mistake.

'Yes, we're just back from a cruise,' Lewis said, his voice heavy with sarcasm. 'It's the perfect relationship.'

'And that's my fault, somehow?'

'Not that,' Lewis said 'But before, yes.'

'I don't understand.'

'Really?' Lewis shook his head. 'You don't remember having a little word with my girlfriend? Telling her that she could do better? That I wasn't good for her?'

'I don't,' Luke said, honestly enough. He could believe he had said those things, or words very like them, but he didn't remember the specific occasion. There were times when he saw the couple out and about, when a few drinks were taken. Not every memory was crystal clear. It really was like a different life. He felt like he was a different man. But he didn't believe that Lewis was hanging onto resentment. Not about that, anyway. 'Since when did you care what anybody said about you?'

The door to the pub swung open. Fiona walked in, holding Hamish in her arms. She was closely followed by Esme. Their cheeks were all pink from the wind and they looked healthy and wholesome in a way that struck Luke anew. It was the contrast with thoughts of his old life.

'This should be good,' Hammer said. He took a sip from his pint and leaned back in his chair.

Esme was standing stock still in the middle of the room. Her gaze went from Lewis to Luke and back again.

Luke stood up to greet her. He realised that Lewis was doing the same. His brother had turned on his charming smile and it made Luke want to punch him all over again.

'Esme,' Luke said, crossing the distance between them as quickly as possible. 'This is Lewis.'

Esme held a hand up in greeting. 'It's good to see you. We've all been worried.'

'Have you?' Lewis cut his eyes to Luke. 'That's nice.'

'Not really,' Fiona said in a matter-of-fact tone. 'This is Hamish.' She hoisted the baby up in her arms and he took one look at Lewis before turning to bury his face in Fiona's shoulder.

'Cute kid,' Lewis said. 'We were just catching up. Would you like to join us?'

'We don't want to interrupt,' Esme said, her eyes on Luke.

'Nonsense,' Lewis started pulling out chairs. 'We were talking about old times, but I'd rather hear all about you.'

Luke felt every muscle in his body tense. He had forgotten that Lewis was smooth.

Esme gave him one of her assessing looks.

The door opened again and Bee walked in.

It was past lunchtime, so Luke didn't understand why the village was gathering. Then he realised that Hammer had been a while at the bar. Plenty of time to text everybody and let them know there was a show on.

'Meeting,' Bee said, dispensing with preamble or social niceties. 'You might want to be elsewhere,' she said to Lewis.

'Why?'

Bee smiled gently, as if dealing with a difficult child. 'Because we'll be talking about you.'

'I'll stay,' Lewis said, turning up the wattage on his smile. 'Then I can answer any questions.' He spread his hands. 'I've got nothing to hide.'

Luke snorted.

ESME KEPT SNEAKING glances at Luke's twin brother. It was stupidly obvious, but she found herself cataloguing their similarities. Even while she knew they were genetically identical, she couldn't stop marvelling at every detail. The matching shape of their earlobes, the exact shade of blue of their eyes.

She had always been fascinated by siblings. Thinking about parents was just too painful and something she had filed away long ago, but siblings. Peers who shared DNA and parents and childhoods. Identical twins were another step closer even than that. She wondered what it was like to share a likeness, as well as all the other stuff. The childhood memories, the verbal shorthand, the shared jokes. Even the irritations, the old arguments and flash points. She envied it all.

Luke looked tense. Lewis looked at ease. They wore their hair in the same style, slightly long and messy, and that added to their striking resemblance. Luke had a scruff of day-old stubble, but Lewis's was almost a beard. Luke had a thin white scar on his left temple. It extended from the corner of his eye upwards and was only visible in certain light. Esme couldn't see it at this distance, but it made her wonder what distinguishing marks Lewis carried. Not that she was worried about mixing them up. Lewis was so clearly not Luke.

Just to be sure, she began cataloguing their differences. Lewis was a fraction bulkier than Luke. Like he lifted heavy things on a regular basis. His smile lifted up a fraction higher on the left, while Luke's was lop-sided to the right.

Seren came out from behind the bar, wiping her hands on a striped cloth. She stood next to Esme. 'Bloody hell, it's freaky.' Her voice wasn't quite quiet enough and Esme winced inside. She understood that this was the flip side of having a ready-made playmate, a sibling that truly couldn't be physically or mentally closer to you. The way that the world would always see something eerie in your sameness. The way you would always be compared and contrasted and judged. Sensing Luke's discomfort, she felt ashamed of her own fascination.

'You should go for a walk,' Luke was saying to Lewis. 'Meetings are for residents.'

'Insiders and outsiders?' Lewis asked. 'I know that game. Surprised to find you playing it.'

'It's not a game,' Luke said stiffly.

Hammer looked at Bee.

'We will ask you some questions and then we will have our meeting. There is a beautiful walk around the bay that you can enjoy.'

Lewis looked as if he was going to argue, but he seemed to think better of it.

Once everyone had taken their seats and Fiona had settled Hamish on a blanket on the floor with a selection of toys, Esme asked Lewis if he was all right.

'I'm fine, thank you for asking,' Lewis replied.

'That's good,' Bee said. 'I know our Luke has been concerned. He is very important to us, to our community. Which is why I offered to help.'

Lewis focused on her. 'You got me out?'

A slight dip of her chin. 'I called in a favour.'

'Well that clears up that mystery,' Lewis said. 'I take it I owe you now?'

Bee didn't answer.

Matteo wrote on his notepad and pushed it across the table. Lewis read it. 'What are my plans? Dunno, mate.'

'Back down south?' Luke interjected.

'I've not really had a chance to think about it,' Lewis said, barely glancing at Luke. Esme could feel his gaze land on her and linger there. Her cheeks flushed.

'But it's you I owe, right?' Lewis asked Bee.

'Why does it matter?' Seren broke in.

'Lydia Crow was there. And then I was released. I need to know if I owe the Crow Family.'

Bee shrugged. 'I called in the favour. You're clear. Unless you made an extra arrangement.'

'What do you do for work?' Seren asked. 'Any skills?'

'Plenty,' Lewis said. He didn't actually wink at her, but he might as well have done.

'Jesus Christ,' Luke muttered under his breath.

'How long have you been here?' Seren asked.

Lewis looked at Bee. 'One night?'

She nodded. 'We have a two-night limit for visitors.'

'Well, that's normal,' Lewis said sarcastically. 'You sound completely—'

Luke interrupted him before he could finish. 'Could you give us a minute?'

'Since you asked so nicely.' Lewis pulled on his jacket. 'I'll go for a stroll, then. Lovely day for it.'

Once the door closed behind him, Esme felt some of her tension ease. It was exhausting being hyperaware, and she realised how little she had to experience that state these days. How relaxed and at home and safe she generally felt.

'So,' Hammer said, directing his question to Luke. 'When's your brother leaving?'

'I don't know,' Luke said. 'You heard him. No plans.'

'He can't stay here.'

'You get to decide that, do you?'

'Don't fight,' Seren said.

'Keep it civil,' Fiona added. 'There's a bairn present.'

'I tried a spell to bring Tobias back,' Esme said. Partly to change the subject and partly because she wanted everyone to know that she wasn't just sitting around. She was trying to fix the situation.

'Did it work?' Seren asked.

'I don't think so. I could tell something was happening. It felt like I was pulling something in, but then the line went slack. It just all stopped.'

Fiona pulled a sympathetic expression.

'Regarding Lewis,' Bee said. She looked at Luke. 'You are our Book Keeper. And he's your flesh and blood.'

Luke's voice was rough. 'I'm glad he's not dead. But I don't trust him.'

Bee nodded. 'Thank you for your candour.'

'Is he dangerous?' Esme didn't know she was going to ask the question until the words were already out of her mouth.

'I don't know,' Luke replied. Miserable.

Matteo was writing. *We all have a past.*

Bee read it and nodded. 'This is a place of sanctuary.'

Esme thought their duty was to provide sanctuary to those seeking it. And they were usually unusual in some way. Gifted or, as in the case of The Three Sisters and Fiona and Euan, not exactly human. Although Luke didn't appear to have any particular ability. Except his affinity with the bookshop. 'Is that what he wants?' She directed this to Luke.

'I have no idea.' His voice was flat.

'Well,' Seren blew out a breath. 'Lewis doesn't seem to have any plans to stay long-term. Maybe we just let him bide a while.'

Fiona raised an eyebrow. 'What about the wards?' She looked at Esme. 'Do you have to do something to allow him to stay?'

Esme shrugged. 'The island chooses. And I guess he's got tonight, anyway. If this is only his second night?'

'That's the answer,' Bee said, and everybody turned to look at her. Without Tobias, she was the de facto leader, Esme realised. 'The island decides.'

TOBIAS WASN'T sure how long he had been walking, but he knew that his throat was dry with thirst and his lips felt cracked. The relentless heat on the top of his head had brought on a pain in his temples that pulsed in time with his footsteps. He knew that he didn't need to feel these discomforts. A long time ago, he had been above such earthly challenges. He was still above them, he knew that, and he only had to remember. But at the same time, the headache was joined with a sharp pain behind his eyes and the sensation drove away the thought. He felt further from the memory and the self that floated above the physical. No, that wasn't right. Not above the physical, but dissolved in it. Subsumed in it.

The self and the physical self. Why had he been thinking about that? The pain pulsed in his head. All matter was just tiny little bits and those little bits didn't have containers. The containers were also made of tiny little bits. Everything was the same small pieces. This seemed like a really important thought, and Tobias tried to hold on to it, but the pain behind his eyes had moved from a stabbing sensation to a white-hot light that filled every part of his vision and every corner of his mind. As his thoughts were burned away by the terrible white light, Tobias had just enough room left for one tiny thought. He ought to be afraid.

CHAPTER FIFTEEN

After the meeting dispersed, Esme asked Luke if he wanted to come back with her.

He shoved his hands into his jacket pockets, his face strangely blank. 'I'd better head back to the shop. I don't know whether Lewis will go back there or...'

'Okay,' Esme said. 'That makes sense.' She wanted to ask if she should go back to the shop with him. She felt as if things ought to be more certain with Luke. They had slept together and that had felt like a seismic shift for her. Maybe it wasn't the same for him, though? Even before that, they had been in an easy routine. Spending evenings together, at her place or his, but there was something about Luke's manner that told her today was different. Of course it was different, she chided herself. His long-lost twin was here.

'I'm sorry,' Luke was pushing a hand through his hair, shoving it away from his face in a gesture that seemed almost angry. 'I can't leave him in the shop on his own.'

Esme's stomach dropped and her skin had broken out in goose bumps. 'It's okay,' she said quickly. She remembered placating Ryan. Trying to placate Ryan. Failing to placate Ryan and all that came after.

Luke looked away, his gaze on the sky above the cottages. When he turned back, his face was softer, more familiar. 'I don't know how to handle this.'

'You two need some time,' Esme said, her speech automatic as she struggled to calm her haywire central nervous system. 'You'll catch up. You'll talk. It will be okay.' She shoved her shaking hands into her pockets.

He nodded, distracted, and already turning away. 'I hope so.'

Once she was home, Esme sat at the kitchen table with a mug of lemon balm tea and talked to Jet. He was sitting on the table, where he wasn't really supposed to be, washing an outstretched leg. She updated him on the arrival of Luke's twin brother and the ensuing village meeting. Then, without realising the words were coming, she told Jet that Luke didn't seem happy to see Lewis. That, after him spending so many months searching and worrying, it seemed a bit of a strange reaction. 'And then,' she finished, 'I wonder if I actually know him at all.'

BEE KNEW she had to approach Lucy carefully. Her youngest sister was skittish. And dangerous. She didn't usually pay attention to the humans on the island, but the arrival of The Book Keeper's twin might be enough to change that, especially with them all off kilter from Tobias's absence. Diana had pointed to the back garden when Bee had asked where she was and so that was where she went.

The day had been overcast, but the sky had cleared in time for the sun to set. Dramatic purple and red bled across the remaining clouds and the air was scented with the undergrowth. Foliage and flowers tangled from the crowded pots and the small mossy green rectangle of the old lawn was dotted with small specimen trees that had grown together, branches mingling until they were one big biomass and it would be impossible to say where one species ended and another began.

Lucy was sitting in the middle, underneath the tangled branches and bright green leaves. Her sister looked well. Her skin was smooth and untroubled, her lips a luscious red. These two facts hardly ever changed. The real indication of her health lay in her eyes. They could become entirely black until they appeared to sink into her pale face like stones beneath a deep lake.

Before Bee could broach the subject of Lewis, Lucy spoke. 'I don't feel him.'

'Tobias?'

Lucy nodded, quick. Her head tilted as if listening for something. 'Do you?'

Bee wished she had a different answer, but she could only give the truth. 'No. Not since he disappeared.'

She turned her face to the setting sun and wondered whether Tobias could see the same one. It wasn't likely, she knew. He was Elsewhere.

'When will he come back?'

'I don't know. The witch tried a spell, but she doesn't think it worked. We might have to get him ourselves.'

She wasn't looking at Lucy, but could sense her fear. 'I know,' she said. 'Hopefully he'll find his own way.'

'Maybe it would be better if he didn't.' Diana had arrived in the garden on soft feet.

'Don't say that!' Lucy rose from her seated position. Her hands were curled into fists.

'I want him back,' Diana said. 'But if Tobias can walk a path back to us, all on his own, that means something else could do the same.'

'We should be looking for him,' Lucy said. 'He would look for us.'

'Would he?' Bee wasn't sure. Tobias was even older than The Three Sisters. And he had been half-asleep for the last couple of centuries. It would be a mistake to assume they knew anything.

'I said we should look,' Diana said.

Bee closed her eyes. Two against one. She knew when she was defeated.

THEY KEPT THE MIRRORS SHROUDED. If any one of them sat in the middle, the other sisters would appear in the mirrors on either side. They didn't need to be physically together, they were always inseparable, but when they sat together, each looking into their own mirror, they could see further than any of them could alone.

'He is Elsewhere,' Bee said as she pulled the thin fabric from the mirrors. 'What more can we hope to know?'

'When he will return,' Lucy said, the pout threatening again.

'You might not like the answer,' Bee said. 'Are you sure you want to know? The islanders are upset as it is. I don't want you making things worse.'

Sharp white teeth in a red, red smile.

'Sisters,' Diana said, placating as always.

Lucy skipped to her place on the left and then looked challengingly at Bee.

Bee sighed. She took her place on the right and waited for Diana to sit in the middle.

They looked at their reflections, three women representing the three stages of life. Some argued there were four stages, wanted to include death, but that had never made sense to Bee. Birth and death were doorways, not stages. You arrived and you departed. Between was everything else.

'When was the last time we did this?' Diana asked.

'Years,' Lucy said with a sigh.

Bee closed her eyes and took a couple of slow breaths. When she opened her eyes, she knew she wouldn't see her reflection. The truth was, Macbeth had been onto something with his walking shadow. Humans strutted and fretted upon the stage, but she and her sisters and Tobias were made to play a different part.

The Three Sisters disappeared from the mirrors. Their images obscured by thick fog, not unlike the haar that had rolled across the island when Tobias disappeared. In the glass, the dark islet rose from an unnaturally calm sea. In the flat water, a mirror image of the island was reflected. It was bright white, the inverse to the black island above.

'Balance,' Bee said.

The black island became darker as they watched. It was the colour of shadow. Of nothing. An absence. The white shape below seemed so white it glowed.

'Tobias has gone through the door to Elsewhere. It leaves a gap,' Diana said. 'On this side. You know what happens when there is a space in a flower bed?'

'The strongest plants take it over,' Lucy said with some satisfaction.

Bee stood up and recovered the mirrors. 'We need to close the door before the vacuum gets filled with something we can't get rid of.'

AFTER THE MEETING FINISHED, Matteo made his way back to the shop. He had waved goodbye to the crowd at the pub, looking a little longer at Fiona. He didn't know if she noticed.

He pottered in his shop, tidying up the already-neat shelves, and then sat on his stool behind the counter and attacked the crossword. He was trying to calm himself after the community meeting. He was pleased for Luke that his brother wasn't dead. That was the right way to feel, so he made sure he felt it. Tried to make it deeper and more true than the competing feeling which told him that Lewis was trouble. That he didn't like change on the island. That new people could mean new problems.

The island was his sanctuary. It had been largely unchanged in the twenty-nine years he had lived there. Now, something felt different. And it wasn't just that Luke's brother had arrived. There had been new people before; Euan's birth, Esme arriving after Madame Le Grys had passed away, and Luke after they lost Alvis. But the island had never felt quite like this. Or perhaps it was him? All of his yesterdays had been the same. Now he wasn't so sure about his future. He felt unsettled, and he couldn't prevent his mind from turning over the most likely reason.

He finished the last clue and folded the paper. There was a card resting on top of the cash register and he picked it up. It was a simple white business card. Bold black type spelled the words 'Crow Investigations' and a mobile phone number. On the back, Lydia Crow had scribbled. 'If you ever go home, call me.'

LUKE MET Lewis on the main street of the village.

'Finished discussing me?' Lewis smiled in the lop-sided way that Luke knew from his own reflection. 'You people need more excitement in your lives.'

Luke didn't dignify that with a reply. He had hated seeing Lewis arguing with Bee and wished his brother would drop the attitude. He was pulled between loyalty to his brother and the deep discomfort of seeing him with the islanders. Lewis had put on a sarcastic and cynical persona a long time ago and Luke wasn't sure he would be able to take it off now, even if he wanted to. One thing was clear – Lewis belonged to the mainland and Luke hadn't realised how much of a gulf that would put between them. He had been so focused on finding him, he hadn't put much thought into what happened next.

He knew that he didn't want Lewis inside the bookshop, but he couldn't see any way around the situation. He had a tent and could ask his brother to camp on the beach, the way he had done when he had first arrived on the island. Lewis had been on the same trips with their father, after all. He knew his way around a tent peg.

The lights in the shop came on as he walked in. Lewis hadn't spoken on the walk from the pub and he didn't say anything now. His gaze roamed the shelves and the counter with the till. Luke wondered what scheme he was conjuring, what he was seeing. Lewis, like their dad, saw the world as split between people who were taking advantage of others and the marks who allowed themselves to be used.

'What's the deal?'

'I run the bookshop,' Luke said. He patted a nearby shelf. It had a new label. Black blocky writing on a piece of white cardboard and yellowed sticky tape that made it look as if it had been on display for years, when Luke knew it hadn't been there a few hours earlier when he had left the shop. *No smoking. No refunds. No hawkers.*

'He hasn't smoked for years,' Luke said out loud.

The lights flickered.

Lewis looked around. 'What was that?'

'Nothing.' Luke went into the back room that held the tiny kitchenette. The fridge contained a block of cheese, a couple of pints of milk and a half-finished dish of lasagne, courtesy of Esme. 'Tea? Coffee? Are you hungry?'

'I'm all right,' Lewis's voice carried from deep in the shop.

Luke shut the fridge and went to find him. Lewis was scanning the bookshelves at the very back of the shop. The sections labelled esoteric and mythology. Luke noted that the bottom row of larger, older books was absent. The sections had been growing steadily with Esme's regular presence, but they had shrunk considerably in the face of Lewis's scrutiny. His brother turned and Luke braced himself for a question about magic.

'Funny little place,' Lewis said. 'Smells.'

Luke's hand shot out to pat the nearest shelf. 'I love it,' he said, partly to assuage the shop, but mainly because it was true and his brother's attitude was pissing him off.

Lewis pulled a face. Luke realised that speaking honestly, using words like 'love', these were all things completely alien to their interactions. He wondered how well they really knew each other now. 'The causeway will be open later.'

'I thought I would stay,' Lewis said. 'For a bit. Catch up with my little brother.'

'There's nothing for you here.' Luke made it a flat statement.

'I don't know about that.' Lewis's attention was distracted by something on a nearby shelf. He pulled out the book. 'I remember this. Mum had it. Do you remember?'

Luke stared dumbfounded at the dog-eared paperback. If he didn't know better, he would have sworn it was the exact copy, the same book his mother had kept in the kitchen. It was an old Collin's guide to garden birds. She had kept it on the counter near to the window and he remembered her picking it up when she had spotted a bird in the garden that she didn't recognise, leafing through the pages eagerly and wondering out loud whether it was possibly a yellow siskin or a greenfinch. His throat was dry as he nodded.

'She always wanted to see a siskin,' Lewis said, echoing Luke's thoughts. His voice sounded odd, as if his throat had gone tight too.

Luke sighed. 'I have a bottle of vodka somewhere.'

CHAPTER SIXTEEN

Tobias had been lying on unforgiving ground. His joints ached and his face was hot on the side facing the relentless sun. When he swallowed, his throat clicked.

He had been thinking something important. Or doing something important. But now he wasn't sure what either of those things might be.

His head still hurt, but he contained the pain, wrapped it into a bundle and shoved that to one side of his mind to open up some space. It was like moving furniture. Those words felt strange. Homely.

And that reminded him that he came from somewhere. That he had someplace he belonged and it wasn't here on his flat plain of red and heat. He belonged somewhere with cool winds and salt water and green things pushing through soil and rock.

Getting to his feet was easier than he expected, and the bundle of pain was smaller. He crushed it experimentally, and it disappeared. The sun was as high as ever, as hot as ever, but Tobias ignored it and closed his eyes. When he opened them, the view was the same and he still didn't know which direction to walk, but he set off anyway.

．．．

Luke woke up with a pounding headache. Lewis was on Luke's camping mat on the floor. He was fast asleep or appeared that way. Luke realised he still didn't trust anything about Lewis to be as it appeared.

He stared at the ceiling for a few minutes and then pulled his pillow out from under his head and threw it at Lewis.

'Morning,' Lewis said, apparently not fazed. He stretched his arms above his head and yawned widely.

Luke wondered when the last time they had been this unguarded with each other was. Lewis seemed almost vulnerable in this sleepy early morning state. But Luke didn't trust that either. 'Causeway opens at lunchtime.'

'You still banging that drum?' Lewis scratched one armpit. 'I'm not in any hurry. Brothers reunited. It's time for us to spend quality time.'

'We did that last night,' Luke said, his head throbbing in reminder. 'I don't drink like that anymore and now I remember why.'

'Lightweight,' Lewis said. There was a pause and then he added. 'Did I say thank you? Last night?'

'I have no idea,' Luke said. His mouth felt dry and disgusting and he reached for the pint glass of water by his bed. 'Doesn't sound like you.'

'No,' Lewis agreed. 'But thanks anyway. For doing that job for Fisher. It feels good to be free and clear.'

He rolled his head to look up at him and Luke was transported back to their childhood. Nights with Lewis on the floor of his bedroom after their mother had died and their father had fallen headfirst into a bottle of whisky.

'And for looking for you for two years.'

'I'm not thanking you for that,' Lewis said, smiling smugly. 'You did a shit job.'

Luke pulled his remaining pillow from underneath his head and lobbed it at his brother.

ACROSS THE VILLAGE in Strand House, Esme woke up alone. Her bed, always her sanctuary, felt bigger than usual. Empty.

Shaking off the longing for Luke, she pulled on her dressing gown and slippers and went downstairs to fetch a morning tea. She opened the door for Jet to go outside, as he usually wanted to if he had been indoors overnight, but he stood on the threshold, back arched and fur standing on end and refused to move.

She petted him, murmuring that it was all right. Jet submitted to a couple of head strokes and even bumped into her hand, looking for more. 'What's wrong? Don't you want to go out?'

He wound around her legs until she closed the door and fed him. Then she took her tea back to bed. She made a nest with her research books and a notebook and Jet settled himself in the blanket at the foot of the bed. The bookshop had given her a textbook by a Scottish archaeological society. It had black and white photographs of standing stones, Pictish carvings, stone circles, brochs and cairns. She leafed through it, wondering which of them looked like the mound on Àite Marbh and at how certain in their faith these early people must have been to labour over these creations. Hauling giant rocks, carving stone, all while they were scratching a living on near-barren soil with driving rain at their backs and winter's chill creeping through their bones. Of course, that was why. When life was hard, you needed something to believe.

One of Esme's foster homes had been with a devout Christian family. The parents weren't terrible people and it wasn't her worst placement, but it still managed to turn her against organised religion. Extensive daily prayer sessions, lasting hours at a time, conducted in strict silence while the biological kids of the family surreptitiously pinched her, were the least of it. When they went to the church and listened to stories about an all-knowing and all-powerful god and his infinite love for them, Esme felt cheated. She had been told to forgive her biological mother for giving her up, told that God had a plan and that all she had to do was accept him into her life and to pray and that all would be well. Esme felt she had been praying, in her own way, for a very long time. And, to her ten-year-old mind, things hadn't much improved.

She had taken to saying 'goddess' rather than 'god' the first time Ryan broke one of her bones. Sitting in the minor injuries clinic of her local surgery, Ryan holding her hand a little too hard, and the pain in her chest blooming with every shallow breath, she willed the nice doctor to accept her explanation and not to make things difficult. If the doctor was suspicious and caused any trouble for Ryan, he wouldn't bring her for medical treatment next time. The fact that she was thinking this calmly, while most of her insisted that he would never do this again, that he had just lost his temper and that he was sorry and that she would know how to avoid upsetting him so much in the future, was a kind of acceptance. She held so many different facts in her head every day it seemed normal.

'Tell me again how you fell?' The doctor was holding Esme's other hand and gently feeling her fingers and wrist. Esme's thumb was swollen and sitting at a strange angle.

'I tripped on the last stair. Thought I had reached the bottom, but I hadn't.' Esme was proud of this lie. The detail of it. The lack of drama. She hadn't 'fallen down the stairs', she had 'tripped on the last one'.

'Nothing else hurt?'

'Just some bruises,' Esme said. She smiled. Still very proud of herself and her performance. Ryan would be so pleased.

'May I see?'

Ryan stiffened next to her.

'Oh, I'm fine. Nothing else hurts.' As if hearing the lie, and objecting, Esme's ribs throbbed in agony. She was pretty sure one of them was broken. There had been a peculiar cold nausea that had washed over her when Ryan had kicked her, something in addition to the sharp pain. And she had heard a crack.

'This might be dislocated,' the doctor indicated her thumb. 'Or there may be a small fracture.'

'Can you sort it?' Ryan asked.

Her kohl-rimmed eyes rested on him for a split second before turning back to Esme. 'You need an x-ray. Take this slip to reception B and they'll book you in. I will see you again after.'

'Can't you bandage her up now? I've got to get to work.'

'That's okay,' Esme said. 'I'm fine to wait.'

'She's in pain,' Ryan said. 'We've been waiting for hours already. Can't you give her something?'

'I'm happy to write you a prescription,' the nice doctor said, still speaking to Esme.

'That's okay,' Esme said. 'I'm taking paracetamol.'

'You can have ibuprofen, too. Take them regularly, according to the dosage on the packet, and it will build up.'

'Can't she have something stronger?'

'If you can manage with the paracetamol and ibuprofen, that's the best.'

'I can manage.'

'And,' the doctor turned and rummaged in a drawer behind her. 'I'll see you again after your x-ray, but you'll most likely need one of these, so I'll give it to you now.' She produced something that looked like a black glove. It had Velcro straps and was stiffened with a thin bar of metal. 'This will help you sleep better at night. You don't want to immobilise the thumb all the time, but you might find it more comfortable to spend time with support.'

Esme thanked the nice doctor and they left the room. Before Ryan had walked swiftly past the reception desk, she had already guessed that they wouldn't be heading down to x-ray. His patience had worn out.

As they walked to the car, Ryan berating her for missing the opportunity to score some 'decent painkillers', Esme was turning over a realisation in her mind. The doctor had given her the wrist brace because she had already guessed that Esme wouldn't be going to x-ray, wouldn't be back in her office. She was, at once, grateful and embarrassed. She had been seen. Her relationship had been seen. And, for a brief and painful second, it made her see it, too.

She wasn't ready for that, so she pushed the incident to the back of her mind. But she did start saying 'thank goddess' or 'all the goddesses' instead of 'thank god'. And when she said it, she didn't see the head of a bearded white man floating in a cloud, but a tired NHS doctor with a kind face and a hijab sitting in an ill-equipped treatment room.

SITTING IN THE RISING MOON, Lewis was looking around like he was visiting an alien planet. 'I didn't appreciate it yesterday, but this place is a real throwback,' he said, just as Seren arrived at their table. She glared at him, and he held up his hands. 'It's a compliment. I like the retro vibe.'

'What's good today?' Luke asked the first thing that came into his head, hoping to diffuse the tension.

'Everything,' Seren said flatly. 'Same as every day.'

'Right,' Luke forced a laugh. 'Maybe a pint to start with while we think about it.'

'Two pints,' Seren said, flicking a glance at Lewis. 'You'll want the venison, then.'

'Yes, sounds good. Thanks.'

'What a ray of sunshine,' Lewis said when Seren had disappeared into the kitchen.

'She runs this place on her own. It's a lot of work.'

'Truly shocking.'

'What?' Luke was regretting bringing Lewis to the pub.

'That she doesn't have a partner with that sunny disposition.'

'I know you've had a rough time, so I'm going to keep things civil. Stop insulting my friends or I will eject you from this island myself and I won't use the causeway.'

'Ooh!' Lewis held his hands up in mock surrender.

Seren returned with their drinks. She put a pint of ale in front of Luke and a pint of water in front of Lewis.

'Excuse me,' Lewis said. 'I'd like a beer too, please.' He gave Seren an entirely fake smile.

She matched his expression with one of her own. 'I'll be right back with that.'

Lewis watched Seren disappear into the kitchen again. 'She's not bringing me that beer, is she?'

'Wouldn't think so,' Luke said, taking a sip of his. He smacked his lips. 'That's the stuff.'

'Arsehole.'

'Wanker.'

. . .

BEE DIDN'T WANT to go to Àite Marbh. She had been very firm with the islanders that it wasn't worth the risk of going to the strange islet and that they wouldn't find Tobias there, but she had been feeling a growing guilt that she ought to at least check it out for herself. She wasn't exactly afraid, but she was wary. They had looked into the mirrors and seen the hole in the world. The doorway had to be closed before something was sucked from Elsewhere. A hole wanted to be filled. That was its nature. It couldn't help it any more than a nettle could help stinging your skin.

Diana was no help. She had point-blank refused to leave the house. It was her sanctuary and Bee understood that, but she had hoped that her middle sister might make an exception just this once.

She borrowed Hammer's boat without telling him where she was going. He didn't question her, as it wasn't unusual for her to head out to the wide ocean, just to have a few hours' peace. She supposed that he understood the impulse.

Bee was experienced with a boat, but she felt a flutter of panic as she approached the islet. The current seemed to alter as she drew nearer, drawing the boat in at an unnatural pace. She jumped out and pulled the boat up onto the sand, her muscles straining with the effort.

Just as Hammer had described, the place was entirely still. It was a dead place. Bee thought she must have been here at least once before, in all her time living on Unholy Island, but she couldn't remember it for certain. It felt like a place she might have seen in a vision or a dream. She put her fingers up to form a frame to look through as she regarded the small hill in the dip of ground. Had she seen it in the mirror with the gilt frame around the image?

She walked down the slope, watching the entrance to

the hill tomb. The emptiness was crushing. Tobias was not here, she was certain of that. But still, she had to check.

The black rectangle in the side of the grassy slope of the tomb was not an invitation. Bee didn't look around as she crossed the flat ground that led to the cairn. It wasn't because she was frightened of what she might see. But that she didn't want to confirm that there was absolutely nothing there. She usually saw things out of the corner of her eye. Visions of the past and future, vying for her attention as if they sensed she was one who could see them and, in the seeing, give them meaning again for a brief and shining moment. It was lonely here and Bee could feel a draining sadness lapping at the shores of her subconscious.

She ignored it and stepped through the angular stone entrance. The light of the world was immediately replaced by darkness. Within a step, it was as dark as being far below the surface. It was like jumping into deep water. Bee strode forward. She could feel her sisters with her, the sharp chaos of Lucy and Diana's warm steadiness, and she realised why Diana had refused to leave the house. Calm and surrounded by her plants, she was at her strongest, and that meant Bee was at her strongest, too. They were three, but they were also one. Bee had been playing at being human for so long that she had started to forget. The thought jolted her.

The passageway had a low ceiling. Hammer would have had to stoop. Several paces in, and Bee estimated she had to be in the centre of the cairn. She trailed her fingers along the stone walls on either side, noting the gaps where side chambers branched from the main passage. If her fingers hadn't been touching either side of the hall, she would have guessed that she was in a cavernous space. Her proprioception insisted that she was in an unbounded cathedral-like building, while her fingers told her that she was in a cramped corridor. The dissonance made her stomach roll.

She took another large step, refusing to allow the space to intimidate her. Her toes connected with an unyielding surface. She reached out and touched the uneven surface of a stone wall, indented in a rectangle shape, as if a doorway had been filled in. End of the road. The words were not her own and she pushed them from her mind with all of her force. Then she waited to see what the cairn would do next.

Was that someone breathing? Something? The wall was still in front of her. Bee put her hands on it and felt cold stone. The surface smooth, as if worn by water and time. As if it had always been here. She hesitated. She could demand to be let through, to the place she was now certain Tobias had gone. But what if she couldn't find him in the Elsewhere? What if she became trapped? He might already be on his way out, and then she would have sacrificed herself and her sisters for nothing.

The moment of uncertainty seemed to give the doorway power. Or perhaps it sensed an opportunity. The wall in front, where her palms were splayed was moving closer. The sides of the passage touching her shoulders. Squeezing in. Closing so quickly that she knew she would shortly be crushed. Like hands clapping to kill a fly. *You idiot*, she just had time to think before the darkness went the colour of nothing.

CHAPTER SEVENTEEN

Bee woke up outside on the grassy slope, her head pounding. The hill tomb looked exactly as it had minutes earlier when she had walked inside. Not minutes, she realised, seeing the sun low in the West. It was late afternoon and hours had passed. She sat up gingerly, scanning her body for signs of injury. She ached all over and her neck had a sharp pain, like she had slept in an awkward position, but she was otherwise unhurt. Lucky, Bee chided herself. You are extremely lucky.

The boat trip back to Unholy Island was fast. As though the winds were helping her to leave the quiet place. The sky was getting darker by the moment and rain began to splatter as she crossed the halfway point to Harbour Bay. She held the tiller of the motor and faced forward, only glancing back once. Àite Marbh was fading into the sea mist and the wake of the boat bumping across the waves was dissolving unnaturally fast, hiding her path. She didn't look back again.

On Harbour Bay, Bee dragged the boat onto the sand. It was a low-lying harbour where the island simply melted into the sea. There was a pontoon for when it was an especially high tide, but they usually just dragged the boat into the water and stepped in once it was floating.

A sleek brown head popped up between the waves further out. It was joined by a second a moment after. Bee watched the seals swimming and then turned to walk up the sand toward the coast path. She hadn't gone very far when she heard Fiona's voice behind her. The selkie was in human form, but with her thoroughly drenched hair slicked back from her face and her eyes looking rounder and darker than they usually did, there was something seal-like about her. Bee raised a hand in greeting and waited for Fiona to catch up.

'Did you see—?'

'No,' Bee cut in quickly, wanting to get Fiona's expression of disappointment over with as soon as possible.

'I thought,' Fiona started, and then she made a garbled sound. Words gone wrong. She shook her head. 'Sorry. Doesn't translate. It takes a wee while when I've been... I'll try again. Did you see any sign of him?'

'Nothing,' Bee said. 'The gateway threw me out.'

'There's an actual gate?'

'A doorway, I suppose. I'm not sure if it's inside the cairn or whether the doorway is the doorway into the hillside. The latter, maybe.' Bee realised that she had felt that she had gone Elsewhere the moment she had crossed the threshold. The line that ran beneath the primitive stone lintel.

'Are you hurt?'

'No.' Bee shrugged, shooting a small smile. 'Just my pride.'

The rain that had started as Bee was sailing was coming in more heavily now. Fiona looked around and Bee followed her gaze. Euan was visible behind Hammer's boathouse, making his way to the pathway ahead of them.

'How is he doing?'

'Better. Now that Oliver is no longer with us. He likes having Hamish around, too. Those two are thick as thieves.'

Bee nodded. She realised she ought to ask after the baby. It was the human thing to do, so she did, even though her mind was still taken up with her failure and what it meant.

'Esme is looking after him.'

Fiona has misunderstood her, Bee realised. She hoped the selkie didn't think that Bee had been criticising her caregiving skills. 'I didn't think you had left him home alone,' she said gently. 'He's a very lucky little boy.'

'Thank you,' Fiona said, mollified. 'But a grumpy gateway doesn't sound ideal. Should we be worried?'

'I don't know,' Bee said. Her calm somewhat restored. That was the thing about humanity. Ask them to name a ship and they'll vote for Boaty McBoatface and tell them there's a tear in the fabric of the reality that they know and they call it a 'grumpy gateway'. Fiona wasn't really human, of course, but she spent the majority of her time living as one. Like Bee. And that had obviously infected them both. Hopefully, with the best that humanity had to offer.

BEE WALKED with Fiona to Esme's bed-and-breakfast. There was a washing-up bowl and plastic jug and cups discarded in the front garden. A note stuck to the door had fallen onto the step and Bee picked it up. It said 'come right in' in rain-streaked letters. So they did.

Following the sounds of voices – Hamish's high-pitched babble and Esme's lower tones – they found Esme sitting on the sofa in the living room with Hamish next to her. They were clearly in the middle of a mammoth reading session with a pile of board books. The coffee table was covered in detritus, including a plastic plate with some soggy strips of toast, some chunky toy cars, and a green Sippy cup.

'Mama!' Hamish launched himself bodily at Fiona the moment she walked into the room. Esme caught the child around the middle to stop him from going headfirst off the furniture and he began to wail.

Fiona scooped him up and the tears stopped. 'Hello wee man,' she said. 'Have you been good for your Auntie Esme?'

'He's been great. We've had a lovely time.'

'I'll put the kettle on,' Bee said, backing out of the room.

'Thanks,' Esme said, stacking the books and removing a strip of toast from the front of her clothes where it had stuck, butter side down.

ONCE BEE HAD MADE three teas and carried them back through, she heard Fiona saying 'Thank you, again,' to Esme.

'Anytime,' Esme said, grabbing a tea from Bee's tray like a woman dying of thirst. 'It was fun.'

'It was exhausting, I bet,' Fiona said. 'You can be honest.'

Esme shook her head and smiled, drinking tea. 'I enjoyed it.' She looked at Bee. 'Is this a social visit or...?'

'I need to talk to you.'

'Should we go?' Fiona glanced down at Hamish, who was sitting on her feet, driving a plastic car across the carpet.

'No,' Bee said. 'You can hear this.'

'What is it?'

'You know the wards and that they protect the island? It's not all they do.'

'Okay,' Esme wasn't looking worried and Bee knew that was about to change.

'The wards protect the world.'

Esme stared at Bee for a beat. 'The wards protect the world,' she repeated eventually. 'I don't understand how...'

'Àite Marbh is a thin place. Like at All Hallow's Eve, but all the time. It's a doorway. The ancient people who lived here sensed it, so that's why they built their tomb where they did. Archaeologists assume it was to honour their high-ranking dead, but it might have been that they sensed it was a place that needed guarding. Maybe things came through at that place that needed to be imprisoned.'

'Or it was a kind of church or temple. Could it have been a sacred place?'

Bee considered the question. 'Why do you ask?'

'I've been reading about cairns and standing stones. Ancient sites.' She shrugged a little self-consciously. 'The only thing I can do is research. It makes me feel like I'm doing something at least. I've felt so useless.'

'You are not useless,' Bee said.

'Sounds like you have the most important job on the island,' Fiona said. Her eyes had lightened, turning fully human on the walk from the beach to Esme's. Now they seemed to be flooding darker again. Bee gave her a warning look until she looked down, composing herself.

'So how do I fix this?'

'There has been a Ward Witch on this island for a very long time. As long as you tend the wards and live on the island, that is all that is required. Just being the Ward Witch is all that matters.'

Esme frowned. 'It's purely symbolic? The gate knows there is a Ward Witch, so they assume the way is shut?'

'Exactly,' Bee said.

'It's sentient?' Fiona asked.

'Kind of. It's hard to explain. But we're pretty sure the things in Elsewhere don't know about it, otherwise they would be trying harder to come through. They would have tested it by now, Ward Witch or not.'

'Well, that's not very reassuring,' Fiona said. 'If they test it, they'll find...' she gestured to Esme. 'No offence, hen.'

'So I'm the symbolic guardian of a doorway between realities? And we've been relying on my title to stop things even trying to sneak through?'

'That's the size of it. But the gateway has been working to keep things locked up, too. It's not exactly sentient, not in the sense you probably mean, but I get the impression that it knows it's not meant to be used. It errs on the side of staying shut in both directions.'

'Well, that's something.'

'So how did Tobias go through?'

Bee looked at the two women. A selkie and a witch.

'I know he's special,' Esme said with a touch of impatience. 'But what is he?'

'Have you ever looked?' Bee asked, curious.

'No,' Esme said. 'That would be rude.'

Bee smiled. She really was very fond of Esme. She patted her arm. 'It's probably for the best. Might have been blinding.'

'What do you mean?' Fiona was looking between them.

'He's a god.'

CHAPTER EIGHTEEN

Fiona and Bee had left, but Esme's mind was still whirling. If Tobias was a god, whatever that even meant, perhaps he couldn't die? It was a comforting thought until her gaze fell upon the pile of books she had borrowed from the shop. Neolithic burial cairns, pagan mythology, death myths from around the world. So many words cataloguing ancient beliefs and a thousand deities. Gods large and small. They weren't all here, now. Which meant they had either been fictitious or they had existed once and then disappeared. Died. She closed her eyes and in the darkness saw a small plant withering, leaves browning and curling and stems drooping until rot set in and the whole thing crumbled to dust.

There was one person Esme wanted to speak to, but unfortunately, he was bonding with his long-lost brother. She didn't blame him, of course, and was glad that Lewis was alive and well. But the timing could have been better. Or maybe it would never be ideal. Would she ever feel good about being shoved aside?

She stopped, surprised at herself. Luke hadn't shoved her aside. He was spending time with his twin, the brother he feared had died. A wave of shame washed over her and she felt a familiar urge to go for a walk, to make some food, to go to her studio and paint until the feeling passed. She took a deep breath and forced herself to look at the place inside herself that hurt, like probing a sore tooth with her tongue. *Luke's family is back. He won't need me anymore.*

And there it was. The orphaned child that lived inside Esme was curled up in the corner, head on her knees, trying not to listen to the happy sounds of a family that she would never be a part of. She had never been adopted, but she had seen families in her foster placements. Knew that they existed for other people. Just not for her. It's not the same, she told that small child. Luke isn't a foster family. They were a couple. He had chosen her.

THE NEXT DAY, the two brothers were walking to the car park. They were moving quickly, long legs eating up the distance, as the sky turned from ominous grey to thunderous black. The weather had been either fog or rain or thundering, with breaks of bright sunshine that felt like a searchlight piercing the thick clouds.

Luke wasn't thinking about the strange weather, though. Wasn't paying attention to the unhappy island. He was waiting for the other shoe to drop, for Lewis to shout 'psych' or initiate another fight. It couldn't be this easy. He couldn't have found his brother and then have him wander out of his life again, no fuss, no trouble, no bomb going off. 'You're really leaving?'

'Try to contain your sadness,' Lewis said, shooting him a wry look.

'Where will you go?'

'Drop me at the nearest train station and I'll work it out from there.'

Now Luke felt bad. His brother wasn't an unexploded bomb, he was a person. His twin. 'You can stay longer if you need to.' He curbed the urge to add 'I think'. He wasn't about to start explaining wards and the two-night rule to Lewis.

'Nah. I have got a lot of catching up to do and it's slim pickings here. Not that your woman isn't delightful, but I get the impression you're not keen to share.'

Luke felt his whole body tense. He knew that Lewis was messing with him, but he still hated it. He unlocked his old Ford Fiesta. 'Stay in touch, yeah?'

'You know me.' Lewis's smile was a smirk and Luke wondered if he looked that annoying. It was one of the hazards of having a twin – you got to see every version of every expression of your own face played out and it wasn't always a flattering experience.

'Is that right?'

Luke had been so distracted by Lewis that he only now realised that something was very wrong.

'How deep is it?' Lewis was looking at the causeway. Or where the causeway ought to be. 'Is that drivable?'

'No.' Luke checked his watch for the third time. The causeway was due to be passable at half three. By four o'clock, it should have been completely visible with the maximum amount of road available and the water receded right out to the guide posts that lined the route. Instead, Luke was looking at choppy waves in an unbroken seascape. 'I don't understand.'

'You got the time wrong?'

'No,' Luke locked his car and turned to head back to the village. His first thought was to visit Tobias and ask for help. Then he remembered that Tobias wasn't an option.

'What do we do?' Lewis fell into step by his side.

'I don't know.'

Lewis was silent for a couple of minutes as they made their way back toward the village. When he spoke, he sounded annoyed. 'Why are you so freaked out? Is it so terrible to have me here for another couple of hours?'

Luke didn't know how to explain just how wrong this was. 'It's the tide. It doesn't just not happen. It's not something that is ever *late*.'

Lewis still wasn't getting it. He scrunched up his face. 'First time for everything, right?'

'Not this,' Luke said. 'Tides are caused by gravitational forces and our rotation with the moon. If tides are messed up, we are basically looking at a cataclysmic change. This weird tide here might mean a tsunami on the other side of the world.'

'I don't remember you being so dramatic.' Lewis looked around at the calm of the island. 'I don't hear anybody else screaming.'

'There's hardly anybody here,' Luke said. 'And the islanders aren't the screaming type.'

Luke meant what he said. He would have sworn the islanders weren't prone to panic, but he still wasn't looking forward to being the bearer of bad news. It made him feel unpleasantly responsible.

Esme flew down her garden path as they approached, her curly hair loose and wild around her shoulders.

'Something doesn't feel right,' she said, out of breath and face flushed. 'I was going to do some painting and I...' She seemed to remember that Lewis wasn't an islander and stopped abruptly.

'The causeway isn't open,' Luke said, reaching out a hand instinctively to touch her shoulder. 'It's high tide.'

'Now?' Esme hooked a stray strand of hair from her mouth and tucked it behind her ear.

'I know it doesn't make sense.'

'It's water, water, every where,' Lewis said.

'Coleridge?' Luke was surprised into asking. 'Since when do you read poetry?'

'I can read poetry if I want,' Lewis said. 'I've had a lot of free time recently.'

'It's not time for poetry,' Esme said, eyes wide. 'I don't know what this is, but it's nothing good.'

'Do you need to check...' Luke remembered Lewis just in time.

'Yes,' Esme said, catching on instantly. 'I'll get my stuff.'

The rain had begun to fall as they were speaking. It wasn't heavy, but there was a wall of sea mist advancing from the north.

'I'll go and speak to the others. I'll drop Lewis at the shop first.' He didn't like the idea of his brother being alone in the shop, but they wouldn't be able to speak freely around an outsider.

Lewis was frowning, following the conversation.

Luke touched Esme's arm. 'Be careful.' He watched her hurry back to the house to collect her rucksack and then steered Lewis away.

As they walked to the village, it was clear that Lewis was unhappy at being kept in the dark. 'You don't need to manage me,' he said. 'Just tell me why you are so freaked out.'

'I'll explain later,' Luke said, not really meaning it. He had to tell the islanders about the causeway. He wondered what Esme would find when she checked the wards.

'Fine. I'll leave you to it,' Lewis said and peeled away in the opposite direction.

Luke swore silently. It wasn't that he thought anybody

on the island was truly in any danger from his brother. Regardless of how much he had changed or what he might have done as part of his criminal life, Luke couldn't believe his brother was a killer. And right at this moment, he had a more pressing problem than the need to babysit his twin.

CHAPTER NINETEEN

Esme was holding her hand over the harbour ward and trying to calm her breathing. If she concentrated, she was usually able to feel if a ward was working. It was difficult to describe, but there was a feeling when she renewed the wards and, after, she could feel tiny vibrations in the air around the ward. It was a skill that made her feel competent and connected to the island in a way that was comforting. She finally felt as if she truly belonged. The news that she was the only thing standing between this world and another dimension hadn't properly sunk in, but she decided she had enough to worry about with this realm for the time being.

Luke's twin, for example, who had walked along the shore to join her and was now staring at her with a puzzled expression. 'What are you looking for?'

'Go and see if Hammer's home.' Esme pointed at Hammer's boat house, hoping to distract him.

Lewis ambled over to the place she had indicated and stood outside for a moment, hands on hips as he surveyed the unusual dwelling. There was a thin trail of smoke coming out of the chimney, but Hammer often left his wood burner banked low when he went out, so that didn't mean anything conclusive.

Esme held her hand over the ward site and confirmed the vibrations. She wasn't going to take any chances. Fat drops of rain marked the rocks and sprinkled dark spots on the sand.

She could hear Lewis knocking hard on the boathouse door. Hammering, really. She wondered if he did everything with the same level of intensity.

'Nope!' His voice was snatched by a sudden squall. Whatever else he might have added was taken by the weather.

Esme pulled the hood of her coat up. She needed to get to the castle ward on the other side of the island. It was a bit of a walk, and she really didn't want Lewis to tag along. Apart from anything else, he was already asking too many questions about what she was doing. When he left the island, he would forget all about it, so on one level it shouldn't really matter whether she told him about the wards. He would think she was kooky or, more likely, crazy, and then he would arrive on the mainland and forget all about her. It didn't matter. But he looked so like Luke. And she realised that she sort of wanted him to like her. To approve of her. He was Luke's family and that made her care what he thought. It was frustrating and confusing and, as the increasing rain reminded her, she didn't have time to be dwelling on her relationship insecurities.

Lewis loped across the sand to join her. 'He's not in. Or he's not answering. What can I do?'

'You want to help?' Esme peered at him from under her hood.

'Don't sound so surprised.' Lewis was hunched into his jacket.

'Go back to the village. The weather is turning and I don't want you to get caught in it.'

'I won't melt in a bit of rain,' Lewis said, frowning.

At that moment, the sky went dramatically dark and there was a roll of thunder.

'If it's going to be so bad, you should come back with me,' Lewis said, glancing out at the sea.

'I'm fine. I'm dressed for it.'

'Well I'm not leaving you. I'm gallant like that.'

Gallant would be doing as she requested, but Esme didn't think it was worth standing in the rain and arguing. Resigned, she turned to walk toward the promontory to Coire Bay. She would check that ward on her way to the castle.

He wasn't keeping step with her and, for a moment, she thought Lewis had changed his mind and decided to head back to the village.

Instead, he was standing on the rocks with one hand protecting his eyes from the rain as he stared out to sea. She followed his line of sight. Àite Marbh. It had been obscured by the fog and the rain of the last few days, but was looming out of the seascape. A dark mass that seemed blacker than it ought to be against the light grey of the horizon. Esme had never liked looking at the dead place, but now she knew that it housed a gateway between worlds, it was even more menacing. What had Bee called it? Elsewhere. And the only thing keeping things from flooding through was her. The Ward Witch.

'What is that place?' Lewis called.

'Just a small island.' Esme moved closer so that she didn't have to yell. 'There's nothing there.'

Lewis looked around the bay. There was a wildness to his eyes that was so different to his usual sardonic expression she found herself taking a step closer to him. 'Are you okay? What did you see?'

He didn't answer, staring back at Àite Marbh as if it was the most fascinating thing he had ever seen.

'Lewis?'

Abruptly, he turned and ran to the place where Hammer's rowing boat was tied up, and began pulling on the rope.

Esme looked around wildly. Lewis was making quick work of releasing the boat and hauling it the short distance to the water. She didn't have time to go and get help, and her only hope was that Hammer would appear, ambling back home just in time.

'Please, stop,' she tried. 'The weather is turning. It's dangerous. Have you even been out on a boat before?'

Lewis didn't answer. He didn't even look at her. He seemed to find it difficult to drag his gaze from the islet.

'Please,' she said again. 'Lewis, please stop.' She grabbed the nearest edge of the boat, towards the back, and dug her heels into the sand, trying to stop it from moving.

Lewis gave her a savage look.

His silence was the worst thing. He had been so chatty, so full of quips and compliments. This was a complete change of personality, as if he was suffering an acute and sudden psychosis.

Even with her efforts, Lewis managed to get the boat into the water. Esme's feet and ankles were soaked, and she was being dragged further in. Lewis climbed awkwardly into the boat and lowered the rotor into the water.

She had been out in the boat with Hammer many times. He had done all the rowing and motor stuff, but she probably had more experience than Lewis. Her mind raced as she tried to decide the best thing to do. Should she go with him? Or run for help?

He was stabbing switches on the motor, frenzied and seemingly at random. He pulled on the starter cord. It didn't catch the first time, but he got it on the second go. Before Esme had made a decision, the edge of the boat was ripped from her hands.

CHAPTER TWENTY

Luke was having a hard time understanding what was going on. All he knew was that Lewis was so desperate to get away from the island – from him – that he had stolen a boat and taken it out in what was fast becoming a storm.

Esme had run into The Rising Moon, where she had found Luke, Bee and Hammer. Seren was in the kitchen, but otherwise the place was empty.

'I'm so sorry,' she said to Luke. 'I tried to stop him.'

'He took my boat?' Hammer asked for the second time. He glared at Luke as if he was personally responsible.

'There was nothing I could do,' Esme said, wringing her hands.

'It's all right,' Luke said, putting an arm around her shoulders. 'It's not your fault. He's a bloody idiot.'

'I think, in this instance, it might not have been your brother's fault.' Bee was speaking gently and it made Esme feel more afraid than ever. 'You said he was looking at Àite Marbh?'

Esme bit her lip, trying to remember exactly what had happened. She had been distracted, thinking about the ward she had just checked and wondering about the next one. The harbour ward had felt fine. She knew she had renewed it when she was supposed to and hadn't found anything untoward. Lewis was looking out to sea, one hand shading his eyes, and then something had shifted. 'He was looking out at the view. We weren't talking or anything. Then he suddenly went running for the boat. I asked him what he was doing. I told him to stop, but he didn't reply. He didn't even look at me.'

'That's not like him,' Luke said, thinking that Lewis tended to be overly charming. Without Luke around to torture, he might not bother to turn the flirting up to eleven, but he would still expect him to be pleasant to Esme.

Bee was listening intently, her eyes boring into Esme's. 'He didn't seem himself?'

Esme pictured Lewis again. The way he dragged the boat as if being chased by a monster. The jerking, panicked movements as he climbed inside and pulled the cord on the motor. 'He was frenzied. Out of nowhere.'

Bee nodded, as if this confirmed her suspicions. 'It called to him.' She gave Hammer a sharp look. 'You know how that feels.'

Hammer's expression went blank, but he gave the smallest of shrugs.

'He might not have been thinking about the islet,' Luke said. 'He might be planning to go around it and on to the mainland. He was going to leave when we found the causeway was flooded... Oh God. What if he doesn't make it? I don't think he's ever even been in a boat before.'

'I'll go,' Hammer said. He got up.

'Should we call for help?' Luke asked.

'There's a lifeboat station at Seahouses,' Bee replied, 'but we've never tried to call them before.'

Hammer was moving toward the door, but he stopped. 'Let me assess the situation first.'

'We'll all go,' Bee said.

OUTSIDE, the rain was still steady. Bee turned around and began walking in the direction of her house. 'I've got a searchlight. I'll go and get it.'

Luke and Esme pulled up their hoods and followed Hammer back toward the bay.

'What did she mean?' he asked Esme. 'How could it call Lewis?'

'Bee said the islet is a thin place. A doorway between realities.'

He pushed his wet hair away from his face, frowning in thought. 'Like the multiverse theory?'

Esme looked at him, surprised. 'I think so. Part of our job is to keep that doorway protected and secret and shut. Apparently, the wards help with that. I'm not sure I really believe it.' Esme laughed self-consciously. 'That's not true. I know it's real. I'm just trying not to panic. I knew I had to keep the island safe and secret, and that was to protect us. The islanders. Tobias and Bee and Fiona and Seren and Hammer. My friends. My family. But now Bee says I'm also protecting the rest of the world from whatever is on Àite Marbh.'

'That's a lot.' He reached for her hand.

'It really is.'

LUKE KEPT HOLDING Esme's hand as they walked down to the harbour. Hammer had fetched a pair of binoculars and was scanning the sea.

'Can you see him?' Luke asked as soon as they were close enough.

'He'll be all right,' Esme said, squeezing his hand. 'It doesn't look too rough.'

'I haven't got another boat,' Hammer said. Clearly not happy.

Luke felt irritated at his lack of care for Lewis. He opened his mouth to say something cutting, but Hammer hadn't finished.

He lowered his binoculars and looked Luke dead in the eye. 'Stupid bastard has taken my only means of helping him.'

'It's okay,' Luke said, even though it wasn't. 'He'll come back. Or he's already reached Berwick and is on his way to the pub. Lewis will land on his feet. He always does.'

'What about my boat?'

'I'll buy you a new one,' Luke snapped. He had no idea how he would pay for that, but that was a problem for future him. In a time when he knew his brother wasn't at the bottom of the ocean and could think about things other than losing the only family he had left.

'No,' Hammer said patiently. 'I forgot about the anti-theft tracker. It's on my boat. We can see where it is.' He swiped his phone and tapped until he had brought up an app. 'It's moving.'

As he spoke, Luke heard the faint sound of a motor. Squinting and shading his eyes with his hand, he could see a shape in the water break away from the small island. It rapidly became clear as a boat with a seated figure.

'Holy shit,' Hammer said. 'He's coming back.'

'Oh thank goddess,' Esme said. She put her arm around Luke's waist and squeezed.

'I'm going to kill him,' Luke said.

They stood together, staring out as the boat got closer,

waves breaking across its prow. Esme spotted Bee walking across the sand, carrying a serious-looking lamp encased in black weatherproof rubber, and went to meet her.

'It's all right! He's coming back.'

Bee's face relaxed and she patted Esme's raincoat-clad shoulder. 'I'll go back and let everyone know. Word has probably spread by now.'

Once Lewis was close enough to the shore, Hammer and Luke waded out to help him pull the boat in.

Esme could hear Luke shouting and she realised that she wasn't afraid. Her reaction to an angry man was hard-wired and she usually panicked, the reminder of Ryan and, before him, coldly furious adults in her group home and foster placements. Right now, standing on the harbour beach with Hammer and Luke and Lewis all yelling at each other – she felt fine.

She could sense they all just needed to expend a bit of energy, to let off the pressure that had built through their fear for Lewis and, in the case of Hammer, his boat. It was like watching Hamish when he was over-excited or in need of a nap. She waited patiently for them to wind down a little and then joined the group. 'When you've all calmed down, you can come to mine for tea. I'll make pancakes.'

ESME HAD a theory that people couldn't stay properly angry when they were drinking a nice cup of tea and eating a fresh crepe with lemon and sugar. She used golden caster sugar, as it had a slight caramel flavour and had cut fresh lemons. Hammer, Lewis and Luke were sitting at her small kitchen table looking like bears at a tea party. The Vikings and the enforcer docilely sprinkling sugar onto their crepes and rolling them up. A warmth spread through Esme's body. She understood why Fiona didn't mind all the work of caring for Hamish and Euan, and why Seren was happy cooking for the island. There was something deeply satisfying about looking after those you loved.

'I don't know what happened,' Lewis said after inhaling three crepes and draining a mug of tea. 'I'm sorry.' He directed this to Hammer, but then looked to his brother. 'I can't explain it. I felt like I had to go there.' He shook his head. 'It was weird. This place is weird.'

Luke and Esme exchanged a look.

'It's just quiet, mate,' Hammer said. 'Makes city people go a bit crazy.'

'I don't think so,' Lewis said. 'It's something else.'

'What did you do there?' Luke asked.

'I didn't even get out of the boat. I don't know how I got there. You know when you drive a familiar route and then you can't remember the journey? I was looking out at the sea and then I was at the island.' He frowned. 'I really don't remember the bit before.'

Luke glanced at Esme.

'What?' Lewis asked. 'What was that look?'

'Nothing,' Esme said. 'You didn't seem yourself when you left, that's all.'

'Did you see anything?' Luke asked.

Lewis shrugged. 'There was a beach. Tiny one. And the boat started scraping on the ground. Then it was like I had woken up. I had no idea why I was there, so I just got out and turned the boat around. Came back.'

'I thought you were trying to leave. Get to the mainland.'

'I wasn't thinking anything,' Lewis said, running a finger around his plate to collect the last remnants of the lemony-sugar.

'Well you don't need to worry,' Hammer said. 'I'll check the weather, but I will be able to take you across to the mainland. If not tonight, then first thing tomorrow.' Jet had climbed up his back and was now settled across his shoulders, tail curled around his neck. It softened his hard man image a little, especially when Jet's tail flicked up and tickled his nose. 'Bloody cat,' he grumbled, but Esme could tell he didn't mind.

'What are we going to do about the causeway?' Luke asked. 'Will it just open again?'

'I hope so. It's got to open at some point.' Esme had hoped to sound calm and in control, but knew the desperation evident in her voice. She didn't know what it would mean if it didn't and they remained cut off permanently. Even a few days would be a logistical nightmare. And what was the strange tide doing in other parts of the world?

Lewis ignored them both and fixed his gaze on Luke. 'I might stay a bit longer. Sleep at yours.'

'It's not up to me,' Luke said.

Lewis scowled. 'Course it is.'

'No,' Esme said. 'We'll have to have a meeting. Decide as a community.'

Lewis leaned back in his chair and regarded them all. 'You know you sound like a cult, right?'

'Cults want new members,' Esme said. 'We're more picky than that.'

CHAPTER TWENTY-ONE

Matteo didn't know if it was Lydia Crow's visit or Tobias's absence making him jumpy, but he sensed a tense atmosphere when he walked into The Rising Moon that evening. Fiona was sitting on a stool at the bar and she greeted him warmly.

Seeming to anticipate the question, she went on. 'Hamish is with Euan. Napping. Hamish, I mean, not Euan.'

He nodded.

'I'm staying here,' Fiona said, leaning in to speak to him in a confidential manner. 'It's a bit serious over there.' She cut her eyes to where Luke, Lewis, Esme, Hammer and Bee were sitting at the middle table.

Matteo took the stool next to Fiona and tried to think of something to say. He pulled his notebook and pen out to get ready, and Fiona glanced at him expectantly.

He's still here.

Fiona leaned in again and Matteo savoured her closeness, and the feeling that they were forming a small unit away from the others. 'He's changed his mind about leaving. Luke isn't very happy.'

Matteo nodded to show his understanding. While Luke had been desperate to find his brother, to know he was alive and well, now that he was here, he had remembered all the old grievances and irritations. Family was tricky that way. He had left his own at nineteen and not looked back.

After they had eaten, Bee called Seren, Fiona and Matteo to the central table. 'We need to discuss something. Take a vote.'

Fiona sighed very quietly and Matteo suppressed a smile.

The tension in the room had eased, and Hammer and Luke were both leaning back in their chairs. Bee had her hands clasped on the table and had a business-like look about her. Esme was just placing her knife and fork onto her plate, and Lewis was scraping the sides of a dish of ice cream, seemingly unconcerned.

'Do you want to excuse yourself while we vote?' Bee asked him.

'I'm fine to stay, if nobody minds.' Lewis carried on scraping the dish, chasing the very last of the melted mint-choc-chip.

Matteo was surprised that Bee was giving him the choice. She had been adamant before that his presence could influence the way people voted. He wasn't interested in rocking any boats, though, so kept his notebook to himself.

Luke clasped his hands on the table and stared at them as he spoke. 'I propose that Lewis stay on the island for a few days. So that we can catch up properly and he has time to work out his next step. He is my brother and I don't want him to be pushed away before he is ready.'

Matteo blinked. That was certainly a change.

Luke raised his head and looked around the table.

There was something in his expression that Matteo couldn't fathom. Uncertainty? Resignation?

'We have no objection,' Bee said, speaking for her sisters at the same time. 'If Lewis is still here by our next meeting, we can discuss the situation again.'

'That's fine with me,' Seren said. She was clearly itching to get up and start clearing plates.

'What do you think?' Hammer asked Esme. He angled his body as if to shield her from seeing Lewis and Luke when she answered.

'He's Luke's family,' Esme said. 'And it's only for a few days.'

Fiona looked around the table. 'If it's all right with Esme, then it's all right with me.'

'That's decided then,' Hammer said. He looked at Matteo. 'Unless you've got an objection?'

Matteo shook his head. He suspected Hammer, like himself, might have reservations, but they were outnumbered. That was the downside of community living. You lived by the strength of your unity, but you also died by it.

AFTER THE MEETING, Esme stood outside The Rising Moon and waited for Luke. Before Tobias had gone missing, she had felt so comfortable with Luke. She still felt the fizzing nerves of early courtship, but he had made everything so easy. Made his feelings for her clear. Always falling into step with her when they left the pub after dinner or lunch, always the first to invite her for a drink or to go back to the bookshop. In truth, it was still very early, too early to call it a routine, but it had felt so definite. So *secure*. Esme realised that she had begun to rely upon it and as she hesitated in the street, the cool damp air cut through her clothes and made her shiver.

Before she could decide whether to carry on waiting or whether to head on home, the door to the pub swung open releasing a blast of sound and warmth. Seren's laughter cut out when the door swung shut again.

Lewis was in the middle of saying something and Esme saw Luke's unguarded smile. The one that crinkled his eyes fully. The one that, in this moment, she realised she had come to think of as hers.

'Were you waiting?' Luke said, catching sight of her. Then. 'Bloody hell. It's got cold.'

'I thought it was supposed to be spring,' Lewis said.

'Yes,' Esme said. She knew she was being awkward, stilted.

Luke didn't seem to notice her discomfort. He turned to Lewis. 'I guess it's linked to the weird tide. Freak weather event.'

'I don't mind about that. I'm happy to stay, even if it is freezing.' Lewis was staring at Esme and she felt prickling across the back of her neck. Like there was somebody standing behind her. She refused to look.

'For a couple of days,' Esme said. 'Then we'll see.'

Luke shot her a confused look, as if he wasn't sure why she was being unwelcoming. 'You might be bored by then,' he said, clearly trying to lighten the atmosphere.

'I doubt it,' Lewis was smiling at Esme. It wasn't quite a leer, but it wasn't entirely friendly either. 'I can see the benefits of island life.'

Esme's skin went hot all over.

'We had better get home before this gets any worse.' Luke hunched his shoulders as a freezing rain began to fall.

Esme knew that was perfectly reasonable, but she still felt the sting of dismissal. 'Right. I'll see you tomorrow.'

'Count on it,' Lewis said. 'Sleep well.'

Luke had started to walk away, Lewis keeping step. He

turned. 'We won't offer to walk you home.' Then he smiled at Lewis. 'Private joke.'

Esme forced a smile. 'Quite right. Night.'

He had already turned away and they loped away together, the thickening rain blurring their matching shapes.

Once she was safe indoors, Esme shut all the curtains. The rain was pelting against the windows as if it wanted to come inside. It was oppressive. She thought about brewing a calming tea, but decided to brush her teeth and go straight to bed instead. She wanted the oblivion of sleep, for this unsettling day to be finally over.

Her phone buzzed just as she was settling under the covers. Her heart lifted as she saw it was a message from Luke.

Going to spend the day with L tomorrow. Hope that's okay.

Esme typed back 'of course' and 'goodnight'.

After a few seconds, a message came back. A smiling emoji and a kiss.

Esme stared at her phone screen for a little longer, willing there to be more.

She wondered if he was annoyed with her for not being more welcoming to Lewis. He knew her role, though, knew that she had to protect the island. And up to a few hours ago, he had been just as keen to see the back of his brother. What had changed?

CHAPTER TWENTY-TWO

It had been decided that Lewis would stay in Tobias's house. When all was said and done, it seemed silly to make Lewis bunk on the floor of Luke's tiny flat above the bookshop, when there was a huge house standing empty. Hammer had asked whether Lewis wanted to have Winter, thinking that the dog might prefer to be back in his familiar home, but Lewis said he wasn't really a dog person. And besides, Winter was still largely glued to Hammer's side and whined pitifully when Lewis held a hand out to pat him.

Over the next couple of days, Lewis spent time with the islanders individually and as a group. He won over Seren with effusive compliments for her food and by eating more than one meal in a sitting because 'it was impossible to choose between the options, they were both so delicious'.

He went fishing with Hammer and, although their time was largely spent in silence, Hammer seemed less hostile towards Lewis after their trip.

He went for a beach walk with Fiona and Hamish and, by the time they were on their way back, he was carrying Hamish on his shoulders. The boy had his hands wrapped around the top of his head, occasionally covering his eyes, and all three were laughing.

Things even seemed easier with Luke. The brothers seemed to have rediscovered their old rhythms and inside jokes.

Esme was still wary. It was impossible for her not to be, but she had to admit that Lewis was easy company. He was quick to smile and, while his charm had made her suspicious, it seemed effortless and instinctive to him and she decided there was no harm to it. She remembered that she had distrusted Luke's charm in the beginning, too, and now she was certain that he had a good heart. She decided to extend the same trust to Lewis. He was, after all, Luke's kin.

Lewis had been on the island for four days. There was no sign of Tobias's return, and the causeway was still closed. The water had receded at times, but not enough to make it passable and nobody could understand it. 'This will happen eventually, but it's not due yet,' Bee said. The islanders were gathered in The Rising Moon for their evening meal. She looked around at the blank faces before explaining. 'Climate change.'

Seren was looking worried. 'Supplies are getting low. Fresh stuff, anyway. I've got plenty preserved and in the freezer, but that's not a long-term solution.'

'Hamish is due his jabs on Friday,' Fiona said. 'Being a wee bit late with them is fine, but I'll need to take him to the mainland, eventually.'

'I can take you in the boat,' Hammer said. 'And pick up some fresh food. Give me a list.'

'It's important for the causeway to open?' Lewis asked, looking around. 'I thought you liked being isolated?' He looked to Esme. 'You said Unholy Island was a sanctuary, cut off from the rest of the world.'

'Not entirely,' Esme said. 'We've always had visitors and we trade with the mainland. We like to stay private, but if someone really needs sanctuary, they can find us.'

'Okay. I understand.' Lewis nodded. 'I will see what I can do.'

'You going to part the sea, pal?' Hammer said.

Lewis smiled, but he didn't seem to be entirely joking. 'Maybe.'

Esme didn't know where he got his confidence. She was supposed to be the island's Ward Witch, she ought to be the one reassuring people. But she hadn't got a clue how to fix the causeway and she wasn't going to start lying.

She looked at Bee to gauge her reaction. The older woman was watching Lewis with quiet intensity. Then she stood up. 'I'm tired. I'll see you all tomorrow.'

'I'm going to head off, too,' Esme said. She looked at Luke to see if he was going to offer to come with her, but he was whispering with Lewis.

Esme followed Bee outside. It was twilight and the houses were clothed in deep shadow. Esme didn't know how she was going to broach the subject with Bee, but she didn't have to wonder for long.

'Something's not right,' Bee said. The lines in her face seemed deeper than usual, and she looked tired.

Esme glanced at the window of the pub. 'I think it's...'

Bee stiffened, listening. 'Not here,' she said. 'Walk me home.'

Once they were safely away from The Rising Moon, Bee spoke again. 'Have you noticed that the fog has gone?'

'The weather is pretty changeable at this time of the year,' Esme replied. 'Do you think it's significant?'

'I'm not certain,' Bee said. 'But the tide is receding. I

think the causeway will be passable again in a day or two. Maybe even tomorrow.'

Esme absorbed this. 'That's good, isn't it?'

'Maybe,' Bee shrugged. 'Maybe not.'

Esme stopped walking. 'What do you mean?'

'Tobias has gone, that upset the balance, and the island closed the causeway. Maybe to protect us. I don't know for sure. But if the causeway is opening, it suggests something has changed. The balance has returned, but Tobias isn't here...'

Esme went cold all the way through. She could see her ruined painting in her mind's eye. The dark shape in the sea like a hole in the world.

'We need Tobias,' Bee said. The frown was back and Esme didn't think she had ever seen Bee look so worried. 'He's the only one strong enough to sort this mess out.'

'We've tried to get him back,' Esme said. 'My spells didn't work and I don't know what else I can do.'

Bee was facing away, looking out to sea. Esme couldn't see her eyes when she said: 'I can look for him.'

'You can't go back to the island. You've always said we should keep away from it. We're not even supposed to say its name.' Esme didn't want to point out that Bee had already tried going to the island and it spat her out.

'Not physically,' Bee replied. 'Tobias is Elsewhere and there is an entrance on Àite Marbh. But there are other ways in for those who can walk outside their bodies.'

'Astral projection?'

'Spirit walking. Astral projection. Soul travel. It has many names. My sisters will have to watch my physical form. Make sure I'm safe. Make sure I wake up.'

'That sounds dangerous.' Esme felt a mix of guilt and relief that Bee was going to do something. Her own spells hadn't been strong enough to pull Tobias from Elsewhere, and she didn't know what else she could try.

'It is,' Bee said plainly. 'I don't want to do it, but I don't see what other choice we have at this point.'

A COUPLE OF HOURS LATER, when Esme was half-way ready for bed and just about to text Luke to say 'goodnight', her landline rang. Luke's voice was always welcome, but the note of excitement sounded a clang of dread in her own heart. 'Lewis has had an idea about how to fix the causeway.'

'What do you mean?'

'A ceremony. He says we need to do it now. We're all meeting at Shell Bay.'

'It's almost eleven.'

'I know!' Luke sounded giddy.

'Bee said that the tide is receding anyway. She thinks the causeway will be open tomorrow.'

'It will be if we do the ceremony,' Luke said.

'I don't understand why you're taking his word...'

'We need the causeway to open, right?' Luke broke in. His voice was soft, and there was an undercurrent of hurt. 'Why can't we try Lewis's idea?'

THE CEREMONY HAD to be that night. Lewis, and nobody seemed to know where he had got this information from, insisted. She had tried to speak to Luke about it once she arrived at the beach, layered up in clothes against the chill of the night air, but he had been oddly quiet. She realised that he was caught between his girlfriend and his brother. She didn't want to be the cause of stress or to make him feel as if she was trying to drive a wedge between him and

Lewis. She remembered one of the families she had been fostered with and how the siblings had closed ranks against her. She knew that blood was the thickest.

Instead, she sought Fiona. She was further down the bay, collecting driftwood for the bonfire. Hamish was wearing a waterproof all-in-one and stacking a pile of pebbles with Euan. His eyes were huge in his face and Esme was surprised that Fiona had brought him out at this time of the night.

Fiona stopped to speak to Esme, clutching her bundle of sticks and turning so that the wind wasn't blowing her hair into her face. Esme tried to explain her reservations but found they were difficult to articulate.

'Isn't it good that he's got an idea? I mean, we need to try something. It feels better than doing nothing.'

Esme felt the stab of rebuke, even though she knew Fiona wouldn't have meant it that way. She was the Ward Witch, she ought to be the one coming up with ideas, she ought to be fixing the situation. 'I've been researching,' she said, 'reading everything I can find in the bookshop and there's nothing about the tides.'

'Well, you looked,' Fiona said. 'That's all you can do.'

'Nothing useful, I mean,' Esme ploughed on. There was something off about Fiona's manner. Something different that she couldn't quite put her finger on. 'There's lots of lore to go along with the science. Myths and stories and spells that are best at certain tide times, but nothing concrete about what to do when you have a high tide that won't recede. And it's huge. If I go in and do the wrong thing, it might make things worse.'

'It's good that Lewis had an idea, then,' Fiona said. 'So you don't have to worry about it.'

Esme frowned. Why was Fiona so calm? 'But what if

he makes things worse? He could flood somewhere or cause a storm.'

'Lewis says this is the best way. He seems to know what he's doing.'

'But how does he know? He's a mainlander. A newcomer. I don't understand why you are so willing to trust him.'

Fiona looked uncomfortable, as if Esme had committed a social faux pas. 'He's our Book Keeper's twin brother,' she said eventually. 'I think that gives him a bit of leeway. And we're desperate for help.'

Again, Esme felt the sting of criticism. 'I wish Tobias was here,' she said.

'That's why it's good we have Lewis,' Fiona said, brightening. 'Are you going to help with the firewood?'

UPSTAIRS in the house of The Three Sisters, Bee lay on her back in her bed. She hadn't gone Elsewhere for a very long time, but she slipped out of her body as easily as breathing. Finding her way between the worlds wasn't quite as simple, but with focus it was possible. Realities were layered like tissue paper and there were places where that tissue had torn. In the end, all it took was patience and Bee had always had plenty of that.

THE FIRELIGHT ILLUMINATED THE ISLANDERS' faces. The fire crackled and sparks flew up into the dark sky. Being so early in the year, night had fallen early. Hamish was standing between Fiona and Euan, each of them holding one of his hands. He was swaying on his feet with tiredness. Next was Seren, who was holding hands with

Lewis. Luke was on the other side of Lewis, followed by Matteo and Esme.

There was no Bee, but when Esme had suggested they wait for her, Lewis had said that they couldn't. 'The time is now,' he had said, lifting his chin and gazing out at the dark sea, as if receiving wisdom from it. The act, and Esme was certain it *was* an act, made her stomach churn.

Lewis smiled encouragingly at Seren and she let go of his hand in order to step toward the fire. She was too close and Esme was about to warn her, when she thrust a hand into the flames.

Esme had a moment of pure horror before her brain caught up and she realised that Seren wasn't screaming in pain and that her hand was back out of the flames. She was wearing a thick glove. The sort she used to tend the fireplace at The Rising Moon.

There were 'oohs' and 'aahs' around the fire. Belatedly, Esme realised that the flames had changed colour. They were flicking green and blue. Seren had to have thrown something in to the fire. A party trick.

Lewis tipped his head back and yelled at the sky. 'Give it back. The causeway is ours.'

If it wasn't for her growing uncertainty, Esme would have laughed. This wasn't a spell. This wasn't magic. This was an overgrown child demanding a toy. The island and the sea weren't indulgent parents ready to cater to your whims, nor people you could bully. Lewis was treating the ritual as if he could intimidate a higher power by yelling at it.

She looked at Fiona, wanting to share a moment of disbelief, but Fiona was gazing at Lewis as if he was speaking in beautiful poetry. Looking around the circle, the rest of the islanders were similarly impressed. Esme wondered if she had stepped into a parallel universe. Or had she suffered a blow to the head? It was as if she was experiencing an entirely different reality to the rest of the group. It was profoundly disorientating.

'It is done,' Lewis said. He put a hand on Seren's shoulder. 'We thank you for your tribute.'

The others filed up and repeated his gesture and his words. Esme didn't and she could feel Lewis's gaze upon her.

Luke was looking at her, confused. That did it. She moved over and put her hand onto Seren's shoulder, repeated the words.

Luke's expression relaxed into a smile.

Lewis was smiling, too, but it wasn't relaxed. He was watching her closely and her instincts told her that she needed to be very, very careful indeed.

CHAPTER TWENTY-THREE

The next day, Esme woke alone. Luke had stayed with her the night before, but he had been distracted and had spoken about Lewis almost non-stop. He had seemed in awe of the fire ceremony and Esme hadn't felt able to question its validity with him. It had meant a slightly strained dialogue before they had gone to sleep. Now, she realised he must have got up early and left before she had woken up. There was a note on his bedside table, confirming this, but it didn't allay her feeling of foreboding. 'Gone to see Lewis. Didn't want to disturb you.' There was a kiss after the last word, but it didn't do much to ease Esme's mind. When had they stopped being a team?

Esme dressed quickly and went downstairs to make tea. The sun was pouring through the kitchen window like it was rehearsing for spring. There were snowdrops in the garden, heralding its coming, and buds appearing on branches. The sea was covered in sparkles from the sunlight and she realised it was later than she had assumed. Her phone buzzed. It was Luke, telling her that he was going to check the causeway.

Esme wanted to ask if Lewis was going to be with him,

but thought it best to assume so. If she asked, she might sound judgemental.

She poured her tea into her insulated travel cup, put food down for Jet, who was nowhere to be seen, and headed to the causeway. She met Luke and Lewis as they appeared from Tobias's house. Luke kissed her cheek and took her hand. Lewis greeted her with impeccable friendliness and Esme didn't know why it made her hackles rise.

Before they had reached the place where the road joined the island, Esme could see that the tide had receded and the causeway was open.

'You did it!' Luke said to Lewis. He dropped Esme's hand to punch his brother lightly on the arm. 'You bloody did it!'

'We all did it,' Lewis said. 'It was a group effort.'

'Nah, it was your idea.' Luke grinned at Esme. 'He'll have a place now, won't he? After this?'

'I told you. The tide was receding anyway...' Esme caught sight of Lewis's expression and stopped speaking. There was something dangerous in his eyes. A warning.

'It was the ceremony,' Luke said. 'I don't know how he knew what to do, but it's a good sign, isn't it?'

Luke looked so happy. Lewis was watching her shrewdly. Esme swallowed. 'It's up to—'

'The community, yeah,' Luke interrupted. 'But we all want him. It's just the island left and it's got to be happy with him now. You saw the fire last night and now this...' He gestured to the causeway.

'I know you don't exactly speak to the wards,' Lewis said earnestly, 'but it would be great if you could see how they feel. See if the island will let me stay. I really feel as if I've got a role here.' He ducked his head and seemed utterly sincere, but there was a shard of ice in Esme's heart.

'How do you know about the wards?'

'Luke told me,' Lewis said, as if it was obvious. Which, of course, it was.

'You don't mind?' Luke asked, frowning. 'After what he did with the ritual and everything. It seemed right.'

'No,' Esme said automatically. 'It's fine.' Did Luke not realise that the ritual had been a nonsense? That the flames had changed colour because Lewis had got Seren to throw something into it? Borax turned flames green, and she was sure there was something else that would produce blue, too. Copper chloride maybe?

Luke took her hand again. 'It's a beautiful day.'

'I think we'll have visitors,' Lewis said, shading his eyes and looking toward the mainland. 'Should make good money in the shop today.'

'Lewis is going to help me out,' Luke said. 'So if you need a hand with your paintings, I'll be able to pop over later.'

Esme had mentioned needing help to hang one of her larger pieces in the hallway. It was taking up room in her studio and she had hopes a tourist might fall in love with it. They usually went for smaller pieces, stuff that was easy to carry, but you never knew. And she could offer to have it delivered to the customer after. They might have forgotten they bought it and have a bit of a surprise, but hopefully it would be a good one.

'Lewis is going to work in the bookshop?'

'Wherever I can be useful,' Lewis said.

At that moment, the sun went behind clouds and the air temperature dropped by a few degrees. The sea went from sparkling blue to forbidding grey.

Luke hunched his shoulders against the chill. 'We should head back. Open up.' He turned and began walking in the direction of the village.

Esme trailed behind the brothers and fretted.

.   .   .

THE DAY AFTER, The Rising Moon was full of tourists. It was always a shock when the new season began after the quiet of winter. Usually it was a good shock. Seeing fresh faces and hearing different voices made a nice change. It reminded the islanders that they were part of a larger world and the renewed sense of 'us and them' buried any small resentments that had begun to build over the long, cold months.

Seren was a blur of movement, carrying plates from the kitchen, taking orders and clearing tables. She had tied her red checked shirt in a knot at her waist and had matching red lipstick. She seemed more vibrant, more alive, than usual. Actually smiling at the tourists, even when they asked whether the mushrooms in the venison casserole were organic.

'Busy,' Esme said, when Seren arrived at her table. 'Do you need a hand?'

'Euan's in the kitchen,' Seren said. 'But thanks.'

'Shall I move to the back room?' Esme was conscious that she had just sat at a table that could seat three, four at a push, and another couple had just walked into the pub, looking in vain for an empty table.

'Lewis is in there,' Seren said and moved away as if that was a complete sentence.

Esme got up from her table and gestured to the couple to take it.

'Are you sure?' one of the women asked. She had a broad, kind face, very suntanned.

Her partner put her bag onto the chair. 'Thanks.' She looked at the blackboard. 'Any recommendations? I don't know what to have.'

'No problem,' Esme said. 'The fish and chips are amazing.'

The back room of the pub held an ancient Space Invaders machine and a dartboard. It usually had seating scattered around the edge, so that people had room to play. There was a decently sized table that lived tucked into the corner. The same table that had been used to hold Alvis's body for her wake. When the pub was very busy, Seren brought in a few small tables from storage and set them up as extra dining spaces. It had happened twice in Esme's memory.

Walking into the room, Esme found the large table had been set up in the middle of the room. Having already thought about Alvis, it was hard not to think about the last time she had seen it in that position. Now, however, it wasn't the body of the island's old Book Keeper, it was loaded with plates and glasses.

Lewis was sat at one end of the table, making good headway on a steak and ale pie. There was a plate of fish and chips to his right and a scraped-clean plate of something else. A smear of gravy suggested the venison casserole.

'May I join you?'

'Sure,' Lewis said, still chewing. He swallowed with some difficulty. 'I don't like eating alone.'

Esme was about to ask about the owner of the fish and chips, presuming they had just gone to the loo, when Lewis grabbed a chip from the plate and stuffed it into his mouth.

He followed this with the last piece of the pie, a large bite that made his cheeks balloon, and was pulling the fish and chips plate forward even as he chewed.

'You're hungry,' Esme said. It wasn't polite to comment on what other people ate, she knew, but the words popped out. Lewis wasn't hungry, though. He was eating like a banqueting king. A banqueting king who hadn't had a morsel for a week in preparation.

Seren came in at that point. 'Know what you want?'

Esme's appetite had fled, but she wasn't about to insult Seren. 'What's the soup?'

'Tomato and lentil. With bread, oatcakes or a cheese scone.'

'Soup and a scone, please.'

'Same for me,' Lewis said, small pieces of potato flying from his mouth as he spoke. 'I'm bloody starving here.'

Esme expected a sharp remark from Seren. She had been known to eviscerate visitors for far less. Instead, she smiled the brightest, sparkliest smile that Esme had ever seen. Her voice, when she replied 'coming right up', was low and warm. As she watched Seren walk out of the room, Esme realised how Seren had sounded. Sultry.

She looked at Lewis. He was a handsome man. He was identical to Luke, so of course she thought he was good-looking. But at this moment, he was not at his best. There was grease on his chin from the battered fish and he was chewing yet another enormous mouthful, his cheeks distended and a kind of stoic blankness in his eyes.

'Are you feeling all right?' Esme could see something was wrong and her instinct, as always, was to fix it. 'May I touch your forehead?'

Lewis shrugged. Not bothering to waste eating time by answering her verbally.

Esme stood up and felt his forehead and the top of his head. He didn't feel hot, but his eyes were definitely glazed. She associated that with fever or drugs or extreme tiredness.

Sitting back in her chair, Esme surveyed the table. In addition to the plates, there were several empty glasses with dregs in the bottom. She had assumed that Lewis had

had lots of company before she arrived, but now she suspected they were all his. Perhaps he was drunk and that explained the glazed look.

Lewis picked up a paper napkin and wiped his face, still chewing. His eyes had come back into focus and he was watching her.

'Did you sleep well?'

He swallowed, washing down his food with a swig of lemonade. 'You don't like me.'

'I don't know why you think that,' Esme said evenly.

He resumed eating, but his pace was more measured, the mouthfuls more modest.

When Seren arrived with the soups, Esme realised that her shirt was knotted higher than before, showing an expanse of skin. She leaned very close to Lewis to collect some of the empty plates, and moved away with a hip-swinging walk.

Lewis watched her leave. 'She likes me.'

His eyes flicked back to Esme. 'Fiona likes me. Matteo likes me. Euan likes me. Luke likes me. But not you.'

'It's not a question of liking,' Esme said. If he wanted directness, she could do that. She wasn't a frightened mouse. Not anymore. 'I don't know you well enough to trust you. That's nothing personal, I'm just very cautious.'

'Trust.' Lewis repeated, as if looking for confirmation.

She shrugged. 'It takes time.'

Lewis smiled. 'Time is okay. Time I can do.'

CHAPTER TWENTY-FOUR

Tobias had lost track of time. Or time had lost track of him. One of those for certain. He had been walking in sand with an enormous sky. For days or years. Now he was somewhere cool and quiet. A forest. The sky was crosshatched with branches and the sun was filtered through pale green leaves. It was a relief. He knew that. And he knew he was looking for something. Or he thought he was looking for something. Unless that was a dream he had had once. His thoughts were slow and there were spaces between them. Spaces that he could lose himself in if he wasn't mindful.

He was just thinking about the word mindful and how it felt to think it and whether it would be enjoyable to say out loud. Whether he could, in fact, still stay things out loud. And that made him wonder at the purpose of such an activity. There was nobody here to hear him and that reminded him that once upon a time there had been others to hear him speak. That he had not always been so utterly alone.

At that moment, the densely packed trees parted into a large clearing. In the centre of the clearing, there was a round hillock. It was covered in grass and didn't look as if it belonged in this forest. Like him. In that moment, he glimpsed a truth. He wasn't supposed to be alone in this forest. And that hill was important.

Esme went to The Three Sisters' house. Bee would understand her concerns, she knew. She hoped Bee had finished her spirit walking. She was the only other person who didn't seem to be taken in by the Lewis show, who hadn't attended the bogus fire ceremony.

There was no answer at the front door. Esme was debating with herself about going around to the back garden and seeing if Bee was out there, when the door opened a crack. Through the opening, she could see a white dress and black hair, and her skin prickled with goose bumps. It was Lucy.

Esme hadn't seen Lucy since she had saved Luke. She opened her mouth to say 'thank you' for that, but something stopped her. Words were powerful and she didn't want to imply any kind of obligation to the youngest of The Three Sisters. Instead, she kept her speech purely factual. 'I'm looking for Bee.'

The door opened wider. Lucy was standing on tiptoe and gazing at Esme with black eyes that sparkled with starlight. Esme felt herself tip forward, as if she would fall into them, and grabbed instinctively at the door frame.

Lucy's laugh was girlish and terrible. She skipped away, leaving the door open. Esme didn't know whether to step inside or not. It felt like a trap. She could see the familiar open-plan space in which she drank tea and practised yoga and meditation with Bee, but it seemed altered in a way that she couldn't perceive with her normal vision. Something menacing was telling her to turn away and go home. Bee was always telling her to trust her gut, so that was exactly what she did. Lucy's laughter seemed to follow her.

BEE WASN'T sure where she had stepped through. The air was warm and humid and she was in an ancient agricultural landscape. She wasn't alone. Farmers were working on the land with hand tools, and there was a small wooden building with a cooking fire outside the entrance. An old woman with a wide-brimmed hat was sitting nearby, hulling beans. She raised her head as Bee approached, and she saw that the woman was blind, her eyes milky with cataracts.

'If I feed you, the food will burn,' the woman said in a pleading voice.

She could sense Bee's presence and assumed she was a spirit. There was a legend in China that ancestors could return as ghosts. They were starving, but if the family member tried to feed them, the food ignited before the ghost could take a bite. They were doomed to see the food, smell the food, even be offered the food, but to never taste a morsel. Like Tantalus. Yet another cautionary tale of the pain that could be inflicted as punishment for wrongdoing in a mortal life.

Bee wasn't sure if she was Elsewhere or had stepped back into her own world but through a tear on the other side of the globe. If she was in her world, then she ought to be invisible. She was walking in spirit only. She turned back to where she had entered. It was a shrine. A pile of stones and a gold statue of a bear. That didn't belong in the China of her world, Bee was almost certain, but the woman had spoken something close to a Beijing dialect.

One of the men in the field straightened up and looked

directly at her. One woman with the sight, who could see her in spirit form, was possible. Two highly unlikely. She was Elsewhere, then.

The farmer was still staring. He had a knife in one hand and Bee knew it was probably intended to frighten weary travellers. She straightened her spirit body and walked over the neatly hoed field to meet the farmer. She wasn't afraid of his knife and he would be her guide.

LUKE HAD NEVER SEEN so many people in the bookshop at one time. Wave after wave of visitors were streaming across the causeway and wandering around the island, browsing the bookshop, buying snacks and drinks in Matteo's and eating at The Rising Moon.

Lewis had helped out for the first couple of days, but he hadn't been very good at it. The bookshop hadn't liked it, either, and had kept hiding even the most prosaic of shelves such as the 'f' section of crime fiction and sporadically switching off lights in different parts of the shop, plunging them into random darkness. On the whole, Luke was relieved that Lewis had found other ways to occupy himself.

He helped a woman find a thriller by C.L. Taylor that she hadn't yet read, and sold a stack of vintage gardening books to a teenager in a washed-out hoodie. 'Nice place,' he said as he paid. When he turned to leave, Luke saw that someone had written 'burn capitalism' onto the back of his hoodie in puffy marker.

Luke appreciated the sentiment, but he could do without burning allusions in his shop. He rubbed at the marks on his chest. They still ached as if they weren't fully healed.

· · ·

At Strand House, Esme had been full for the week. When one set of people left, another lot arrived. Nobody was staying more than the two-night rule, but she had never experienced this level of turnaround before. By Thursday, demand for accommodation was too high, and Lewis said that he would start hosting people at Tobias's house. 'It's the only way to maximise. If people can only stay such a short time, we need to pack them in while the weather is good.'

That was the other thing. The weather wasn't particularly good. It wasn't quite as dramatic as it had been in the first few days after Tobias's disappearance, but it was standard early spring on Unholy Island. Extremely changeable, in other words. Cold and wet as often as it was dry, misty, chilled, grey on many of the others, with occasional moments of sunshine in a cloudy sky.

Esme objected to Tobias's private space being opened up to strangers, but she had been in the minority. 'It's good to make money while we can' had been Matteo's pragmatic response. Even Hammer had shrugged. 'I don't think Tobias would mind. Besides, he's not using it at the moment.'

She had tried to get Luke on his own to talk about it, but he was either busy in the shop or spending time with Lewis. It was good that they had regained their closeness and she didn't begrudge him time with his family, but she missed him too. And worried that this distance between them would turn out to be more permanent.

It was almost midnight, and Esme was in her kitchen. The guests had all, finally, retired for the night and she was enjoying the peace and quiet. She knew she would be tired tomorrow – it would be another early start to make the guests' breakfast – but she wanted a few minutes to drink tea in her home and to pretend that things were normal. Jet was out, no doubt hunting. Or sulking. One of the families that was staying had a small girl who had grabbed his tail earlier.

She had brewed chamomile and valerian and added a spoonful of honey. The bread was proving in a basket on the side and she had a tray of breakfast muffins ready to bake. Small pots of bircher muesli were already assembled and in the fridge. There was clean folded bedding in the laundry basket ready for the bed changes and no reason to feel unsettled. All was well.

Esme yawned. She was more tired than she had realised, or the tea was working quickly. She put the mug on the side and turned to make her way to bed.

She did not notice the figure in her garden, staring through the window at the tableau inside.

THE WARMLY LIT KITCHEN. The sleepy witch. Lucy prowled around the grass in her bare feet. The island didn't feel right. The humans were dreamwalking, not properly awake. Lucy didn't usually concern herself with the people, didn't have the patience or the interest, but her skin was itching with the wrongness that had stolen over the island. Something was not right, and the witch was drinking tea. Oblivious.

CHAPTER TWENTY-FIVE

Luke was meant to meet Lewis for lunch, but the shop was too busy to close. He texted him to let him know that he would see him at dinner instead. The reply came back quickly.

Bring it to the house.

'Yes, your highness,' Luke muttered, but at the appointed time, he went via the pub and collected the take-away order that was waiting.

'I'll pop round later to clear up,' Seren said.

'You don't have time for that,' Luke said, confused. 'And Lewis doesn't need looking after. Are there dishes in here that need returning?' He hefted the bag, realising that it was heavier than he would have expected. There had to be enough food to feed all of the visitors, too. Luke wondered whether Lewis was paying for it himself.

'I'm happy to do it,' Seren said, waving him on. 'Go on, before that gets cold.'

There was a stone in Luke's stomach. Something wasn't right, but he didn't know what it was. The thought was slippery, and it slithered away before he could grasp it.

The windows were wide open at Lewis's house.

Tobias's house, he mentally corrected himself. Luke could hear the music as he approached and someone was laughing loudly in the garden. A couple were sitting on the formerly neat lawn, which was now muddy and torn-up in places. They were smoking and talking, and the woman was laughing in an unconvincing way that set Luke's teeth on edge.

Luke didn't bother knocking as the front door was wide open. There were people in the hall and, going into the kitchen to find cutlery and plates, more people again. He didn't know any of them and hoped they were all aware that the causeway was going to close for the day in just over an hour.

He heard Lewis's voice before he walked into the living room. He was sitting in Tobias's chair by the empty fireplace. A group of six were sitting on the floor, gazing up at Lewis. Luke had the distinct impression that he had interrupted something important. A story. Or a service. The word was strange. His brother wasn't a priest, had never been religious, but there was something fervent and charged in the atmosphere.

Lewis smiled at him, though. He stood, raising his hands. 'Time for a break, my children. Go into the fresh air and breathe deeply. The island will whisper its secrets.'

The group didn't seem thrilled, but they stood up obediently and filed out of the room.

'Thank Christ,' Lewis grabbed at the bag of food, his voice reverting to its usual tone. 'I'm starving.'

'My children?'

'Cringe. I know.' Lewis didn't look up from his task of peeling back the cardboard lid from a foil container. 'They like it.'

Luke put a plate and set of cutlery onto the small side table. He remembered Tobias putting his tea tray onto the same space and the memory was sharp. Like it was trying to pierce something. Break through. 'It's weird,' he said out loud, as his mind tried to chase the line of thought.

'Your face is weird,' Lewis said, flashing Luke his old smile. He looked like his brother again. Normal. Then he noticed that the grate was filled with cold ash. The fire was always burning in this room, he'd never seen it out while Tobias was here. Fire in the grate and frost on the windows. It was another reminder that all was not as it ought to be. Something wasn't right. Tobias wasn't here, that wasn't right. Lewis was here and that wasn't... well, it wasn't wrong. He was his brother. He was glad he was safe and whole and with him. But something wasn't quite... 'What are you saying to them?' Luke managed. 'Why are those people looking at you like that?'

'Like what?' Lewis was intent on the food. He had spooned some curry into his mouth already, as if he couldn't wait to plate it up.

'And how did you get Seren to make you curry?'

'I asked,' Lewis said around his mouthful.

Curry in Tobias's living room. That was another sharp thought. A shard of glass that cut through the muddle in his mind. Tobias's room was a place of tea and cake. A fire in the grate and frost on the windows and Winter lying on the hearth rug. Now there were containers of curry and dead ashes in the fireplace. And a group of random strangers roaming the garden like zombies, waiting until their master called them back inside. A moment of clarity. Luke felt the wool in his head part to reveal a single thought – he had to get out of this room.

TOBIAS WAS STILL in the forest. He had walked for a while, away from the clearing with the grassy hill, but had arrived back at it again. He had touched the hill and felt vibrations through the palm of his hand. There wasn't a way inside the hill. He was frustrated and not used to the feeling.

He knew that the hill ought to have an entrance. He knew it in the way that he knew his own name. Horrifyingly, he realised that he didn't know his own name. Did he have one?

Moving away from that troubling question, he returned to the hill. Beat his fists on its grassy slope. There should be an entrance. A doorway. But it was just a hill.

Defeated and exhausted, he sank to his knees. The ground was wet and he dug his hands into the soil and dead leaves. He thought about lying down. He was so tired and had been walking for so long and now he was here, the place he remembered, the doorway, and he couldn't walk through. Something like despair crept through his mind and he felt it steal away his will. He thought about closing his eyes and going to sleep.

Luke left Tobias's house and went to the first person he always wanted to see, in good times and bad. And, incidentally, the only person he trusted.

Esme was unpegging sheets from the washing line in her garden. She looked happy to see him, but he thought he could detect a wariness, too. The clarity was holding, and he knew why she was concerned. He had been thinking over the last few days as he walked from the mayor's to Strand House, and he was mildly horrified. He had been following Lewis around like a sheep. He had given him free rein in the bookshop. He had barely spoken to Esme and had only had time for Lewis. When Esme had raised a concern about his brother's effect on the islanders and visitors, he had turned away from her. His face burned hot with shame. 'I'm sorry,' he blurted.

She dropped a handful of pegs onto the washing in the basket at her feet. 'What's happened?'

'I was at Tobias's house. And I started remembering him. I think being in the living room there just made the memories stronger. I don't think I've thought about Tobias for days. And then I realised how wrong it all is. It's not right, is it? What's happening?'

Esme's relief was obvious, but she was still cautious in her reply. 'It's unusual. And you know I objected to Lewis staying in Tobias's home. That doesn't feel right to me.'

'I haven't been thinking clearly, but I think the fog has cleared.' He crossed the grass in a couple of strides and took hold of Esme's hands. 'Forgive me?'

She smiled up at him. Properly this time, and his heart squeezed in relief.

'If you help me with the rest of this.' She kicked the laundry basket.

AFTER BRINGING IN THE WASHING, folding the sheets, and kneading bread, Luke and Esme hatched a plan to go and speak to the islanders. The sun had set and the cool air was refreshing on his skin. It helped to anchor him in the here and now, although his thoughts were still strangely slow. Dreamlike.

'Shouldn't we go to Bee first?' He asked on their way to Fiona's house. 'She will know what to do.'

His phone buzzed before Esme could answer. It was Lewis, and he held it out to show Esme. 'Should I answer?'

She shrugged, and he could sense she was still wary. 'It's up to you.'

He wondered how honest to be. He could feel something tugging at the edges of his mind. A desire to speak to Lewis, to be near him. He was thinking clearly, he was almost sure, but there was the impression of fog at the edges of his mind. He would feel it there like when you felt the atmospheric pressure before the weather changed. 'Bee will help,' he said out loud.

'She can't,' Esme said. 'Not right now.'

His phone buzzed again. Lewis. At once, he felt the pull to be with his twin, stronger than he had ever felt it before.

'I'm going to...' He had pressed the button and had the phone to his ear before he finished speaking.

'I miss you,' Lewis said. There was a plaintive note that cut through Luke. How could he have left Lewis? What was he doing on the other side of the village?

He was walking away, phone pressed against his skin, before the thought had even completed.

ESME WATCHED HELPLESSLY as Luke strode away from her. He was going back to Lewis, that much was clear. His moment of clarity had burst the moment his brother had spoken.

She felt like turning around and going home. She was the lone voice. What could she do? But she was close to Fiona's and she owed it to her friend to check in. And perhaps Fiona's unusual nature would protect her from whatever strange effect Lewis was having on the other humans.

When Fiona opened the door, Esme saw she wasn't alone. Matteo was sitting on the sofa, Hamish cuddled on his lap and half-asleep.

'Sorry, it's bedtime, I didn't think...'

'Come in,' Fiona said. 'It's all right. I'm glad you're here.'

Esme sat on the floor cross-legged and waited for Fiona to settle on the sofa. She stroked Hamish's head and smiled encouragingly at Matteo. 'You've got the knack.'

'Is Euan out?'

'He's working. Seren is run off her feet.'

'I was supposed to be here with Luke. But he's gone to see Lewis. We were going to talk about what's going on...'

Fiona looked up. 'What do you mean?'

Esme took a deep breath. 'Lewis is gathering people to him like the Pied Piper. And nobody seems to find it odd.'

Matteo carefully laid Hamish on the sofa cushion next to him, where he promptly snuggled into Fiona. He took out his notebook and wrote something before showing it to Fiona and then passing it to Esme.

Silver blood in Luke's family?

'Not that I know of. His mother's maiden name was Brown.'

'Is that why you're not affected?' Fiona asked Matteo.

He shrugged and then took his pad back to write: *I am. Feel too calm. Sedated.*

Fiona's eyes lit up in recognition. 'That's it. Exactly.' She looked at Esme. 'Until you turned up, I wasn't even thinking about it.' Her expression clouded. 'We should be worried.'

'And all these visitors. They are obsessed with him. There is turnover at the moment, the wards are holding, but what if that stops? What if some decide they want to stay with Lewis for longer?'

'You'll look after the wards,' Fiona said, as if she was comforting Hamish.

Matteo tapped his notepad. *We voted.*

'We did,' Fiona smiled dreamily. 'It will be all right. He's The Book Keeper's brother. All will be well.'

LEWIS PICKED at the food on his plate and then handed it to a waiting woman. He was surrounded, as always, by his acolytes. A woman with a sleek grey bob and red-framed glasses was curled up on his feet. A man who had the tanned skin and toned physique of an Instagram influencer was leaning against his chair. His hand kept roving onto Lewis's knee and Lewis kept removing it with a kind of tired monotony. The woman who had taken his plate held it aloft and carried it ceremoniously out of the room, presumably to the kitchen. Although, given the strange glazed look in her eye, Luke wasn't sure. Perhaps she was going to add it to a Lewis-themed shrine. He would no longer be surprised.

'This can't go on,' Luke said. He decided to ignore the several elephants in the room and to focus on Lewis himself. 'You don't look well.'

He turned mournful eyes to Luke. 'I'm so hungry.'

Lewis had been eating well. Too well, really, for several days. Now he seemed to be unable to eat more than a few small bites.

'I could pop along to the pub and get some soup. Something easy to—'

'It won't help.'

'What do you mean?'

'I tried,' Lewis flapped a hand, barely lifting it from his lap. 'I ate until my stomach hurt, but I was still hungry. It doesn't make any difference.'

'Perhaps you should get checked out. Medically.'

The door opened and a couple walked in. They were holding hands, but only had eyes for Lewis. The woman gasped and put a hand to her mouth. The man did a strange sort of bow and then another, deeper one.

'Where are all these people sleeping?'

'Wherever I am,' Lewis said, brightening a little. 'I don't like to be alone, so they stay with me.' He reached out and patted the head of the influencer, who made a weird little cooing noise.

BEE FOLLOWED her guide out of the fields and along a dusty track. They passed a loaded cart dragged by oxen with gold horns and no driver, and a group of young women who watched them silently from underneath jewelled headscarves. At the end of the track, the landscape changed abruptly. Featureless red earth stretched out as far as the eye could see to a flat horizon. Bee looked at her guide and shook her head. She opened her mouth to tell the farmer what she needed, but found she could not. Her lips were sealed shut by some power greater than her own.

Her guide was smiling in a way that suggested she was in trouble. He had led her the wrong way on purpose, she realised, too late. There was no such thing as too late, though. That was something Bee knew in her bones. Whatever she could see in the future, there was only ever right now. And right now could not be too late. It was all there was. Bee bowed her head and dropped into a deep curtsey. She couldn't draw on her sisters, not this far from home, but she was still the eldest. And experience counted. When she straightened, she told the guide what he would see and what he would hear, using the strength of her own conviction.

The guide's eyes widened in understanding. She no longer required lips to form a command.

CHAPTER TWENTY-SIX

L uke woke up in his room above the bookshop. His first thought was Lewis and he realised he had been dreaming about his twin. Dreaming that they were together and now he had woken up alone and it felt all wrong. How was Lewis feeling? What was he doing? He sat up and pushed a hand through his hair. Why hadn't he just stayed with Lewis the night before? Then he would be near him.

He forced himself to think through his actions the day before, to pinpoint the moment he had left his brother, his twin, his other half. Esme. He had been with Esme before he had gone to be with Lewis. He remembered that there hadn't been anywhere to sleep. The house was full and Lewis was surrounded. Luke had gone upstairs to find a bed and then had experienced the nagging feeling that he had forgotten something important. It had been enough to spark the desire to go home to the bookshop to sleep. He had been doing something with Esme. But he couldn't hold on to the thought long enough to remember what.

That was a tiring line of questions, so he relaxed against his pillow and thought about his brother. Lewis had been asleep in Tobias's chair. He had been snoring. One of the visitors was draped in his lap, wide awake and watching Lewis's every breath as if it was the most fascinating sight.

Sunlight was streaming through the big window at the front of the shop and Luke knew it was past opening time. He couldn't run the shop and see his brother, though, so the customers would have to be disappointed. The front door refused to open and the lights in the shop flickered.

'I've got to go and see Lewis,' Luke said out loud. He tried the door again, but it was stuck fast.

He walked back to the main room. There was a large book on the counter. It was a rich royal blue leather with embossed scrollwork, the spotted remains of gilt, and a tarnished brass latch. There wasn't any text on the outside of the book, but when he flipped it open, an ornately illustrated title page informed him it was a collection of Russian folktales. It was a book for Esme, he realised. The shop had been supplying her with an endless parade of reading material and this was exactly the kind of volume that he had become used to finding in the stockroom or waiting for her on the counter.

His comfortable bubble of calm popped. Memories rushed in. He had been walking with Esme. They had been going to speak to the islanders about Lewis. About the stream of visitors, and the weird way they seemed drawn to Lewis. Obsessed with him.

'Thank you,' he said. The lights flickered in answer and he heard the front door unlock.

LUKE DIDN'T WANT to go back into Tobias's house. Not until Tobias was safely home and sitting by his fire. He messaged Lewis and asked him to walk with him. Then he left his phone in the bookshop. He wanted to be able to control when he spoke to Lewis.

The sun was setting over the waves. A path of sparkling water leading to the horizon, like a trail leading to a distant land.

He wasn't sure whether Lewis would come. And, if he did, he half-expected him to have his entourage with him.

When he saw the familiar figure walking alone, he let himself believe that all would be well. He knew Unholy Island wasn't the life that Lewis had dreamed of. He was a city man. He liked clubs and restaurants and pavements thronged with people. He liked opportunities and buzz, the feeling that he was at the centre of everything. Whatever weird thing was going on, Lewis was still Lewis, and he must be getting restless by now.

'Nice out here,' Lewis said cheerfully when he caught up to Luke. 'Good idea.'

'It gets claustrophobic,' Luke said. 'The small community. I need to walk sometimes.'

'You seem snug as a bug,' Lewis said. 'Tucked in that little shop.'

'I didn't say I didn't like it. But I'm me. I'm surprised you're still here.'

'Not this again.' Lewis's good humour died.

'I'm happy to see you. You know that. But that doesn't mean I'm not surprised. Thought you would be bored out of your skull by now.'

'Maybe I've changed.'

They walked for a few minutes in silence, falling into step together as they always had. Shoulder to shoulder, same length of stride, their footsteps in the sand forming two identical trails.

'I'm not talking about you leaving,' Luke began, feeling his way into the conversation.

A sidelong look from his twin. Suspicion.

'But you have to get those people to leave. It's not healthy.'

'What do you mean?'

'All those people crowded in Tobias's house. You were invited to stay there. They shouldn't be there.'

'I thought you said unhealthy?'

'Well, it is.' Luke kept his gaze forward, looking toward the headland. He was trying to keep the conversation easy, not be too confrontational. Lewis had never been at his best when he felt cornered. 'I'm just saying... Do they seem all right to you? They're all obsessed with you. You've got to admit it's a bit weird.'

'Are you jealous?'

'No! That's not what...' Luke rubbed his brow, feeling a headache taking root. A few more steps, another deep breath. 'Surely you can see that this isn't normal behaviour?'

'Nothing about this place is normal,' Lewis shot back. 'Why does everyone leave after two nights? I'm just getting to know them and they go? They don't want to go, they don't talk about going, but they do. Regular as clockwork.' Lewis narrowed his eyes. 'Is it something to do with the witch?'

'What?'

'You know. Esme. You told me that she's a witch.'

Luke frowned, trying to remember.

'I don't think we need those wards anymore,' Lewis continued. 'Let people stay if they want, that's what I reckon.'

A coldness crept into Luke's stomach. 'No. The wards keep the islanders safe.'

'It's a power grab.' Lewis stopped walking and faced Luke. 'I respect it, but that's what it is. Your missus wants everyone controlled and beholden to her. She stops outsiders from staying too long, means she keeps control of the island.'

'That's not...' Luke trailed off. He felt as if he was losing the thread of his thoughts.

'It's smart.' Lewis lifted his chin. 'But I'm saying it's not the only way for things to be. We could have loads of visitors all the time. Everyone would make more money. Your little shop might turn a profit for once. Or there would be other opportunities. I know people who could use a bolt-hole. Somewhere quiet to do business.'

'It won't be quiet if you break the wards,' Luke said. 'Not that you could.' He hoped that was true. On one level, he knew that Lewis was wrong, but part of his mind was insisting that he made a kind of sense, that Luke ought to listen, to obey.

'I bet Esme would break them for you. If you asked. That woman is head over heels. God knows why.'

That sounded more like the brother he knew. Luke was simultaneously annoyed and relieved, and he felt clarity returning. He bared his teeth and punched his brother on the arm. Not all that lightly. 'I won't ask. And neither will you.'

BEE HAD WALKED AWAY from the farmland, leaving the guide far behind. She had crossed the vast red desert by telling the world that it was no more than a narrow strip of sand. Now, she told Elsewhere that she required shade and water. Her mouth was dry and her eyes felt hot and sore. She knew those were sensations from her body, locked back on Unholy Island. Still, a copse of trees rose up on the brow of the next hill. Bee headed for their cool green embrace.

CHAPTER TWENTY-SEVEN

E sme was in her kitchen. She had just shaped the bread and put it on the tray ready to bake, and had taken a lemon and poppy seed loaf cake out of the oven to cool. She saw the shape of the Viking in the garden seconds before the knock at the door. Luke.

Heart leaping and blood fizzing, she opened the door to him.

The man on her doorstep was wearing Luke's jacket and t-shirt. He had Luke's face and gentle smile, but every part of Esme was screaming at her that it wasn't him.

She had already stepped back to let him inside, and the man crowded into the kitchen. He didn't take his boots off. If Esme had been in any doubt as to whether this was Luke or not, that would have clinched it.

'What do you want?'

'To see my girl,' Lewis said, leaning in for a kiss.

Esme took a deliberate step back. 'You're not Luke.'

He frowned. 'What do you mean?'

'Stop it,' Esme said. 'I'm not fooled. You can't put his clothes on and expect me not to be able to recognise you. What are you after?'

Belatedly, her words sunk in and Esme realised what a man might be after. Had Lewis thought he could pretend to be Luke and sleep with her? Surely not. She felt a thrill of pure fear in her blood.

'That's so sweet,' Lewis said, dropping his Luke act. 'I love that you know him so well. You really are smitten with my little brother, aren't you?'

Esme's heart was racing. She took another step back and tried to remember where she had left her mobile. Her landline was in the dining room, a retro thing that was fixed to the wall by the doorway. Could she get to it before Lewis caught her? Call Luke?

Lewis was smiling widely. His words didn't fit his expression. 'I need your help.'

There was pleading in his tone. And an honesty that didn't fit his actions or the instinct that was telling her he was a threat. That she was in great danger. Esme had learned to trust those instincts, but she knew she could see clearly, too. She pushed down her fear and made herself look into Lewis's eyes.

Something slithered away.

Lewis's smile relaxed. His stance changed and he shrugged easily. 'Can't blame a guy for trying. And Luke and I have always shared our toys.'

'That's not true,' Esme said, her voice even. 'I'd like you to leave now.'

'Maybe I like it here.'

'That's not my concern.' Esme slipped a hand into her pocket, praying to all the gods and goddesses that her mobile phone would somehow be there. It wasn't, of course. There was no such thing as divine intervention. She knew better than that.

Her fingers closed around something. Not the welcome smooth rectangle of a mobile phone, but a few items, rough and round. Allspice berries from when she had been making spiced tea. It was a recipe from one of the books that the shop had gifted. It was a brew meant to warm both your heart and hearth, but Lewis didn't need to know that.

She rolled the dried pods between her fingers and then drew them out with a flourish. 'Leave, or I will hex you.'

Lewis laughed, but he stopped moving toward her.

'You don't want me to do that. I'm not very good yet, and you'll probably just spend the next twenty-four hours in the bathroom. You'll be exploding from both ends. But it might be worse. I'm not really sure.' Esme stretched out her hand, her fist around the pods. 'Shall we find out?'

'You're crazy,' Lewis said, but there was a shard of uncertainty in his voice.

'Luke told you I'm the Ward Witch. He believes me.'

Lewis took a step back. 'I'm going,' he said. 'But not because of that,' he indicated her fist, 'just because it's polite.'

He backed out of the kitchen, keeping his eyes on Esme, before ducking out of the door. He didn't shut the door behind him and Esme listened to his steps on the path and the squeak of the garden gate before running through to use the landline to call Luke. Her hand paused halfway through dialling. Luke was connected to Lewis. He seemed to have been having more clarity, had said he would speak to his brother about leaving. But had he? Maybe he had gone back to the bookshop and instantly fallen back under whatever spell Lewis was weaving. She hung up and dialled a different number.

Esme knew she had to be careful. The islanders seemed to be in some sort of thrall to Lewis. Hammer wasn't too badly affected, and he had agreed to stay at her house with

Winter, sleeping downstairs in case of any trouble. She had told him about Lewis trying to impersonate Luke and he had been briefly angry, but that seemed to have faded. He was happy to stay to protect her from the visitors, though, and that was better than nothing.

Esme wondered how the rest of the islanders were doing. She went to The Rising Moon to see who was around, and grabbed the opportunity to speak to Seren. She had dark circles under her eyes from lack of sleep, but was still rushing around the pub with a fervent energy. The latest set of visitors had just left to cross the causeway back to the mainland. Esme had passed a couple who were bickering on their way back to the car park. Neither of them wanted to leave and they were taking their confusion out on each other. Esme was relieved that the wards were holding, but for how long? They had never been tested like this.

'Can I help?' Esme asked, picking up some empty glasses from one of the overflowing tables.

'Thanks, yes,' Seren said. 'I don't know where Euan's got to.'

'I haven't seen Fiona today either.' It occurred to Esme that they couldn't be out swimming together, not without someone to look after Hamish.

Once they had made a decent dent in the dirty crockery and the glass washer was filled and switched on, Esme tried to raise the subject of Lewis.

Seren's eyes immediately went a little unfocused as she gazed into the middle distance. 'He's easy on the eye.'

Esme stared at her for a moment, not saying anything.

It took Seren a second to realise the significance of her words. 'Oh shit,' she said. 'I don't mean that Luke is... I know they look similar, but I don't think—'

'It's all right,' Esme said, smiling to show that she

wasn't upset. 'They are both extremely easy on the eye. You'd have to be blind not to notice.'

'But there's something about Lewis,' Seren said. She trailed off. 'Sorry. Ignore me.'

'No. What?'

'I feel like I've known him for a long time. Longer than I have. He just reminds me of someone.'

'Luke?' Esme was trying not to sound sarcastic.

Seren laughed nervously. 'No. Yeah, I mean, you would think? But not Luke. Someone else, but when I try to think who, I get sort of...' She trailed off.

Esme waited for her to continue, but she picked up a stack of clean plates and began putting them away.

'Have you felt differently? Since Lewis has been here?'

Seren straightened up. 'Don't be silly. I have a bit of a crush, but it's nothing serious.'

Esme forced a laugh. 'You're not the only one.'

'What do you mean?' Seren wasn't smiling.

'Just that he's very popular with the visitors.'

'No,' Seren said. 'He's not interested in them. What has he said?'

'Nothing,' Esme said quickly. 'Nothing.'

Seren's knuckles were white as she gripped the edge of the steel countertop. 'He's ours. Not theirs.'

'Right,' Esme took a step back. 'I'm knackered. Think I'll head home.'

'Straight home? Or are you going to see Lewis?'

'Straight home.'

Seren stared at her for another moment. 'You're still with Luke, right?'

'Right.'

'You still like Luke? Happy with him?'

'I love Luke,' Esme said. 'Don't have eyes for anyone else.'

Seren seemed to relax. 'Thanks for your help. See you tomorrow.'

HAMMER HAD GONE OVER to Strand House as soon as Esme had called him. It had been far too busy on the island for his liking, with people everywhere he went with their loud chatter and curious glances, but at least he had his own private house to escape to. He knew it had been non-stop customers at the bed-and-breakfast, and he didn't know how Esme had been coping. She hadn't sounded fed up or frustrated on the phone, though. She had sounded afraid.

Winter had been reluctant to leave the boathouse, but Hammer had managed to coax him along the shore and up the path. That evening, he kept Esme company in the living room.

'They mostly spend the day with Lewis,' she said, 'just coming back to sleep. It could be worse.'

At that moment, there was a crash from the dining room.

A table being turned over, if Hammer had to guess. 'Stay here,' he said.

In the dining room, one table was on its side and a woman was standing behind it screaming at a man who was in the middle of the floor. He had a knife and, for a moment, Hammer thought it was a domestic violence situation. Then the man held the knife to his own throat.

Hammer crossed the room in two strides. He got hold of the arm with the knife and twisted his wrist until he dropped it. Then he got him in an easy lock-hold. He kicked the knife away and held onto his struggling form. The man was crying and speaking at the same time, it was hard to make out what he was saying.

'He's gone mental,' the woman was screaming. It wasn't helping.

'That's not helpful,' Esme said and Hammer realised that she had joined the party. She was looking at the woman, speaking calmly. 'You need to stop.'

The woman stared back with wild eyes, but she stopped screaming.

As soon as she did, Hammer could hear the man more clearly. 'Why doesn't he love me?'

'Who?' Esme asked, but Hammer already knew. Lewis. He felt a pang. Lewis didn't love him, either. He was confused by the thought and the accompanying pain. For a moment, he thought he might let go of the man and go and see Lewis. Just to see him. To be close to him.

Then he saw Esme's stricken expression and the exhaustion around her eyes and he tightened his grip on the deranged man. He couldn't leave Esme alone with these nutters.

TOBIAS DIDN'T KNOW how long he had been in the forest. Long enough that the welcome shade had become a damp cave and the dense foliage felt like a prison. He was lost again. There had been something important, he knew that much, but he couldn't remember what it was. And now there was a shuffling sound. Something was approaching through the undergrowth. For the first time in a very long time, Tobias felt something like fear.

CHAPTER TWENTY-EIGHT

After speaking to Lewis, Luke had returned to the bookshop and bolted the door against the visitors who were wandering around. He felt woolly-headed and had experienced a worrying urge to follow his brother to Tobias's house. He had the strong sense that he would feel more himself if he spent time in the shop, surrounded by the comforting shelves of books and the smell of old paper.

The lights flickered in greeting, and he patted the counter. His foggy thoughts were becoming clear again, but a wave of tiredness was flowing over his whole body. He felt weak with exhaustion and he didn't think he could stand up for another second. He sank into his reading chair, promising himself that he would just close his eyes for a few minutes. Just a short nap. Then he would walk to Esme's and they could work out what to do.

ESME WOKE up to a strange new sound. Silence. For days, she had become used to Strand House being full of visitors with all of their life and noise. Doors opening and closing, toilets flushing, showers running, random coughs and voices and feet on the stairs. Now there was nothing.

She got dressed and went downstairs. The door to the yellow room was ajar and Esme peeked inside. The bed was still made from yesterday and it was clear that Mr and Mrs Carter hadn't come back last night. Their bags were still in the room, though, which suggested they hadn't checked out.

Then it hit her. The Carters ought to have left the island. It was their fourth day. Had they fled across the causeway without bothering to pick up their belongings? Or had they broken the two-night rule? The wards ought to have prevented that, unless they weren't working. She shoved the thought away violently. The wards were fine. This was a mistake. She had miscounted. She was exhausted with the tension and not sleeping properly and the weirdness of it all. She would check the wards and find they were working. They had to be working. Esme packed her rucksack with shaking hands.

Hammer was asleep on a camping mat on the living room floor. She knew he didn't fit on the sofa, and he had assured her that he was perfectly comfortable. Winter was lying along his side. He raised his head when she walked in and whined softly.

Jet was asleep in the kitchen and he began winding around her legs as soon as she entered the room. She fed him and stroked his blunt head and then wondered whether to bother setting the breakfast tables. There didn't seem to be anybody around.

Hoisting her rucksack onto her back, Esme walked away from the village and Tobias's house. The sky was blue, mocking her state of mind, as she looked out at the sea. The harbour ward was the nearest, and it took her no more than fifteen minutes to get there and check that she was alone. Holding her hand over the stones, Esme willed the ward to reply. But the answering tone was absent. The stones were silent.

The knowledge that had been growing was a lead weight, but she went to the church ward. If only one ward was broken, it was possible that she had made a mistake in the last renewal. It would be fixable.

The causeway was visible from the church ward and a line of cars were snaking onto the island. The sun caught the shined surfaces, reflecting back light from an endless stream of polished metal and glass. Whatever she had seen behind Lewis's eyes was getting more powerful. It was drawing more and more people to him.

She held her hand over the stones. There was no answering tone. No vibration in the air that told her the ward was working. Esme unpacked her supplies. It wasn't time to renew the wards, but she didn't know what else to try. She pricked her thumb with a clean needle and squeezed a drop of blood onto the stone. It didn't do anything. She couldn't feel the island.

Her legs moved automatically, taking her to the next ward. She knew what she would find, but felt she had to check. For the sake of thoroughness. She wanted to laugh at herself. As if diligence mattered now? She couldn't make up for her failure with attention to detail. Still, she walked to the ward at the far end of Coire Bay.

Cleaning her thumb with an antiseptic wipe, Esme's mind was blank. She had failed. She was the Ward Witch, but without Tobias, she wasn't enough. The island was no longer responding to her blood and the wards were broken.

. . .

Hammer was in the living room of Strand House, stroking Winter. It was calming for both of them. He really wanted to go to Lewis's house to see how he was doing. Or, he could admit this only in the quiet of his own mind, to see him. Which was confusing. He still didn't particularly like The Book Keeper and didn't understand why he was being so tolerant of his twin. He didn't think he had always felt this way, but when he tried to remember that version of himself, it refused to come into focus.

He held onto the things that were certain and felt right. Esme had asked him to stay with her, to protect her. So he wouldn't leave. And Winter refused to leave the boundary of Strand House, whimpering when Hammer tried to get him past the garden gate, and he wasn't going to abandon Tobias's dog. Tobias. *Where was the mayor? And why did he keep forgetting about him?*

Winter lifted his head and barked an alarm.

Hammer got to his feet. He heard a door open and then a voice. Like Lewis's, but not as pleasant. 'Esme?'

Hammer went to meet Luke. He was standing on the mat by the back door.

'She's not in,' Hammer said.

'What are you doing here?'

'Looking out for her. It's been fucking bedlam round here.'

The lane leading past the mayor's house was packed with people. Visitors from the mainland kept arriving and, with the wards broken, nobody was leaving. Esme had thought things were easing, as the visitors had left Strand House, but it appeared they hadn't gone far. She recognised the couple who had left their luggage. 'Mr Carter,' Esme said. 'What are you doing?'

The man didn't answer. Didn't appear to hear her.

His wife was on tiptoes, trying to see over the heads. At that moment, there was a scuffle and a wave of movement from somewhere inside the crowd. A scream, cut off. If this was how bad it was outside, Esme didn't want to think about what it had to be like inside the house.

Then she heard a familiar voice and saw a flash of a red checked shirt. Seren was in the middle of the crowd, determinedly working her way to the front door.

Esme called her name several times, but Seren either didn't hear her or wasn't listening.

Standing in the pale sunshine with the signs of spring just beginning to burst from the ground and the cacophony of a crowd of strangers, crazed by their blank desire, Esme felt hot tears build. She had failed the island. She had failed these people. She was supposed to protect them all, and she wasn't strong enough. The wards were broken, which meant none of these people would leave. She could only imagine the state of inside the house. How many people were squeezed in? How long had they gone without food or water as they worshipped at Lewis's feet?

She couldn't see Seren's shirt any longer. She must have fought her way inside. Esme couldn't see a way she could rescue her. The tears fell hotly onto her cheeks, and her face burned with shame. She wasn't a powerful witch. She was as useless as she had always been.

CHAPTER TWENTY-NINE

Luke couldn't understand why Hammer and Winter were in Esme's house. A bolt of jealousy helped to further clear his mind, and he bowed his head. He had let Esme down. He tasted bitterness on his tongue as the unpleasant truth fell into place. He had failed her.

'Are you all right?'

Luke lifted his head in surprise. It wasn't like Hammer to ask after his wellbeing. He wanted to ask how Hammer had managed to hold on to his priorities, how he was resisting Lewis. He wanted to demand where he had been sleeping and what, exactly, protecting Esme had involved. But he knew that was stupid. He was the one at fault. He still couldn't believe he had been tired enough to fall asleep in his reading chair, that he had been out cold for over twelve hours.

The sound of the gate made them both look out of the kitchen window.

Esme was returning, looking exhausted and carrying the rucksack she used when she renewed the island wards.

Luke opened the door, not wanting her to be shocked

when she stepped inside. Wanting her to feel safe, but knowing he had forfeited his right to provide that safety.

Her wary smile cut him through his chest. 'I'm sorry,' he said. He wanted to step forward, to take her in his arms, but he felt unsure. Something that had seemed as natural as breathing just a few days ago now seemed impossible.

'Are you alone?'

'He's not here,' Hammer said. 'It's just us.'

Esme nodded. 'Good.' She looked at Luke.

'I know it's not just Lewis. It can't just be him. Something really weird is... I was so tired after spending time with him, like all my energy had been drained. I've left my phone at the shop so he can't call me. I'm going to stay clear. We've got to do something.'

'Oh thank Goddess,' Esme said.

At Coire Bay, Fiona made it back to the shore before Euan. He was younger and needed a longer swim, and she was glad he was taking the time. He had been working flat-out in the pub helping Seren and the rest of the time he was either playing video games or spending time with Hamish. She knew that he needed the time and space to stretch his muscles and to be in his other skin.

Her thoughts were jumbled as she readjusted to human language, her mind switching along with her physical form. As she did, she felt the strange pull to visit The Book Keeper's brother. It was a small impulse, an itch on her skin and nothing more, and she pushed it easily to one side.

Seren had agreed to watch Hamish so that she and Euan could swim, and now Fiona was excited to see her baby boy. She had left Seren and Hamish playing on the carpet, and when she opened the door to her cottage, she expected to be greeted by his adorable smile and happy babble. The house was silent.

AT STRAND HOUSE, Esme was swinging between hope and despair. The flicker of hope had been ignited the moment she had seen Luke in her kitchen, but it wasn't enough to light the darkness of the broken wards. She knew she had to tell both men that she had failed, but the words were stuck in her throat.

'Have you spoken to Bee about Lewis?' Luke asked. 'Is he going to be okay?'

'He's fine,' Hammer said. 'It's the rest of humanity we need to worry about.'

Luke let out a shocked sound that was halfway to a laugh. 'Bit dramatic, don't you think? He's not that bad.'

'I don't think he's himself,' Esme said, putting a hand onto his forearm. 'I think there's something on board. Riding the Lewis train.'

Luke looked stricken. He didn't speak for a moment and, when he did, his voice was strained. 'That makes sense.'

'You looked at him?' Hammer asked.

'I did,' Esme said. She swallowed hard and avoided Luke's eye. 'I looked into his eyes and something else looked back at me.'

'Whatever it is, it's hungry.' Hammer said. 'Seren has barely been able to keep up with his demands for food. She's exhausted.'

'It's the thing inside him. You must have seen him change? Since he came back from Àite Marbh, he's been different. And people started responding differently to him. Doing what he wants. Wanting to be near him. The visitors that don't want to leave his side. Seren feeding him.' Esme thought about seeing Seren in the crowd. Had she been taking yet more food to Lewis?

'Seren feeds everyone,' Luke said, a touch defensively.

'None of us can help it. There is something inside Lewis and it is calling to us. Making us think things, do things, feel things.'

'You've been feeling things for Lewis?' Luke asked.

'Not me,' Esme said quickly. 'But look at the people gathered around him. They are infatuated.'

'I'm not,' Hammer said.

'No,' Esme said, a frown creasing her forehead. 'And you're human. You should be.'

'I haven't thrown him off the island, though,' Hammer said thoughtfully, as if it had only just occurred to him. 'Or punched him.'

'For you, that probably counts as infatuation,' Esme said, smiling.

Hammer growled. 'Not bloody infatuated. Never liked him.'

Esme patted his arm.

FIONA WALKED into The Rising Moon, calling for Seren. Her voice sounded higher pitched than usual and was rough with worry. She didn't understand why Seren would have taken Hamish back to the pub rather than staying at Fiona's, where all his toys and equipment lived. Perhaps she had realised she had to take something out of the freezer or do some prep work for the dinner rush. But she shouldn't be multitasking. Fiona expected babysitters to do one thing only – look after her son.

Once she had walked through the rooms of the pub and gone upstairs to the accommodation above, confirming that neither Seren nor Hamish were anywhere to be found,

Fiona felt the edges of her fear expanding. She let go of the mild ticking off she had been preparing for Seren, accepting that this was more serious. And that realisation made her weak with panic. Something was seriously wrong.

CHAPTER THIRTY

Tobias was afraid of what was moving in the forest. The sun had gone and it was dark and cold. Leaves and branches shook and parted, and a figure appeared. It was an exceedingly old woman with thin white hair plastered to her scalp, hunched over with a spine that was twisted. Her eyes were rheumy, set into a deeply wrinkled face, and she wore a simple white shirt and trousers. Clothes that didn't seem to go with the rest of her appearance. Tobias felt he had seen a picture in a book long ago of this sort of figure. That she ought to be wearing a black dress. She smiled, gaps in her mouth where teeth ought to be. 'There you are,' she whispered.

'Who are you?'

The old woman reached into the neck of the loose linen shirt and pulled on a gold chain. There was a round jewel on the chain, and she held it up for Tobias to see.

He took a step closer. It wasn't a jewel. It was a mirror.

Esme still didn't trust Luke's clarity, kept expecting him to give in to the pull of Lewis's charm. To turn from her and walk out of the kitchen and back to his brother. She could feel it herself, the urge to be near to Lewis, tugging at the edge of her mind with a terrifying persistence.

'What would Tobias do?' Luke asked.

'I don't know.' Esme wrapped her arms around her middle, holding herself together. 'I've thought and I've thought, but I really don't know. There's something else...' Before she could speak, the landline began to ring.

'Don't answer it,' Luke said. 'It might be him.'

'I'll be all right,' Esme said, hoping she was right. She went into the dining room, where the phone was attached to the wall.

It was Fiona, not sounding like herself. It took Esme a moment to realise that she was crying. 'Is Hamish with you?'

Esme went cold. 'No.'

'I left him with Seren, but she's not here. She's not at mine or at the pub.'

'I saw her going into the mayor's house.'

'With Hamish?'

'I don't know. I couldn't see. She was in a crowd of people. There was a bit of a crush...'

A strangled sound.

'Don't go to the house without me,' Esme said, but she was speaking to dead air.

She replaced the receiver and found that Hammer and Luke had followed her into the dining room.

'Seren?' Luke asked. 'Is she all right?'

'She was going to Lewis,' Esme said. 'She's looking after Hamish.'

'Why would she take Hamish there?'

An awful thought had fallen into Esme's mind, so terrible she couldn't voice it. What if Lewis was hungry for something other than food? He had been gathering people to him, feeding off their attention, their energy. What if that was more than metaphorical?

'Esme?' Hammer was a stoic sort. Impassive, unless you knew him well enough to read the minute changes in his expression. Right now, he looked terrified. 'Why would Seren take the baby to Lewis?'

'I don't know,' Esme said, pushing down the awful possibilities. 'But I think that whatever is in Lewis is as strong as Tobias. It's filled the gap that he left.' She took a breath before delivering the final piece. 'The wards have broken.'

FIONA BANGED down the receiver at The Rising Moon. Her mind was filled with one thing only; the need to get to Hamish. To hold him in her arms and protect him from whatever was going on. She was out, the door banging shut behind her and her feet flying up the main road to the mayor's house.

There were people standing outside in the garden, gazing up at the windows with yearning expressions. 'Have you seen my baby?'

Nobody looked at her. It was as if they were all drugged.

A young woman opened the door after a few minutes of Fiona hammering on it and yelling.

'Wow,' she said, in a voice that couldn't have been more laconic if she had been asleep, 'you're very loud.'

'Where is my son?'

'Son?'

'My baby. Hamish.' At that moment, she heard a wail and she pushed past the woman and into the house.

There were too many people, and they were crammed

into the entrance hall and up the stairs. She was hit with the smell of human sweat. Fiona could hear Hamish crying in the living room, but the press of people was too great to move through. She tried to fight her way through, but they were immovable. One man shoved her back when she tried to squeeze between him and another. It was a hard shove and she would have fallen if it wasn't for the people that had filled the space behind her. She stood, breathing heavily and trying to work out what to do.

The people weren't moving. They were all clearly desperate to get as close to Lewis as possible and he must be in the living room. Images of Hamish being crushed carelessly by these slack-jawed, hypnotised cattle made her chest squeeze painfully and her heart thud faster. She had to get Hamish back. Now she had been absorbed into the crowd, she didn't know if she could get out. She couldn't move. It was terrifying. 'Please,' she said to the people nearest. 'Please let me through. My baby is in there.'

Nothing. Blank stares. One woman was moaning softly and Fiona realised that she was hurt. She was cradling one arm in the other and her skin was a waxy colour. But she was still upright and staring toward the living room door. The cold fear was creeping across Fiona's skin. In the water she was strong, but here in this form, she was a middle-aged woman of average height. She was too weak to push through and, if she wasn't careful, she was going to get crushed herself. The bodies around her were pressing in, squeezing.

She managed to manoeuvre her phone from her pocket. She didn't usually bother with a mobile. The reception on the island was patchy at best, but since Matteo had started texting her, she kept it on her. Communicating via text message was perfect. They were even in writing. And being at a distance made it feel both safe and exciting. She tapped out a short message. *Help. At T's. Hamish danger.*

Waiting was the worst thing that she had ever endured. Previously, she would have given that to the seconds after her ex-husband had blamed Euan for Alvis's death, the time when the protective veil she had pulled around her marriage fell away and she could no longer pretend that he was a good man who was struggling. That she had, in fact, been harbouring a monstrous person in her home and her bed. Allowing him to spread his toxins throughout their family home and infect her precious boy. She could not fail to protect a child of hers. Not again. And Hamish was a baby. He was so vulnerable. He could be harmed through carelessness or stupidity, there didn't need to be evil intent. Her phone buzzed in her hand, and with difficulty she manoeuvred it to see the screen. In the minutes since she had texted, the bodies had shifted and her arms were pinned in place. She had almost got it twisted into position when somebody let out a howl of longing and there was a violent surge from the back. Fiona's phone slipped from her grasp and she knew she had no hope of bending down to get it. She didn't dare sink to a crouch, either, as she would be easily toppled. If she ended up on the floor, these people would walk over her. It was a single, awful thought, that there was a very real danger of being trampled to death in Tobias's hallway.

The front door slammed open, and a gust of fresh air blew through the throng.

Fiona heard the same laconic voice say 'hey'. Her heart leapt, but before she could call out, she heard an unfamiliar voice. It was a man's voice, deep and extremely compelling. She felt it thrum through her body as if he were standing next to her and her head was on his chest, feeling the vibrations of his speech.

223

'Walk through this doorway and stand in the garden of this house.'

Fiona couldn't see what was happening, but the pressure of the massed bodies seemed to be easing. She took a full breath and realised that she hadn't been able to for a few minutes.

She could feel something else... a desire to walk through the front door of the house and stand in the garden. The idea of the fresh air and the sunshine on her skin, of being in the open, it all seemed extremely appealing. She turned in that direction and Matteo appeared in her line of vision. He frowned at her and mimed putting her fingers into her ears. She did so and then felt the vibrations of his voice again, and the muffled rumbling of speech.

The people in front, blocking Fiona's path to the living room and Hamish moved back. Their faces were confused, glazed eyes sparking into life as they fought the impulse to be near Lewis with the instruction from Matteo.

Fiona didn't know why Matteo's words had such an effect. Truthfully, she hadn't known he was capable of speech, but at this moment, she didn't have time to ponder it. Grabbing the opportunity with a grateful heart, she ran into the living room. It was roasting hot and Hamish was on Lewis's lap, held in a firm embrace that didn't seem to be physically harmful but was clearly upsetting to the small boy. Hamish was squirming to escape and his face was bright red and streaked with tears. Her heart squeezed painfully and she felt light-headed with relief. He was alive. He was well enough to cry. He had just opened his mouth for another plaintive wail when he saw Fiona, and the desperate relief seemed to halt everything in his small body for a split second. Then his mouth opened wider and he let out a roar that was part distress, part excitement, and part pure fury. There you are! it seemed to say, in that way that only a toddler can manage.

Fiona was suffused with such a powerful rage that it coursed through her body and gave her strength she had never had before. She felt as if she could lift Lewis bodily from his chair and wrestle Hamish from him, but she was also wary of frightening Hamish more than he already was, and of him getting hurt in a tussle. Despite the exodus of people, the room was still filled. And Lewis's arms were like a cage around her child.

She realised that Seren was close by, gazing at Lewis with naked adoration. There was anger somewhere inside, for the woman who had brought her baby into this hellish place, but it would have to wait. Her only focus was on Hamish, on getting him to safety.

'Hello, darling,' she said in a singsong voice. 'It's okay, my love. I'm here to take you home.'

'No.' When Lewis spoke, every head in the room leaned forward, as if afraid they would miss a precious syllable. Seren reached a hand out and joined it with Lewis's, adding to the barrier that kept Hamish on Lewis's lap. 'I need him.'

Keeping her voice light and not looking at Seren, Fiona said, 'what do you mean? He's just a bairn.'

'So much,' Lewis said. 'He has so much...'

'Potential?' a woman with frizzy hair and sweat patches on her pale blue t-shirt asked.

Lewis's gaze snapped to her. For a moment, Fiona thought he was angry, but then his expression relaxed and he smiled at the woman. 'Exactly. Well done.'

The woman sighed in a breathy, over-the-top way. It was overtly sexual and Fiona felt the prickle of discomfort to go along with her terror and fury.

'He's my baby,' Fiona said. She smiled at Hamish,

beaming as much reassurance as she could while physically shaking. 'It's all right, poppet, we're going home.' Her throat was tight and she forced herself to swallow. To Lewis she added, 'you're not yourself.'

Lewis still hadn't loosened his grip and Hamish had begun to cry in a thin, desperate kind of way. She wondered when he had last been fed, whether he had been given anything to drink. He could be dehydrated. There was a strong smell in the room and it wasn't just sweat or even Hamish, so she was pretty sure some of the adults hadn't been able to leave the room to use the bathroom.

She felt a touch on her arm. It was Matteo. He pushed his way to Lewis and leaned in, cupping his hands around his ear. Seren gasped and attempted to push him away, but Matteo held on. Lewis's eyes shut as Matteo whispered.

Fiona wondered if he would be able to hear above the sound of Hamish crying and the moans, articulations from the crowd. She wondered if it would have the same effect that it had on the other people or whether Lewis would prove immune.

It seemed to be a struggle. There was tension in his shoulders and his jaw clenched, muscle ticking. Lewis seemed to be trying to move, and a strange shudder went through his body. Seren began wailing, a sound of pure distress that was soon echoed by the others in the room. It was as if they weren't able to think for themselves and had become merely reactive to each other and to the object of their fascination.

Matteo held out his arms and spoke again, loud enough that Fiona could hear him, even above the wailing and crying. That strange sensation from before ran through her body, the vibrations of his voice seeming to come from far away and also inside her mind, as if Matteo was simultaneously everywhere. 'Lewis. Give Hamish to me.'

CHAPTER THIRTY-ONE

Lewis's face twisted. His teeth were clenched and he shook his head violently, but his arms were opening in a robotic manner.

Matteo swiftly grabbed Hamish and spun around to walk out of the room. He handed Hamish to Fiona, and she felt the relief of holding him, of his body in her arms. It was like having a piece of herself returned. Within seconds she was outside the fug of the house, and her face was wet with tears. Hamish's little body was shaking, and he held pudgy hands up to her face, squeezing her cheeks on either side as if frightened her face would disappear if he didn't hold on to it.

'It's okay, my love, it's all right. Everything's all right.'

Esme was just hurrying up the path. She stopped when she saw them. 'What happened? Is he all right?'

'Matteo's inside.'

'He's gone to Lewis?'

'He had Hamish,' Fiona said, every part of her wanting to run, to take her baby as far away from the house as possible.

Esme's lips went into a straight line. Fiona didn't think

she had ever seen the mild-mannered Esme look so angry before. 'Go to mine. I'll check him over. If you want?'

Fiona was already moving away, her body hunched as if to shield Hamish from attack, her muscles obeying the primeval part of her brain that was telling her to move her child far from the threat.

ESME COULDN'T BELIEVE Seren had taken Hamish and wasn't able to think about what Lewis had wanted with the baby. Matteo was still inside, so she pushed her way into the house. There were people in the garden, but more still in the hallway of the house, and more were turning around and heading back inside, moving as if sleepwalking. The smell hit her first. Sweat. Human waste. And a scent she knew as infection. Matteo was just leaving the living room. He shook his head when he saw Esme and gestured for her to leave with him.

'These people,' Esme said, unable to process the horror of the silently staring mass. One woman was cradling her arm and crying. It was clearly broken but when Esme tried to speak to her, to offer help, the woman hissed at her.

Esme made to push through into the living room. Matteo blocked the way, shaking his head. She caught a glimpse through the gap between his body and the door frame. Lewis was sitting in Tobias's favourite chair by the empty fireplace. The room was packed with bodies and the smell coming from the crush was like a physical blow.

The scrum around Lewis was moving feebly. Seren was lying across the top of a pile of bodies. She was stretched out, her checked shirt riding up and one hand managing to grasp the material of Lewis's t-shirt. Her eyes were shut and she was panting as if she had just run a race.

'Seren!' Esme shouted to her, but she didn't respond.

She began pleading with her, calling and cajoling, but Seren's fingers flexed on Lewis's t-shirt, gripping tighter.

Her eyes opened and she shot a hate-filled glare at Esme. 'You can't have him!'

The scene was ripped from her sight as Matteo towed her out, through the congested hallway and into the garden. Some of the people standing outside were beginning to move. One man took a hesitant step back toward the house.

Matteo had his notebook out of his pocket and was writing something:

We must go

HAMISH CLUNG to Fiona and Esme didn't want to pry him loose in order to check him over, so she did as good a job as she could while he sat on her lap. She gently touched his head, parting his hair to check for bumps or bruises, and did the same for each of his limbs. 'Is it okay if I check his tummy?'

Fiona nodded and lifted his t-shirt so that Esme could visually inspect his skin and then gently feel his belly.

She had filled a sippy cup and Hamish had drained it. She knew he ought to be taking small sips and that if he was dehydrated, it should be a solution with electrolytes, but it was a start at least. Hamish's eyelids were heavy.

'He's kept the water down,' Esme said. 'Do you think he would like some milk?'

She warmed a half cup of milk and Hamish drained it as if he were starving. For a moment, Esme thought of the ravenous thing inside Lewis and fear clutched her heart. He was just a toddler, though. With a tiny stomach, and who knew how long it had been since he had had anything to eat or drink. It would be more worrying if he wasn't thirsty.

Fiona was staring at Hamish with a fixed intensity that Esme had never seen before. It was as if she physically couldn't look away. She put a hand onto her friend's shoulder. 'He's all right. He's not hurt.' Mentally, she crossed her fingers that she was right. 'We can take him to the mainland to be checked out properly, though. Just to be sure.'

'No.' Fiona shook her head. 'I trust you.'

'I'm not a doctor. I'm not even a qualified nurse...'

'I trust you,' Fiona repeated. 'You can see what is really there. Look at him.'

Esme took a deep breath. She had done all the health checks she could think of. The child was exhausted, thirsty and hungry. He hadn't needed the bathroom yet, but she would ask Fiona to let her know once he had. That would confirm that his digestive and urinary system were working. He didn't have a fever. His eyes were clear and there were no signs of concussion. He had no marks on his body and no areas of pain. Now, she closed her eyes and slowed her breathing by counting. When she opened them again, she looked at Hamish. He had a sleek head, grey markings on his fluffy body and large brown eyes with no pupils.

'He's a beautiful seal pup,' she said out loud. And then snapped her jaw shut.

Fiona finally looked away from Hamish, smiling into Esme's face. 'You can see that?'

Esme blinked. Hamish was a human-shaped toddler again. He was sucking furiously on the Sippy cup that was now empty. He would take in air and give himself a tummy ache. She removed the cup. 'I'll get you some more of that milk, wee man.'

·   ·   ·

In the kitchen, Winter was wedged underneath the small table, his head pressed against Hammer's legs. Jet was on the windowsill, staring haughtily out at the world, as if challenging it to a fight. Luke was leaning against the counter near to the kettle.

'We need to get Seren,' Esme said. 'You will have to physically force her. She won't come easily.'

'I can carry her,' Luke said.

Hammer shook his head. 'You can't go near him.'

'He's right,' Esme said. 'And she'll just go back to him the moment you put her down.'

In amongst the preserves and the bread making, the cake baking and endless laundry, Esme had been working on another project. A cocktail of prescription medication that would put someone into a deep sleep. Esme hadn't completed her nursing training, but she had learned just enough about titrations and dosages to be dangerous. The issue, naturally, was going to be getting to Seren in order to dose her and then to physically get her out of the house. Esme couldn't carry a woman on her own and she couldn't trust Luke or even Hammer to withstand Lewis's influence at such close quarters. She explained the issue, trying to keep her language as neutral as possible.

'We can't drug her,' Luke said, still fixated on the first part of the problem.

'We *shouldn't* drug her,' Esme corrected. 'But we might have to. If she's gone like the others, she'll be obsessed with staying close to Lewis. The others, the visitors, you know what they're like. They won't leave his side. They don't eat, they don't sleep, they just worship him and now the wards have broken so they won't ever leave.'

'Is it really that bad?'

Esme closed her eyes briefly. 'There was a distressed man in the dining room yesterday. He had a knife.'

'What the hell? Are you all right? Why didn't you tell me...'

'You weren't in your right mind. And I'm fine. He wasn't threatening me.' Esme didn't want to think about the mania in the man's eyes, the desperation that rolled from him and seemed to have a physical stench.

'What did he do?' Luke's jaw was clenched.

'He was intent on killing himself, but I talked him out of it. With Hammer's help.'

Luke seemed to absorb this. 'Good.'

'He has been sleeping in the living room. With Winter.'

'I told him,' Hammer said.

'There have been so many strangers, so many people in the bed-and-breakfast. Hammer agreed that I should have a security presence. He got the knife off the guy and we calmed him down. Convinced him that he didn't need to end it all just because Lewis hadn't looked at him.'

'I should have been here. I'm so sorry.'

'It's all right. You haven't been yourself.'

'It's not all right. I let you down.'

'It's not your fault,' Esme said again.

Luke addressed Hammer. 'Why have you been thinking clearly and not me?'

Esme had been wondering the same thing. Not everyone on the island was affected by Lewis to the same degree. Hammer seemed to have such a natural aversion to strangers and to Lewis that it counteracted the hypnotic effect, while Seren had been firmly 'team Lewis' for a while.

'Lewis is your flesh and blood. Your twin. It's possible that you are linked in some way. That might increase the effect of his charisma on you.'

Luke squared his shoulders. 'Should we speak to Bee?'

'You don't know?' Esme spoke before she realised how daft she sounded. Of course he didn't know. Even more than the rest of the villagers, Luke had been in a bubble. Lewis's influence corroding his ability to think, to act rationally. 'She's in a trance. Trying to find Tobias mind-to-mind.'

'We're on our own, then.'

CHAPTER THIRTY-TWO

Tobias stared into the small mirror offered by the old woman. He saw his own eye and in that eye was a truth he had somehow forgotten. In an instant, he remembered who he was. *What he was.*

He awoke with a splash of cold. He was no longer in the dark green prison of the false forest, but deep underneath the cool salt water. The old woman had gone, but he felt the lingering sense of gratitude for her help.

Sunlight was filtering from above and the scene wavered. He was standing on the rock of the seabed, a dark mass that stretched out for miles in every direction. He wasn't under the sea by the island. To have this much unbroken vista, he would need to be really deep in the ocean and then he wouldn't see the sunlight. This place wasn't off the coast of Northumberland, this place was somewhere else.

He had stepped between worlds, he realised. Like putting his foot through tissue paper, he had broken through the thin place Unholy Island guarded. It was hard to explain in words. None of them quite did the thing justice, but it was easiest to think of it as a doorway. And doorways could be used in both directions.

That was a comforting thought. He clasped it gently, like he was cradling a moth.

Esme couldn't get the smell of Tobias's house out of her nose. She had even made a steam inhalation with cloves and ginger to clear her sinuses, imagining the scented steam scouring away any lingering odour particles, but kept catching the scent. It was in her mind, she knew, and that wasn't so easily scrubbed clean.

Hamish was safe and well. The baby was back with his mother. She closed her eyes, thinking about all the people packed into the house, the people who weren't so lucky. Fiona had told her that Matteo had spoken. That the people in the house had done what he had told them to do, and that was how he had cleared enough of a path to get to Hamish. But that by the time they were leaving, the effect had worn off and they were pushing back into the house. Their need to be close to Lewis overriding whatever magic Matteo held in his voice.

Matteo wasn't the answer. Esme looked at the pile of spell books from the shop and knew that there was no point in her reading them again. The things she had tried hadn't worked. The wards were broken and she hadn't managed to fix them. She was only human, and had never felt it so keenly. She needed help.

Taking the long way around the village, to avoid walking close to Tobias's, Esme arrived at The Three Sisters's house. She knocked on the door several times, keeping her fingers crossed that it would be Diana and not Lucy who answered.

Once inside, she asked to see Bee.

Diana raised an eyebrow. 'That is not possible. You know what she is doing.'

'She is still asleep? I need her.' Esme had allowed herself to hope on her way to the house. She knew that Matteo couldn't keep all the people away from Lewis and she had begun to believe that Bee would be able to help instead. She tried to explain to Diana. 'Lewis, or whatever is inside him, is affecting everybody. It's like an infection. We can't just treat the symptoms, we have to treat the cause.'

'Cut it out at the roots,' Diana said. 'I understand.'

'But I can't do it. The wards have broken.' She swallowed hard. 'I need help.'

Diana dipped her chin. 'Bee is looking for Tobias. You know this, witch.'

'It's been days,' Esme said, another thought hitting her. 'You have to wake her up. It's been too long.'

'We can't.' Diana was gentle and sad. It was worse than anybody shouting or stamping.

Esme had been so engrossed in the Lewis problem that it hadn't hit her immediately. Now it did. Diana was upset. Her eyes reflected a pure pain that terrified Esme.

'We can't,' Diana said again, her voice almost a whisper.

'But she will die if she doesn't eat. If we can't wake her, we need to get her to hospital. They've got the equipment to keep her hydrated and... everything.' Esme had been going to say 'alive'. But that conjured the opposite word and that couldn't apply to Bee, so she refused to say it.

'You know we're different?' Diana's voice was still soft.

'She still has a body,' Esme said stubbornly. 'And a body still needs to be awake and moving and drinking water.'

'She's in between.' Diana made a gesture with her

hands. 'We can see and touch her physical presence, but she's not fully here. Part of her is Elsewhere and that means time isn't passing for her body in the same way that it is for us. She isn't hungry or thirsty.'

'She can stay like that forever?'

A look of regret passed across Diana's beautiful face. 'Forever is too far to see. But a very long time, yes.'

ESME WAS SITTING up late at her kitchen table. Jet was not a lap cat, but he pressed against her legs in a companionable way. She picked up her mug of tea and discovered it was cold. Luke was upstairs in her bed. Asleep with one arm thrown above his head. He looked so vulnerable. Her Viking. Her giant of a man. His face was barely relaxed, even in sleep. He had been looking pale and drawn for days as his concern about Lewis grew.

Lewis was pulling people to him, and the thing inside was draining them of their energy. But Lewis himself hadn't looked good, either. When she had seen him at the house, surrounded by his adoring fans, he had clearly lost weight. He looked haggard, with dry skin that was cracked and peeling at the corners of his mouth. She wondered how long his physical body would hold up and what would happen when it failed.

There was a sudden noise from outside. It sounded like a woman's voice, but it could just as easily have been a fox. She got up and opened the door. Moonlight spilled across the back step. The garden was still, not a leaf stirring in the unnatural quiet. And then a figure unfolded from the shadow of her rowan tree.

'We need to talk.' Lucy stepped lightly across the damp grass, almost dancing.

'Where is Diana?'

Lucy waved a hand. 'With her plants. She's upset. She doesn't understand why you aren't helping.'

'I don't know what I can do. I can't go to the Elsewhere.' What Esme wanted to ask was why didn't Lucy go in after Bee, pull her back out? But perhaps she couldn't. Perhaps that was Bee's skill. She still didn't really know how The Three Sisters worked. She knew they were connected. She knew they weren't human. She knew they were terrifying. Lucy most of all. And now Lucy was standing in Esme's garden, her head tilted to one side and an intensity to her gaze that made Esme want to run and bolt the door.

'My sister will come back when she is ready. Where is The Book Keeper?'

The change of subject was alarming. Esme didn't want Lucy to focus on Luke in any way. He still owed her his life and Esme was worried for the day when Lucy would decide to collect. 'Asleep,' she answered.

'Good. He won't like this.'

Esme was shivering. She hadn't noticed and wondered when it had started. 'What won't he like?'

'You know,' Lucy said, her gaze intense. 'You know what we must do. What you have to do.'

'Lewis is still a person,' she said weakly. 'And it's not his fault.'

'There is a hungry spirit inside that man. It must be stopped.'

Esme didn't need to ask what Lucy meant by 'stopped'. She shook her head, as if that was going to help.

'It will never be full. Never be satisfied. It will eat and eat and eat until it consumes everything.'

'The island?' Esme felt sick.

'Certainly.' Lucy smiled, showing far too many teeth. 'Perhaps the world.'

CHAPTER THIRTY-THREE

Once upon a time, tales of witches were dark and scary. They spoke of ugly old women doing evil things. Putting children into ovens. Cursing the young and pure with poisoned apples. The world had found witches in ordinary women. Women who talked back to their husbands, helped others with medicine and advice. Women who didn't want to get married or have children or embark on a life of drudgery for others. This wasn't witch-finding, of course. It was misogyny. It used the old stories as excuses. And none of it came close to naming true witchery.

Now, Esme looked at the prone form of Lewis and felt she had strayed back into one of those old myths. She was the evil crone. By rights, she ought to be cackling. Showing a mouthful of broken teeth. An ugly shell to match the darkness in her heart.

Lucy had helped her to draw a circle in the sand and they had laid the picnic blanket out upon it. Lewis had been happy to come to the Harbour Bay beach for a picnic, seeming to accept their invitation at face value. Matteo had been stationed in the garden, where he repeatedly told the people trying to follow Lewis that they had to stay within the boundary of the house. Esme had played her part, chatting animatedly to Lewis, asking him questions about himself and gazing at him adoringly, until he had relaxed on the blanket and tucked into the food. He bolted down half of the apple pie before getting too sleepy to continue eating. Lucy had stayed hidden behind the rocks but was now moving around the circle, muttering to herself.

Esme wished that Lucy could take over. She didn't want to do it. Didn't want to hurt another human being. Couldn't believe, in fact, that she was going to become a killer.

'Do it.'

Esme thought that Lucy was in front of her, but her voice came from behind.

Lewis was asleep. The mixture that she had fed him via the apple pie had done its work. He looked peaceful.

Mixed with the horror of her actions was a more selfish pain. She would never be with Luke. He would never look at her with love in his eyes. While he had understood her reasoning and could see that there wasn't an alternative, there was a world of difference between logic and reality. Once she had done this thing, there would only be pain and revulsion. And anger.

This last thought brought a shiver of fear. But it would be no more than she deserved.

Lucy's voice was next to her now. Whispering into her ear with urgency. 'It's the only way. The thing inside needs a host. Kill the host, you kill the thing.'

They had been over all of this, of course. Esme had asked whether the hungry spirit might survive long enough to flow into another host. They were pretty sure it couldn't find a home in Lucy, which was why it hadn't jumped aboard Bee when she had visited Àite Marbh. But, just to be certain, Esme had to be the one to kill Lewis. Lucy would not allow it to take root in Esme.

'I'll make it quick,' Lucy had assured her. 'But it has to be you. If I kill the boy and the thing does, somehow, slip inside, you won't be able to stop me. You're just a human.'

Esme couldn't shake the unsettling feeling that Lucy was enjoying herself. That she wanted Esme to have to do this terrible thing. But no matter how much she thought about it, nothing altered the facts. This was the safest option, and it was for the greater good. But that truth did not crowd out the other, darker one. That killing a person was wrong. That killing the only family that the man she loved had left was evil. That, if she even survived this night, she would be forever changed. No longer Esme the Ward Witch, but something twisted and terrible. Her soul stained black.

She looked toward the causeway, the sun glinting off the cars that were queued along the road, and reminded herself that this had to be done. The thing inside Lewis had to be stopped, the cause of the infection had to be cured.

'I will do it if you can't,' Lucy said, her voice slightly mocking. 'You can just watch.'

And that's when it hit Esme. The solution. If she threatened Lewis's life enough, the thing might jump into her before he actually died. And then Lucy could kill her to finish it off. It wouldn't be pleasant for Lewis and it was still risky, but he should survive. She would be dead, but she would still be her. And if there was a place that souls went after death, hers would still be recognisable. Largely unstained.

She ran over the plan, trying to find the right words to convince Lucy that this was a better idea. And that it meant only one person had to die. Her voice was steady, and she was proud of herself and her resolve. Lucy didn't stop moving around the edge of the circle. Esme could hear her light footsteps and sense her movement, but she couldn't see her clearly. When she appeared in front of Esme, far closer than Esme expected, she flinched in surprise.

'I don't like it.'

Esme was touched for a microsecond.

'Safer to kill the boy. Many a slip betwixt cup and lip.' Lucy glanced inland. 'And we haven't got much time.'

Esme followed her gaze. There were figures on the path that led to the bay. Too far away to identify, but she had to assume Matteo hadn't been able to contain all of Lewis's followers. Or they had come directly from the carpark. Esme knew that Lucy would be able to keep a couple of humans from interfering, but she didn't think she would be gentle about it.

'I can hold the spirit. Once it's inside me, I'll keep it. And you'll kill me quickly.' Esme had been learning to trust her intuition. All the meditation with Bee had given her an understanding of her inner landscape, and she was sure she would be able to locate and distract an interloper. She wouldn't need to do it for long. 'Please.'

'We will have aggravated it.' Lucy's voice was flat. 'If it doesn't work—'

'Please,' Esme said again.

'What if I don't agree?' Lucy stepped up to Lewis's prone form. Her eyes were hungry. 'It would be better to just finish the boy. I could do it for you. If you don't have the stomach.' She clicked her fingers. 'It's not so hard.'

'No.' Esme spoke firmly. She channelled Bee, the tone she had heard her use with Lucy. 'We will try everything else first.'

Lucy pouted. 'No fun.'

'You'll get to kill me.' Esme was trying to be brave. She

was playing the part of the Witch. The brave woman who would do anything to save her island and wasn't afraid of death.

Lucy brightened. 'Better than nothing.'

'There you go.'

THERE WAS a tiny thread of blood in the water. A thin red ribbon that twisted and spun. And then another and another. Tobias remembered that the blood was the Ward Witch's. It meant the island was nearby. If he kept walking, he would get there. He had been here before, a very long time ago. When the rock that formed the island was still at the bottom of the sea. The wisp of red danced in the black water. He was so deep there was no light, but his eyes didn't need light to see. Not down here on earth that had once been in the air with legged creatures stepping across it, and was now under water with the few deep-sea fish, and would, perhaps, be in the air once again.

He was dragging his body against the press of the water, the pressure was intense down here, but it was becoming easier with every step. He was adjusting, finding the way to move through this particular arrangement of the tiny bits of matter. In the past they had been something else, behaved in a different way. In the future, the pieces would form something else. It was just a question of working with the way they were right now. He took a bigger stride and startled a grey no-eyed fish.

Time wasn't all that important, except when things were happening. Then it compressed and became very important indeed. The future was pressing upon Tobias with urgency. Something was happening or about to happen. He could feel it.

Whatever force had blocked the entrance to the

doorway on Àite Marbh hadn't realised something very important. Tobias was a god and gods can make their own doorways. Tobias was going the long way around but, luckily, he had infinite patience. And it was a beautiful day for a stroll.

THE FIGURES on the path were closer. Esme could see that it was two people. A man and a woman, and they were moving slowly but steadily toward the beach. 'I will carry on the plan, as if it hasn't changed,' Esme whispered to Lucy, as if the thing inside Lewis might be listening. She was imagining it, she realised, not as a spirit, but as a parasite. A thick maggoty worm that had burrowed inside Luke's brother and made its home. Her stomach rolled and she tried to replace the image with something less physically revolting. A cloud of smoke. Something ethereal. Something that she would inhale as easy as breathing. 'The thing should panic and jump into me.'

'You will have to be convincing,' Lucy said. She looked over her shoulder, toward the approaching couple.

Esme didn't much like the idea of half-smothering Lewis. It wasn't quite as terrible as the original plan of smothering him to death, but it was fraught with danger. 'I will have to be really careful with the timing. If I get it wrong, I could kill him by accident.'

'Don't do that then.'

'Helpful,' Esme snapped, forgetting, for a moment, who she was speaking to.

Lucy didn't seem offended. Her blood-red lips stretched into a delighted smile. 'You have claws. I like claws.'

That was enough of a reminder. The half moon scars on Luke's chest. Souvenirs of Lucy's attentions. And that had been her saving his life. Goddess only knew what a person would be left with if she was trying to harm them.

'I'm just on edge,' Esme said.

'You'll get used to it.' Lucy stepped closer to Lewis and trailed a fingernail down his cheek. 'Shall we begin?'

And there it was. She had no choice. If there was a way to avoid killing Lewis, she would take it. But she didn't want to die. And she hadn't had a chance to say goodbye to anyone. Not Luke. Not Fiona. Or Hammer. Not Tobias, of course. She spared a thought for him, hoping that he would make his way back. She was sorry she had failed to help him. Sorry she had failed to protect the island. But this would work, she told herself. This would stop the thing that was squatting inside Lewis and stop it from wreaking havoc on the wider world. In this moment, however, it was hard to care about the wider world. It seemed very amorphous and strange. Blank, while her own life was springing to mind in perfect multifarious detail. The faces of the ones she loved, the quiet rhythms of her life, the view of the sun on the water, it all seemed impossibly dear to her. Every breath she took, now that they were among her last, was sharply, agonisingly precious.

'That's the will to survive.' Lucy's voice was quiet. It didn't have its usual mocking tone. 'Humans have a lot of it. Too much, some might suggest.'

If there was one thing that Esme knew she would always do, it was this: the right thing. It occurred to her that this was the true meaning of being a witch. You had to do the right thing. Even if you weren't sure what that meant, even if you were filled with doubt, even if you were scared. She was the Ward Witch and it was her responsibility. At the moment, at any rate. Whoever came after, whoever moved into Strand House and took over her role, well, they could make up their own mind about what being a witch meant.

At least she wasn't running away. She wasn't flinching from the pain and difficulty. She was facing it head on and doing what she thought was right, not what seemed the least scary. And something else dawned upon her as she climbed on top of Lewis, knees pressing into the sand on either side of his waist. She wasn't panicking and anxious. She didn't want to die, but she wasn't frightened. She was in control and she was choosing to walk this path. It was a one-way journey, and all she had to do to take it was to cover the achingly familiar face with the pillow and press down. She looked at Lewis's face for a beat longer and then withdrew the pillow from underneath his head.

CHAPTER THIRTY-FOUR

Luke was sitting on the sand at Shell Bay, watching the sunrise. The pink streaked sky did nothing to ease his mind, but he couldn't spend another moment inside the four walls of Esme's bedroom. Alone and angry and frightened.

The air was chilled and damp and he could taste salt on his lips. He had been crying earlier, but now he knew it was salt from the sea. He didn't have an alternative plan, that was the plain truth. Nothing to offer. His mind had run endless circles, and there was no way out. Esme had explained the ramifications of letting the thing live. What would happen to Lewis, the island, the mainland. Maybe even the world as who knew how far the hungry thing would spread. It would never be satisfied. Never be full.

It would keep his brother alive for as long as it could, but he would only ever be a vehicle. Esme said that the longer the hungry spirit inhabited his body, the less of himself Lewis would remember. Eventually, there would be nothing of his brother left. He swallowed painfully past the lump in his throat.

There was something out at sea. A dark shape in the

waves. Luke thought it would be a seal. He didn't think it was Fiona, but it could be. Euan was capable of looking after Hamish, after all. But he imagined them all together. Euan on one side and Fiona on the other, Hamish safely tucked between them. That was what he would want to do if Hamish was his. After Hamish had been taken from them and endangered, they would want to stay close to him, not let him out of their sight. An image of lying in a double bed with Esme, their baby between them, made his head drop with a fresh wave of grief. He loved Esme. He understood what she was doing, and that she was doing the only thing possible. She was saving the world. He knew that. But he didn't know if he would be able to look at her without seeing his dead brother's face. He hoped he would be strong enough and that they could be together, with children of their own and all the happy days of their lives stretching out in front of them, but he did not know. It was the first time he had felt any uncertainty about his place by Esme's side and it rocked him to his core.

The dark shape in the sea was getting bigger.

He blinked the tears from his eyes to clear his vision, sniffing hard and wiping his face with his hand. Another minute later and Luke could see that the shape was human. A person was emerging from the waves and he could see a head and now, shoulders. Another minute and it was clearly a man wading out from the cold North Sea. A tall man with impressive upright posture and neatly cut silver-white hair. A man wearing, impossibly, a tweed suit that appeared to be bone dry even as he was still up to his knees in swirling salt water. Tobias.

Esme had held the pillow firmly and pressed down. She had known she was doing it right as Lewis's body had begun to jerk. She had been prepared for this, which was why she had climbed on top of him. It was the best way to ensure she could keep the pillow in place. She was leaning with all of her bodyweight and it was only just enough to stop him from dislodging her. His hands had come up and were pushing at her shoulders, fighting for his life. She felt sick.

She was counting, too, knowing that he would need to be at the point of falling into unconsciousness, and that would happen before he died. She wasn't an expert. Nursing was rather more about keeping people alive than knowing how to suffocate them, but she knew that she needed him to be at the brink of death and that meant the moment he dropped down into a deeper state of unconsciousness. The theory was that the thing inside him would sense he was about to die and would jump into the nearest living host.

She realised she had lost control of her careful count. Her stuttering mind had lost focus for a split second and now she wasn't sure what number she had been on. If she got it wrong, she might kill Lewis after all. That couldn't happen. She was so close to fixing this, to getting everybody out alive. She kept the pillow pushed down and tried to feel if Lewis was still struggling. Had he blacked out? She was so close to success. Of doing her job and protecting the island and the people on it. She had to keep believing that she could do this, that the plan would work.

She just had to keep her fai—

The thought didn't have a chance to complete. It was drowned out by a roaring sound that filled her mind. It was so loud and rough, it vibrated inside her skull and made her teeth thrum and ache.

When the sound faded, it left a background hum. A strange pitch that was unlike anything Esme had heard before. She tried to focus on it and work out whether it was coming from outside or inside her head. Maybe her ears were ringing from the big sound and it would clear soon.

She was still sitting on top of Lewis. He was a handsome man. His body felt warm and solid underneath her, and she squeezed her thighs experimentally. It felt good. So she did it again.

'Esme?'

There was a voice that belonged to another person. Lucy. Youngest of The Three Sisters. Why was she thinking like that? As if she were answering a question? She knew who Lucy was. Why had she thought, for a moment, that she hadn't?

And it came to Esme. There was something else in her head. It was the thing that was rubbing her body along Lewis's and enjoying the sensation in its nerve-endings. Her nerve-endings. She stopped the movement with an effort and began to climb off Lewis.

'I'm all right,' she said, unable to focus on Lucy. Telling her muscles what to do was an effort. And the thing inside her didn't want to move off the handsome man. There was something about him that promised more good feelings. Something to fill the time. Something to fill the...

'I'm okay,' Esme said. Her legs felt wobbly, but she finished climbing off Lewis and straightened up. The sea was shushing in and out on the shoreline. She was kneeling beside the outstretched man. Her hand was on Lewis's chest, caressing the breadth of his pecs and shoulders. She pulled it away and pushed both hands into her pockets.

'Did it work?' Lucy was bending over so that she could look into Esme's face. Her eyes were on her. Burning into her own. Searching.

Esme wanted to say 'yes' but the new thing that was in her head seemed to know what that would mean. She supposed it could access her thoughts and memories or, perhaps, it just had an instinct for danger. Self-preservation had to be important, otherwise it would never have been alive for so long. Now that it was inside her, Esme could tell it was old. Old beyond counting. And very alone. A whistling sound joined the background hum. It was wind in a mighty cavern, miles of rock pressing from all sides and the faintest trickle of water. Water that had found its way through the tiniest crack and would eventually widen that crack into a fissure. Something wide enough to follow.

Esme blinked. 'I'm sorry?'

'Did it work? Esme? Look at me. Open your eyes.'

Esme didn't want to open her eyes. She felt sad. And alone. And very, very hungry.

LUKE COULDN'T QUITE TAKE in the scene. Tobias had marched to Harbour Bay, seeming not to hear any of Luke's words as he had tried to speak to him. They passed a couple of visitors on the edge of the sand, walking slowly and steadily in that zoned-out way Luke had come to recognise.

Tobias and Luke powered past them to the far corner of the bay. The tide was out and there was an expanse of sand before it became muddy. There were some rocks, a fire, and two figures. As they got closer, he realised there were three figures. His brother was stretched out on a picnic blanket, the cheerful checked material incongruous in a scene that included Lucy with her hands around Esme's throat.

'Stop!' Luke yelled.

'It's in her,' Lucy said, not looking at them. 'This is the only way.'

'You will stop,' Tobias said, his voice carrying easily over the distance.

Lucy's hands stopped moving instantly. Her eyes widened in surprise.

'I will take it from here,' Tobias said, sounding more like his usual self. He crossed the remaining distance and placed his hands over Lucy's. She let go of Esme and stepped away, her expression impossible to read. Her red lips were curled back from her teeth and Luke didn't think he had ever seen her look less human.

Tobias began to drag Esme to the edge of the water. She was half-walking, half-stumbling beside him, scrabbling for purchase on the soft sand.

Luke wanted to step in, stop the mayor from restraining her, but the mayor wasn't quite the old gent he remembered. He was wearing his usual tweed and he looked the same, but there was something different... something that Luke couldn't even name.

As they reached the sea, Esme began to pull away from Tobias in earnest. She made a low keening noise that made every hair on Luke's body rise. Her eyes opened and found his. 'Help me.'

And that's when his body overtook his mind. He put himself in Tobias's path, cold seawater splashing up to his calves. 'What are you doing? Let her go.'

Luke was used to Tobias's presence as a tweed-clad comfort. A sprightly and sharp elderly gent who gave Luke grandfatherly vibes. Not that he had ever had a grandfather, but Tobias was the kind of thing he had been led to expect from television.

Now, however, Tobias was terrifying. His skin was still wrinkled, but his whole face was glowing with a subtle light. It was like the man was being filtered by a kindly app. The light seemed to be smoothing out his skin and brightening his eyes until he was no longer a well-kept man in his twilight years, but a young man, no more than thirty.

As if that wasn't disconcerting enough, Tobias appeared to be far taller than he had been a moment earlier. And there was a strange humming sound that was getting steadily louder. Luke didn't know if the sound was coming from Tobias himself, but he knew it wasn't a sound that he had heard before. The hum was both high pitched and low at the same time and he realised it had to be many sounds all at once, combining to make one weird, deeply vibrating hum. His skin was prickling, his hair raising with tiny electric sensations running across his skin, and his lips starting to feel numb.

'You will not stand in my way.'

'I'm sorry.' Luke didn't know whether apologising was going to do the trick, but he figured it was a decent place to start. He stepped aside. 'Please don't hurt her. Don't hurt Esme.'

Tobias seemed to shrink, to become more human again. 'Trust me.'

Esme was still pulling hard on his arm, leaning back with all her weight to try to yank herself free. It didn't seem to have any effect. It was as if she was trying to topple a tree.

Tobias began walking again, his face turned to the sea. Soon, he was up to his knees in the freezing foam. Now that she was deeper into the water, Esme seemed to calm down. She was no longer leaning back, putting her weight into trying to break Tobias's grip on her hand, but she was shaking and wailing. An awful sound that cut Luke to his soul.

Only then did he realise that Lucy had wrapped her thin arms around his waist and was anchoring him to the sand. 'Let them go,' she whispered in his ear.

The water was up to Esme's waist, now.

'Esme,' Tobias said sharply, his voice carried back to the shore by the wind. 'I know you know that this must happen.' And, with that, he pushed her underneath the waves.

CHAPTER THIRTY-FIVE

Burning in her lungs, the desperate need to breathe, eyes stinging and head pounding. Esme was herself, in her own body, but she didn't much like it. Everything hurt. And then she broke through to the surface. She took a breath and then another, dragging oxygen into her body.

'You're all right.' That was Tobias's voice. She opened her eyes, blinking through the salt water, and realised that the mayor was holding her upright and patting her back.

They were on the sand. She didn't have a clear memory of coming out of the water. Perhaps she had blacked out? Her mind was stuttering, but there was Tobias. He was back. He was right there, smiling in a kindly way.

Before she could say anything, a violent cramping overtook her body. She doubled over, feeling as if she was turning herself inside out. A stream of water came up, the salt burning her nose and throat. She coughed and coughed and wiped at her face.

'You're alive,' Lucy said from somewhere to her right.

She sounded slightly disappointed, which, improbably, made Esme laugh. It sounded slightly hysterical, but it felt good. A release. Once she could speak and had wiped the tears from her eyes, she smiled warmly at Lucy. 'You can't drown a witch. Everyone knows that.'

Luke could not believe that Esme was making jokes. His head was spinning and he felt sick with relief. He dragged one of the blankets from underneath his sleeping brother and wrapped it around Esme. Then, because it felt so good to be holding her, he wrapped his arms around her too.

'Is it gone?' Esme asked Tobias.

'It has,' he said, his eyes crinkling.

'The wards...' Esme began and then her voice cracked. 'I failed. The wards are broken...'

Tobias stepped close and put a hand onto the witch's shoulder. 'You didn't fail. We are all needed to keep the balance. I wasn't on the island and that meant it was only a matter of time before the protection dissolved.'

'Bee said it's my job,' Esme said. 'I am supposed to—'

'It is your job,' Tobias said gently. 'And it's my job to be the mayor, and it's Luke's to be The Book Keeper. We're all needed. The roles must be filled to keep the wards strong.'

Luke hugged Esme close, wiping tears from her face. 'It's not your fault,' he said. 'None of this is your fault. You've saved everyone.'

'Your blood was in the water,' Tobias said. 'It helped to guide me home.'

His words seemed to cut through her distress and she took a deep breath, looking more her usual self.

Lewis made a small sound in his sleep, as if he was dreaming.

'Is he all right?' Esme turned to Lewis. She crouched

down, one hand knotted in the corners of her blanket cloak and one reaching to check Lewis's forehead, his pulse.

Luke had already checked on his brother, but he guessed Esme had been too distracted to notice. She had been busy being possessed. A wave of nausea threatened to engulf him, and his limbs suddenly felt watery. The danger of what she had done, the risk she had taken. All to avoid harming Lewis.

The couple that had been making their way steadily across the bay had arrived at their little group. The man had a black eye and scratches down one cheek. The woman didn't have visible injuries, but her face was drawn with exhaustion. Neither of them looked as though they had slept or eaten in a long time. They weren't moving toward Lewis anymore, and were looking around in confusion. It was as if they were waking up from a nightmare.

Esme moved as if to speak to them, but Tobias put a hand on her shoulder. 'You should go home, get into some dry clothes.'

Lucy was scowling at the people, probably frustrated that the need for violence had passed. For a moment, Esme wondered if she would attack somebody anyway. There was always the feeling she might spring at any moment and this was a particularly tense time.

'Go on home,' Tobias said to Lucy, noticing the same risk.

She stared at the mayor for a moment, black eyes wide and red lips stretched to reveal white teeth. Then she shrugged and skipped away across the sand.

Luke spoke quietly to Tobias. 'Is that thing really gone?'

'It will be unable to hold itself together in the vastness of the sea, or it will be pulled back to Àite Marbh and the gateway to its home. Now that I am back, there is no longer a space for it to occupy. It simply cannot stay.'

Luke stared out at the waves, wondering what they concealed. 'What if it survives in the water and someone goes swimming?'

Tobias smiled gently, as if reassuring a small child. 'I do not believe that is possible.'

Luke was going to argue that believing something wasn't possible wasn't enough, that Tobias ought to be certain, but then he had second thoughts. Tobias was The Island God. If he believed something, maybe that was better than certainty.

OVER THE NEXT TWO DAYS, the visitors that had clogged the streets and footpaths of the island quickly dispersed. Esme's guest house went from full to empty in one blessed afternoon and she sat on her back step with a mug of tea, enjoying the sun on her face and the enchanting sound of birds and insects, the breeze ruffling the leaves, and not a single human voice.

SEREN PUT a closed sign on the door of the pub, which was pretty much unheard of, and took to her bed. She slept for thirteen hours and spent the rest of the day lying in bed and watching The Walking Dead and reruns of Hell's Kitchen. Once she felt sufficiently recovered, she visited Fiona to apologise. Trying to put into words how awful she felt about taking Hamish and the extent to which she hadn't been in control of her actions. 'Can you ever forgive me?'

'Already done,' Fiona said warmly.

Back at the pub, it occurred to Seren that Fiona hadn't

invited her into the house. She knew, in her heart, that Fiona would need a little more time to truly forgive her actions, but for the first time since she had regained her senses, she felt hopeful.

MATTEO OPENED the shop as usual, but was extremely relieved to have no customers. He tidied up the shelves, reordered the dated goods, and gave everything a thorough clean. Restoring the shop to order gave him a sense of deep peace. He swept up the mess that had been trampled underfoot when there had been more people than physically sensible moving around the small space, and then wiped down the edges of the shelves. He was alone in the shop until closing time, without a single interruption, and it was bliss. Although he was now looking forward to dinner and he hoped Seren had reopened The Rising Moon. He wondered if Fiona would be there.

LEWIS GOT out of the car. He stretched until his spine cracked and looked at the suburban street where Luke had parked. They were on the outskirts of Alnwick, which wasn't very far away from the town centre. But there was a bus station and it was on the A1 which led to cities down south.

'I can take you further. You don't have to take the bus.'

'That's all right. You've done enough.'

Luke wasn't sure if that was meant to sound reassuring or like an accusation. He wondered whether the awkwardness between them would ever completely dissipate. It was, he reflected, a little better than it had been. They had overlaid their shared childhood and the subsequent chaos of their teenage and young adult years with new experiences. Those experiences included Lewis being possessed by an apocalypse-capable spirit from another reality, and Luke's future wife almost killing him in order to save mankind, but at least they were adult memories. And not rooted in old patterns. These were, Luke thought, entirely new patterns. And, yes, he had just thought of Esme as his future wife. He just hoped she agreed.

'I'll stay in touch,' Lewis said, a little self-consciously. They didn't do polite or sincere.

'You better had. You know I'll come looking.'

'I do.' Lewis's shoulders hunched and he looked away, south and toward whatever adventures were calling him next. 'Thanks.'

'Sorry?' Luke wasn't being a dick, he was genuinely unsure he had heard Lewis properly and the word slipped out.

Lewis darted a look at his face. 'For looking out for me.'

'Of course,' Luke said.

Lewis took a step closer and Luke did the same. They hugged. Quickly and awkwardly, but it didn't end in a wrestling match, so that was a win.

TOBIAS SAT with his old friend and waited. The window was open and the curtains moved in the fresh sea air. Presently, Bee began to stir. Her breathing became shallower and her right foot twitched. She was waking up. But first, Tobias knew, she had to sleep. Normal, restorative sleep. Bee was not quite human, but she was alive and would need to rest after her long journey. He was grateful to her for meeting him in the forest, for reminding him of himself. He did not like to consider how long he might have languished in Elsewhere, half-asleep and stumbling. He squeezed her shoulder gently, and she moved in her sleep, curling over onto her side.

Back at his house, newly cleaned with help from the islanders, Tobias settled into his favourite chair. All had been put back as it ought to be. The sofa was unsalvageable, but Fiona had helped him to order a replacement on the internet. It would be delivered in a couple of weeks' time.

But right now, he had a tea tray with a proper china cup and saucer and a small milk jug. He poured the amber liquid and inhaled the familiar scent, added a dash of milk and stirred with the spoon.

Winter lifted his head and checked that Tobias was still sitting in the same place. He was doing this with decreasing frequency as his canine brain began to accept that Tobias was back and not about to disappear. He yawned widely, tongue lolling, and then laid his head back on his paws and went back to sleep. Tobias added another log onto the fire and looked deeply into the flames. He took another sip of the tea and contemplated a piece of short-bread. It was good to be home.

ALL WAS peaceful at Fiona's house. Euan and Matteo were sitting on the sofa in companionable silence. Not complete silence, as Euan was playing a video game and would occasionally make a comment or explain what was happening to Matteo.

Hamish had taken a little longer than usual to settle for the night, clinging to her and crying when she tried to say 'night-night' and leave the room. Fiona had allowed an extra story and had stayed sitting on the floor by the door to the room until he had drifted off. She knew it was probably setting a bad precedent and that he might demand it in the future, but she still felt raw from the worry of losing him and needed the reassurance of his presence just as much. He would be all right. She made the vow as she leaned against the wall and watched his sleepy eyelids lose the battle to stay open. She would never let anything scary happen to him ever again. No sooner had she finished the thought than she knew it was pointless and impossible and, probably, undesirable. To never feel fear was to never take a risk. To never feel sadness was to never feel happy. To never lose was to never love. Her throat was suddenly tight and her eyes hot with tears. Fiona wasn't a crier, as a rule. She was practical and she carried on. She got on with things.

So, she would get on with this, she decided. She would give Hamish love and stability so that the knowledge that his birth mother had given him away would be a mere detail in the story of his life, overshadowed by his loving family and happy childhood on the island. She would fill his days with memories of laughter and games and books and cuddles and nourishing food and swimming in the dark and beautiful waves, so that the memory of being taken and held by a maddened stranger, was overwhelmed by the goodness of his young life. She couldn't protect him from all the bad, but she could make sure it was heavily diluted, to the point of safety. Like a single drop of poison in all the oceans of the world.

Having crept out of Hamish's bedroom and softly closed the door, Fiona wiped under each eye with a finger and went to find her older child. Standing in the doorway, she was caught by Euan's relaxed position. He was usually hunched in on himself, shoulders tense, face closed. But now he was laughing at something on the screen and then telling Matteo about it in a burst of chatter that reminded her of when he was a small boy and full of guileless enthusiasm.

Matteo wrote something and nudged Euan. He read it and laughed again. 'Right. All the time.' Catching sight of Fiona, he added, 'come and see this, mum.'

Matteo turned, too, and she saw the uncertainty in his handsome, dear face.

'You stay put,' she said to him. 'I'll sit on the floor.'

And she did. With Euan on her left and Matteo on her right, her back against the sofa and something incomprehensible on the screen.

ESME WAS HOLDING Hamish's hand as he lurched from one part of the bookshop to another. He seemed to know instinctively that these books were not for hauling off shelves and, while he occasionally collided with a book-laden wall, he didn't deliberately put hands onto anything. 'He's got clean fingers,' Esme said out loud.

'Sorry?' Luke called from the front of the shop. 'Did you ask me something?'

'Nothing,' Esme called back. 'Just letting the shop know that I wiped Mr Sticky here before letting him anywhere near the books.'

As if in reward, Esme caught sight of some brightly coloured shelves low to the ground. She guided Hamish to the alcove, which also had a thick soft rug and a large comfy-looking floor cushion. It definitely hadn't been there the last time she had been in this part of the shop. 'Thank you,' she said, as Hamish moved delightedly to the row of picture books that were placed at Hamish-height. He held a hand out and hesitated, just momentarily, his head lifted as if listening. Then he grabbed a book about friendly skeletons going on holiday to the seaside and held it out to Esme.

'Would you like me to read it?'

Enthusiastic nodding. Esme sat cross-legged on the cushion and Hamish plonked himself into the nest made by her legs. The simple trust made her eyes prickle with tears.

She had read the book from cover to cover, twice, and then one about a pigeon and was halfway through The Enormous Crocodile when she realised that Luke was standing opposite the alcove, watching.

'What time did Fiona say?'

'Twelve,' Esme replied and carried on reading.

At the appointed time, Fiona arrived at the shop. Her hair was damp from the sea and she had a pink glow. She thanked Esme and Luke and accepted Hamish's bag, which Esme had packed with all his things. He had a book clutched in one hand.

'You need to put that back,' Fiona said. 'It belongs to the shop.'

'He could borrow it, if you like?' Luke said. 'I'll put it in the ledger.'

'Doesn't it need to be a swap?' Fiona asked.

'Not for the under-fives,' Luke said. He looked around at the shop. 'New rule.'

The shop didn't seem to object.

ONCE THEY WERE ALONE, Luke offered Esme a coffee or tea.

'I'm fine, thanks. I was thinking we could go for lunch soon?' Her stomach was just beginning to let her know it was time to eat.

Luke flipped the closed sign. 'How hungry are you?'

'Middling,' Esme said.

'I was thinking,' he said, sliding his hands around her waist and dipping his head to kiss her, 'that we could go upstairs for a little while first.'

'Upstairs?' Esme felt breathless from the kiss, which had been excellent. 'Yes, please.'

After, as they got dressed, Luke caught Esme and kissed her again. So thoroughly that she wondered whether they might just skip the food portion of their lunch break and climb back into bed. Luke's stomach took that moment to growl loudly, and they both laughed.

'I've been thinking about something,' Luke said, his voice uncertain.

Esme was wearing her skirt and tights and finished pulling her cotton jumper over her head.

'I want us to stay together.'

For a wild moment, she thought he was going to propose. That would be too soon, though. And surely not? She was getting ahead of herself. 'I want to stay together, too,' she said. Her voice was quiet and she reached for him, for the comfort of his body.

They kissed and, when they had stopped, their heads stayed close and they smiled at each other. Luke was holding her as if she were precious and, at the same time, as if she were unbreakable. Esme felt strong and cared for and, while she knew that there were still a great many things she did not understand and many more that would frighten her, in this moment she felt safe and whole and very, very happy.

Luke's eyes were warm, watching her, and she felt suddenly emboldened. She had faced scarier things than speaking the truth of her heart. 'I think I might love you.'

'That's a relief because I definitely love you, Esme Gray.'

'Oh.' Esme wasn't sure she had ever felt a happiness like this. Her insides were warm and she felt as if she were expanding, as if the joyful feeling could not possibly be contained in the vessel of her body. It was her spirit, she realised. It had unfurled all around her, finally free.

'And I know it's too early to propose, but I want you to know that I want to marry you. I want us to be a family.'

Esme's breath caught in her chest.

'And I would like to have children with you. If that's what you want. But neither of those things if you don't want, although I really hope you do.'

'I do,' Esme said. 'Although maybe not quite yet on the children thing.'

'No, of course.' Luke was smiling and his eyes were shining and all she could see was happiness and love and a little relief. And, maybe, just hovering around Luke like a haze, his beautiful spirit that, like hers, had broken the confines of his body from the sheer and complete joy of the moment.

'I'd like a bit more practice at the thing you have to do to get children,' Esme said, feeling her smile stretching wider than it had ever done before.

'Now that,' Luke said, 'is a very wise suggestion.'

'I'm a very wise woman,' Esme said, and she stepped into his arms with no hesitation at all.

THE END

THANK YOU FOR READING!

I am busy working on my next book. If you would like to be notified when it's published (as well as take part in giveaways and receive exclusive free content), you can sign up for my FREE readers' club:

geni.us/Thanks

If you could spare the time, I would really appreciate a review on the retailer of your choice.

Reviews make a huge difference to the visibility of the book, which make it more likely that I will reach more readers and be able to keep on writing. Thank you!

ACKNOWLEDGMENTS

First off, thank you for reading. Without you, this book wouldn't exist.

The Island God was a blast to write and I want to thank my muse, the characters, and all the writing gods for that!

To my writing coven, Hannah Ellis and Clodagh Murphy, thank you for everything. I can't wait for our next trip! Thanks also to Nadine, Sally, LK, and Julia, plus the many other authors I know from groups and podcasts. I love our community.

Thank you to Stuart Bache for another fantastic cover, and to the team at Siskin Press. Many thanks to my brilliant ARC readers for their early feedback:

Desiree Arnold, Melissa Balmer, Lynda Brown, Sue Bruce, Elizabeth Butcher, Ronnie Calderwood-Duncan, Sherrill Cormany, Wendy Ellis, August Enger, Cathy Evans, Beth Farrar, Deborah Forrester, Brian Francis, Erin Gately, Jenni Gudgeon, Karen Heenan, Mel Horne, Michelle Hunter-Gray, Kathryn Jamieson-Sinclair, Sandra Keller, Christina Lindholm, Carmel McMillan, Katja Milants, Eva Merrick, Caroline Nicklin, Lizzie Noblett, Kristen O'Loughlin, Gill Othen, Elizabeth Ottosson, Andrew Peachey, Paula Searle, Patrice Smith, Jacquie Thornber, Amba Wade, Walt Wallmark, Fiona Ward, Sara Wolfe.

I am very lucky to have understanding and supportive friends and family, who cheer me on, pour me wine, and forgive me when I disappear into a book for months at a time. Thank you to you all.

As always, thank you to my wonderful children, Holly and James, and my lovely husband, Dave. You are my favourite people.

ABOUT THE AUTHOR

Sarah is a bestselling author of contemporary fantasy and magical realism. She writes the Crow Investigations series, a London-set urban fantasy featuring private investigator Lydia Crow.

Having always been a reader and a daydreamer, she now puts those skills to good use with a strict daily schedule of faffing, thinking, reading, napping and writing – as well as thanking her lucky stars for her good fortune.

Sarah lives in rural Scotland with her husband and extensive notebook collection.

Head to the website below to sign-up to the Sarah Painter readers' club. It's absolutely free and you'll get book release news, giveaways and exclusive FREE stuff!

www.sarah-painter.com

facebook.com/SarahPainterBooks
twitter.com/SarahRPainter
instagram.com/SarahPainterBooks